IN RIDES
TROUBLE

BLACK KNIGHTS INC.

JULIE ANN
WALKER

sourcebooks
casablanca

Published by Sourcebooks Casablanca, an imprint of Sourcebooks, Inc.
P.O. Box 4410, Naperville, Illinois 60567-4410
(630) 961-3900
Fax: (630) 961-2168
www.sourcebooks.com

Printed and bound in the United States of America.
VP 10 9 8 7 6 5 4 3 2 1

To my kick-ass agent, Nicole Resciniti. You gave me the chance to chase my dreams, and then you ran with me all along the way. There are no words to express my gratitude, so I'll simply say this: You're the best. This book is as much yours as it is mine.

Look into a soldier's eyes and you can tell how much war he has seen.

—William Henry

Prologue

"WE'RE DEFINITELY CHANGING THE NAME." FRANK "BOSS" Knight pulled the Hummer up in front of the sad little pre-fab building and glanced at the hand-painted wooden sign screwed over the front door: BECKY'S BADASS BIKE BUILDS.

"Too much alliteration for you?" Bill Reichert snickered from the passenger seat while unbuckling his seat belt and throwing open the door. The frigid winter wind whipped into the interior of the vehicle, prompting Frank to grab his black stocking cap from the dashboard and tug it over his head and ears before zipping his parka up to his chin.

If this thing actually worked out, Chicago winters were definitely going to take some getting used to. Of course, freezing temps were a small price to pay for a good, solid cover for his new defense firm. And joining Bill's kid sister in her custom Harley chopper business, posing as mechanics and motorcycle buffs, promised to be a freakin' phenomenal cover for all the guys he'd recruited away from the various branches of the armed services. Especially considering most of them were bulky, tattooed, and—without regulation military haircuts—just scruffy enough to pass for their own chapter of Hell's Angels.

He pushed out of the Hummer and had to lower his chin against the gust of wind that punched him in the face like an icy fist. Shoving his hands deep in his coat pockets, he trudged up to the front door through the path someone had shoveled in the thick blanket of snow.

Bill applied a gloved thumb to the buzzer, and five seconds later, a familiar noise sounded from the behind the metal door, making the hair on the back of Frank's neck stand up.

How do you know you've been in the business too long? When you recognize the sound of a .45 caliber being chambered from three feet away, that's how.

"Who is it?" a deep, wary voice inquired from within.

"I thought you said she knew we were coming," Frank hissed over Bill's shoulder.

"She does." Bill grinned. "But she also knows she can never be too careful in this neighborhood."

And that was no lie. The graffiti tagging every vertical surface for six blocks in each direction announced that they were smack dab in the middle of some very serious gang territory. The Vice Lords ruled the roost, and they wanted to make damned sure everyone knew it.

Raising his voice above the shrieking wind, Bill yelled, "Open the damned door, you big ape! We're freezing our dicks off out here!"

And that was no lie either. Frank couldn't even begin to explain to his family jewels why he hadn't jumped into a pair of thermal underwear this morning and instead opted to go commando.

Big mistake. *Huge.*

One he sure as hell wouldn't be making again.

The front door swung open with a resounding clang, and they were met by a giant, red-headed man who looked like he should be wearing a face mask and leotard while smashing a folding chair over some guy's back.

Frank could almost hear Michael Buffer shouting, *Arrrrre you ready to ruuumbllle?*

"Manus," Bill said, stepping over the threshold and motioning Frank through, "this is Boss. Boss, meet Manus. He and his brothers work security for my sister."

Frank waited until Manus tucked the .45 into the waistband of his jeans before cautiously stepping into the small, tiled vestibule. The walls were covered in rusted motorcycle license plates, and as soon as the door closed behind him, the aroma of motor oil and burning metal assaulted his nostrils.

"You the guy who wants to partner with Becky? Invest some money and learn to build bikes?" Manus asked while pumping the hand he offered, a smile splitting the big man's ruddy face and making all his freckles meld together.

Yeah, that was the story they were tossing around until he could get a look at the set-up...

"I haven't decided yet," he answered noncommittally, and Manus's smile only widened.

"That's only because you haven't seen Becky's bikes," he boasted. "Once you do, you're gonna want to give her all your savings and have her teach you everything she knows."

Frank lifted a shoulder as if to say *we'll see* and watched as Bill opened the second set of glass doors.

His ears were instantly assailed by a wall of sound.

The pounding beats of hard-driving rock music competed with the hellacious screech and whine of grinding metal. He resisted the urge to reach up and plug his ears as he followed Bill into the custom motorcycle shop, skirting a few pieces of high-tech machinery.

And then he wasn't thinking about his bleeding eardrums at all.

Because his eyes zeroed in on the most beautiful, outlandish motorcycle he'd ever seen.

It was secured on a bike lift. The paint on the gas tank and fenders was bright, neon blue that sparkled iridescently in the harsh overhead lights. It sported a complex-looking dual exhaust, an outrageous stretch, and intricate, nearly whimsical front forks. It also had so much chrome it almost hurt to look at it.

In a word: *art*.

It made the work he'd done restoring his vintage 1952 Harley-Davidson FL look like amateur hour.

And just when he thought he couldn't be any more blown away, the sound of grinding metal slowly died down and a young woman emerged from behind the bike with a grinder in one hand and a metal clamp in the other.

He nearly swallowed his own tongue.

This couldn't be…

But obviously it was. Because the instant the woman caught sight of them she squealed, clicked off the music pouring out of the speakers of an old-fashioned boom box, and dropped both tools on the bike lift before jumping into Bill's arms, hugging him tight and kissing his cheek with a resounding smack that sounded particularly loud in the sudden silence of the shop.

This was Rebecca "Rebel" Reichert, Wild Bill's little sister.

Little being the operative word. If she stood two inches over five feet Frank would eat his biker boots for dinner.

He didn't quite know what he'd expected of a woman who ran her own custom chopper shop, but it wasn't long, blond hair pulled back in a tight ponytail, intense brown eyes surrounded by lush, dark lashes, and a pretty, girl-next-door face that just happened to be his own personal weakness when it came to women.

Something about that wholesome, all-American thing always managed to bring him to his knees.

Well, hell.

Bill finally lowered her to the ground, and she came to stand in front of Frank, small, grease-covered hands on slim, jean-clad hips. For some inexplicable reason, he felt the need to stand up straighter.

It was probably because she had the same unyielding look in her eye that his hard-ass drill sergeant always had back when he'd been in Basic.

"So." She tilted her head until her ponytail hung down over her shoulder in a smooth, golden rope. "You must be the indomitable Frank Knight. Billy has told me so very *little* about you."

And that voice…

It was soft and husky. The type that belonged solely in the bedroom.

"Everyone calls me Boss," he managed to grumble.

"I think I'll stick to Frank," she said with a wink. And for some reason, his eyelid twitched. "After all, there can be only one boss around here, and I'm it. Now, I hear you want to get into the business of building bikes?"

"I'm considering it." He couldn't help but notice the way her nose tilted up at the end or the way her small breasts pressed against the soft fabric of the paint-stained, long-sleeved T-shirt she wore.

Kee-rist, man, get a grip.

"Well, then." She nodded, pushing past him as she made her way toward the front door, "let's go take a look at that bike you brought with you and see if you have any talent at all."

For a split second, he let his eyes travel down to the gentle sway of her hips before forcing himself to focus on a point over her head as he followed her back through the various machinery. Bill was right behind him, which helped to keep his eyes away from the prize… so to speak. Because the last thing he wanted was to get caught ogling the guy's kid sister.

Talk about a no-no of epic proportions. Especially if he didn't fancy the idea of finding one of Bill's size-eleven biker boots shoved up his ass.

Once they reached the first set of glass doors, she pulled a thick pair of pink coveralls off a hook on the wall. Balancing first on one foot then the other, she stepped into the coveralls and zipped them up before snagging a bright purple stocking cap from a second hook and pulling it over her head.

She looked ridiculous. And feminine. And so damned cute.

He gritted his teeth and reminded himself of three things. One, she was way too young for him. Two, if things worked out, then despite what she thought now, *he* was going to be *her* boss. And three, he'd made a promise not to—

"How much money are you thinking of investing?" she interrupted his thoughts as she pushed through the double doors and into the vestibule.

As much as it takes…"We'll talk more about that

later." He held his breath, waiting to see how she'd respond to both his authoritative tone and his answer. It was a test of sorts, to determine if they had any hope of working together.

She regarded him for a long second, her brown eyes seeming to peer into his head. Then she shrugged, "Suit yourself."

When she opened the outer door, he once again had to dip his chin against the icy wind. The three of them slogged through the snow to the small, enclosed cargo trailer hitched to the back of his Hummer, and he fished in his pocket for the keys with fingers already numb from the cold. Once he opened the trailer's back door, she didn't wait for an invitation to jump inside.

He and Bill were left to follow her up and watch as she walked around his restored bike before squatting near the exhaust.

"You do all the work yourself?" she asked.

The bike he'd been so proud of thirty minutes before seemed shoddy and unimaginative by comparison.

"Yes," he admitted, amazed he actually felt nervous. Like maybe *she* wouldn't want to work with *him*.

"Your welding is complete crap," she said, running a finger along a weld he'd thought was actually pretty damned good. "But it's obvious you're a decent mechanic, and that's really what I need right now, more decent mechanics. Plus," she stood and winked, "it might be nice to have a big, strong dreamboat like you around the place day-in and day-out. Something fun to look at when my muse abandons me."

He opened his mouth...but nothing came out. He could only stare and blink like a bewildered owl.

Holy hell, was she *flirting* with him?

He was saved from having to make any sort of answer—*thank you, sweet Jesus*—when Bill grumbled, "Cut it out, Becky. Now's not the time, and Boss is definitely not the guy."

"No?" She lifted her brows, turning toward Frank questioningly.

And now he was able to find his voice. "*No.*" He shook his head emphatically, trying to swallow his lungs that had somehow crawled up into his throat.

"Well," she shrugged, completely unflustered by his overt rejection, "you can't blame a gal for trying." She offered him a hand. "I'm in, partner. That is, once I know exactly how much you're thinking of investing."

"Bill will get back to you with the specifics," he hedged, taking her hand only briefly before releasing it, more eager to get the hell out of there than he'd care to admit.

Again she did that head-tilt thing. The one that caused the end of her ponytail to slide over her shoulder. She regarded him for a long moment during which time he thought his heart might've jumped right out of his mouth had his lungs not been in the way. Then she shrugged and said, "Fine. Go ahead and do that whole mystery-man thing. I don't really give a rat's ass as long as you're good for the green."

And with that, she hopped down from the back of the trailer.

He moved to watch her traipse through the snow to the front door of her shop. Only once she disappeared inside did he turn to Bill. "You sure she's trustworthy enough? She seems a bit impulsive to me."

Impulsive and arrogant and bold and...way too cute for her own good.

Bill smiled, crossing his arms. "Despite all evidence to the contrary, Becky's as steady as they come. We can depend on her to keep our secrets. You have my word."

"And what about the hierarchy? How's she going to react once she realizes I'm the one calling the shots?"

Bill clapped a heavy hand on his shoulder and chuckled. "I have no doubt you can handle her, Boss."

Uh-huh. He wished he shared Bill's certainty. Because there was one thing he could spot from a mile away, and that was trouble.

And Rebecca Reichert?

Well, she had trouble written all over her...

Chapter One

Three and a half years later…

Pirates…

Wow. Now there's something you don't see every day.

That was Becky's first thought as she ducked under the low cabin door of the thirty-eight foot catamaran named *Serendipity* and stepped into the blazing equatorial sun. Her second thought, more appropriately, was *oh hell*.

Eve—her longtime friend and owner of the *Serendipity*—was swaying unsteadily and staring in wide-eyed horror at the three dirty, barefoot men holding ancient AK-47s like they knew how to use them. Four more equally skinny, disheveled men were standing in a rickety skiff tethered off the *Serendipity*'s stern.

Okay, so…*obviously* they'd been playing the oldies a little too loudly considering they'd somehow managed to drown out the rough sound of the pirates' rusty outboard engine motoring up behind them.

"Eve," she murmured around the head of a cherry Dum Dum lollipop as her heart hammered against her ribs and the skin on her scalp began crawling with invisible ants. "Just stay calm, okay?"

Yep. Calm was key. Calm kept a girl from finding herself fathoms deep beneath the crushing weight of Davy Jones's Locker or under the more horrifying weight of a sweaty man who didn't know the meaning of the word *no*.

When Eve gave no reply, she glanced over at her friend and noticed the poor woman was turning the color of an eggplant.

"*Eve*," she said with as much urgency as she could afford, given the last thing she wanted was to spook an already skittish pirate who very likely suffered from a classic case of itchy-trigger-finger-syndrome, "you need to breathe."

Eve's throat worked over a dry swallow before her chest quickly expanded on a shaky breath.

Okay, good. Problem one: Eve keeling over in a dead faint—solved. Problem two: being taken hostage by pirates—now *that* was going to take a bit more creativity.

She wracked her brain for some way out of their current predicament as Jimmy Buffet crooning, "Yes I am a pirate. Two hundred years too late," wafted up from inside the cabin.

Really, Jimmy? You're singing that now?

Under normal circumstances, she'd be the first to appreciate the irony. Unfortunately, these were anything but normal circumstances.

The youngest and shortest of the pirates—he wore an eye patch...*seriously?*—flicked a tight look in her direction, and she threw her hands in the air, palms out in the universal *I'm unarmed and cooperating* signal. But a quick glance was all he allotted her before he returned the fierce attention of his one good eye to Eve.

She snuck another peek at her friend and...oh no. Oh *crap*.

"Slowly, very slowly, Eve, I want you to lay the knife

on the deck and kick it away from you." She was careful
to keep her tone cool and unthreatening. Pirates made their
money from the ransom of ships and captives. If she could
keep Eve from doing something stupid—like, oh, say
flying at the heavily armed pirates like a blade-wielding
banshee—they'd likely make it out of this thing alive.

Unfortunately, it appeared Eve had stopped listening
to her.

"Eve!" she hissed. "Lay down the knife. *Slowly*. And
kick it away from you."

This time she got through.

Eve glanced down at the long, thin blade clutched in
her fist. From the brief flicker of confusion that flashed
through her eyes, it was obvious she'd been unaware she
still held the knife she'd been using to fillet the bonito
they'd caught for lunch. But realization quickly dawned,
and her bewildered expression morphed into something
frighteningly desperate.

Becky dropped all pretense of remaining cool and
collected. "Don't you even think about it," she barked.

Two of the men on deck jerked their shaggy heads
in her direction, the wooden butts of their automatic
weapons made contact with their scrawny shoulders as
the evil black eyes of the Kalashnikovs' barrels focused
on her thundering heart.

"You don't bring a knife to a gun fight," she whispered, lifting her hands higher and gulping past a
Sahara-dry knot in her throat. "Everyone knows that."

From the corner of her eye, she watched Eve slowly
bend at the waist, and the unmistakable *thunk* of the
blade hitting the wooden deck was music to her ears.

"Look, guys," she addressed the group, grateful

beyond belief when the ominous barrels of those old, but still deadly, rifles once more pointed toward the deck. *That's the thing about AKs*, Billy once told her, *they buck like a damned bronco, are simpler than a kindergarten math test, but they'll fire with a barrel full of sand. Those Russians sure know how to make one hell of a reliable weapon*—which, given her current situation, was just frickin' great. *Not.* "These are Seychelles waters. You don't have any authority here."

"No, no, no," the little pirate wearing the eye patch answered in heavily accented English. "We *only* authority on water. We Somali pirate."

"Oh boy," Eve wheezed, putting a trembling hand to her throat as her eyes rolled back in her head.

"Don't you dare pass out on me, Evelyn Edens!" Becky commanded, her brain threatening to explode at the mere thought of what might happen to a beautiful, unconscious woman in the hands of Somali pirates out in the middle of the Indian Ocean.

Eve swayed but managed to remain standing, her legs firmly planted on the softly rolling deck.

Okay, good.

"We have no money. Our families have no money," she declared. Which was true for the most part as far as she was concerned. Eve, however, was as rich as Croesus. Thankfully, there was no way for the pirates to know that. "You'll get no ransom from us. It'll cost you more to feed and shelter us than you'll ever receive from our families. And this boat is twenty years old. She's not worth the fuel it'll cost you to sail her back to Somalia. Just let us go, and we'll forget this ever happened."

"No, no, no," the young pirate shook his head—it

appeared the negatives in his vocabulary only came in threes. His one black eye was bright with excitement, and she noticed his eye patch had a tacky little rhinestone glued to the center, shades of One-Eyed Willie from *The Goonies*.

Geez, this just keeps getting better and better.

"You American." He grinned happily, revealing crooked, yellow teeth. Wowza, she would bet her best TIG welder those chompers had never seen a toothbrush or a tube of Colgate. "America pay big money."

She snorted; she couldn't help it. The little man was delusional. "Maybe you haven't heard, but it's the policy of the U.S. government not to negotiate with terrorists."

One-Eyed Willie threw back his head and laughed, his ribs poking painfully through the dark skin of his torso. "We no terrorists. We Somali pirates."

Whatever.

"Same thing," she murmured, glancing around at the other men who wore the alert, but slightly vacant, look of those who don't comprehend a word of what was being said.

Okay, so Willie was the only one who spoke English. She couldn't decide if that was good or bad.

"Not terrorists!" he yelled, spittle flying out of his mouth. "*Pirates!*"

"Okay, okay," she placated, softening her tone and biting on her sarcastic tongue. "You're pirates, not terrorists. I get it. That doesn't change the simple fact that our government will give you nothing but a severe case of lead poisoning. And our families don't have a cent to pay you."

"Oh, they pay," he smiled, once again exposing those urine-colored teeth. "They always pay."

Which, sadly, was probably true. Someone always

came up with the coin—bargaining everything they had and usually a lot more they didn't—when the life of a loved one was on the line.

"So," he said as he came to stand beside her, eyeing her up and down until a shiver of revulsion raced down her spine, "we go Somalia now."

And she swore she'd swallow her own tongue before she ever even thought these next words—because for three and a half very long years the big dill-hole had refused to give her the time of day despite the fact that she was just a little in love with him, okay *a lot* in love with him—but it all came down to this…she needed Frank.

Because, just like he always swore would happen, she'd managed to step in a big, stinking pile of trouble from which there was no hope of escape.

She absolutely hated proving that man right.

—∿∿—

Briefing room onboard the navy destroyer, USS Patton
Six days later…

Sometimes Frank hated being proved right.

"Well Bill," he said as he skimmed through the plans detailing Becky and Eve's rescue for what seemed like the umpteenth time. No way was he letting this op go off with even the slightest hiccup, not with Becky's neck on the chopping block. "It appears your little sister has finally landed herself in a big, stinking pile of trouble. I always knew it'd happen."

Bill sat at the conference table with his desert-tan combat boots propped up, placidly reading a dog-eared copy of *The Grapes of Wrath* as if his kid sister wasn't currently in the hands of gun-toting Somali pirates.

Un-fucking-believable.

But that was Bill for you. The sonofabitch was the epitome of serenity, *always*, even when balls-deep in the wiry guts of an IED. Which was why two hours after Frank made the decision to open his own private shop, he'd recruited Bill from Alpha Platoon. The commanding officer of Alpha still hadn't forgiven him for that little maneuver, but Frank didn't much care, considering it was a known fact within the spec-ops community that no one knew his way around things that went *kaboom* like Wild Bill Reichert. And Frank accepted nothing but the absolute best personnel—the elite of the elite—for Black Knights Inc.

"It's not like she *intentionally* put herself in the path of Somali pirates, Boss," Bill murmured as he licked his finger and turned a page.

"I don't care if she *intentionally* put herself in the path of Somali pirates or not." He nearly popped an aneurism when the words evoked a starburst image of Becky in the merciless hands of those ruthless cutthroats. "The fact remains, she should've known better than to travel to this part of the world."

"Seychelios waters are considered secure. Pirates have never attacked a vessel so close to Assumption Island, so it is reasonable to assume the women believed they would be perfectly safe," rasped Jamin Agassi.

Frank glanced over at one of Black Knights Inc.'s newest employees and, not for the first time, felt a shiver of trepidation run down his spine. How could you trust a guy who knew the adjective form of Seychelles was Seychellios?

And it didn't help matters in the least that Agassi

had been dubbed "Angel" by Becky because the man's features were so perfect they were almost unearthly. Of course, the plastic surgeries he'd undergone after defecting from the Israeli Mossad and before Uncle Sam decided to conceal him within the ranks of Frank's Black Knights no doubt had something to do with the perfection of the man's mug.

Goddamn pretty boy.

Which only served to remind Frank of all the other goddamned pretty boys who worked for him. The ones who'd been out on assignment when the call for Becky's ransom came in, leaving him to catch the next transport onto the USS *Patton* with only Bill and the FNG—the military's warm and fuzzy acronym for the fucking new guy.

"Yes, *Seychellios* waters," he unnecessarily emphasized the word, "have never before seen pirate attacks, but military ships from across the globe have increased patrols and secured the shipping lanes around the bottle-necked Gulf of Aden, which anyone with a smidge of gray matter will tell you has only chased the pirates farther south around the Horn of Africa. So it stands to reason that it was only a matter of time before the waters around the Seychelles and Madagascar started seeing pirate activity."

See, just because he didn't know the adjective form of Seychelles didn't necessarily mean he was a slavering idiot. He knew some shit about some shit even though his vocabulary—liberally sprinkled with four-letter words on a good day—tended to indicate otherwise.

"It's not really their fault, you know," Bill said quietly, never taking his eyes off the text as he turned another page.

"Of *course* it is," Frank rumbled, throwing his hands in the air and wincing when his trick shoulder howled in protest of the sudden movement. Damn, getting old sucked...hard. "She didn't have to go on this asinine vacation halfway around the world to potentially pirate-infested waters. If she wanted to get some sand and sun, I know of some very nice beaches in Florida and California, on *U.S.* soil," he emphasized as he rolled his shoulder and reached into a zippered pocket on his cargo shorts to pull out his trusty bottle of ibuprofen.

He was never without the pain pills these days...

Goddamnit.

And that fun little fact was beginning to make him feel like he was just one step away from Metamucil and Viagra, and *that* just pissed him off.

"I wasn't talking about Becky," Bill said, "although you know as well as I do a mere weekend stroll along a beach in Florida or California wasn't going to do it for her. She needed to get away, *far* away, to clear her head."

Ah God. Why did no one agree with his decision to keep Becky from risking her fool neck by becoming an operator? Had everyone suddenly gone completely kill-the-bunny crazy?

Obviously. Because before he'd found out and eighty-sixed their activities, a few of the Knights had been teaching her—upon her repeating wheedling, no doubt—such dubious skills as computer hacking, sniping, explosives, demolitions, FBI investigative techniques...and God only knew what else. He was still mulling over some really inventive ways to kill his men for that.

She was supposed to be their *cover*. Nothing more. End of story.

Of course, she'd become so much more to him. The bane of his existence and the fantasy he didn't dare allow himself to fully contemplate all rolled into one.

"When I said it's not really their fault, I was talking about the pirates," Bill continued.

Say what?

Frank stopped with a couple of pain tablets halfway to his mouth. "What the hell do you mean by that? Of course the pirates are at fault."

"I'm not giving them a get-out-of-jail-free card, but Somalia hasn't had a functioning government in twenty years," Bill explained, keeping his place in the novel with one callused finger. "As a result, its fisheries were nearly poached dry by foreigners. Not to mention that the tsunami in 2004 washed ashore tons of toxic waste."

"The snot-green sea," Angel murmured. "The scrotum-tightening sea."

What the hell? Frank thought.

Bill's head snapped around, his expression shocked. "*Ulysses?*"

Angel shrugged. "Seemed appropriate."

Okay, so they were talking about a book? *Now?*

"For fuck's sake!" Frank roared, incredulous. "Can we all just get back to the point?"

"Yes," Angel agreed, "Bill's point is that, because of the pollution and tsunami and overfishing, early episodes of piracy close to the coast were a form of self-preservation. Simple people protecting their only economic resource. The sea."

"Exactly." Bill nodded toward the ex-Mossad agent.

"Great! Just fucking great!" Frank threw the pills in his hand to the back of his throat and swallowed them down without benefit of water. "Of all the Knights who could've been between missions, I get stuck with Plato and Aristotle. And I swear to God, if you two keep bobbing your heads like that at each other, we're going to start buying you matching outfits."

He could *maybe* understand Angel's ability to disassociate himself from the situation long enough to get a good long peekaroo at the big picture, but *Bill*? The man's baby sister was in the hands of Somali pirates and had been for nearly a week!

"Not that I won't happily blast them all into the welcoming arms of Allah if they harm one little hair on my sister's head," Bill added, a darkly menacing smile tilting one corner of his mouth.

Frank did a double take, then stared at Bill in astonishment.

Folks thought *he* was scary with his fiery temperament, but hearing how calmly Bill spoke of killing the pirates after he'd just been proselytizing on the raw deal they'd been handed? Now *that* was truly bloodcurdling.

It was the difference between holding a live grenade in your hand and stepping on a bag of trash on a roadside in Kandahar. The first was going to go off, no doubt about it, so you throw it as hard as you can and let it do its worst. The second looked totally innocuous until it suddenly blasted you into a hundred bloody bits.

Huh. Well, there you go. Frank was just happy ol' Billy Boy was on *his* side.

"And you?" he turned to Angel. "You have a problem killing poor Somali pirates if it comes to that?"

The mysterious Israeli lifted one perfectly shaped brow. "Not in the least."

Good. At least he could depend—

The door to the briefing room swung open and Commander John L. Patterson ducked inside.

———

"Why do you keep writing those notes?" Eve asked as Becky closed her spiral notebook, shoving a felt-tip marker inside the wire rings at its spine.

"Because," she craned her neck around to make sure One-Eyed Willie wasn't within earshot, "the surveillance drones flying overhead have crazy accurate cameras. I'm just letting the guys know what's up, keeping them informed as best I can. I don't want Billy or any of the others to worry too much."

Eve tilted her head back and gazed into the spotless blue bowl of the sky, then slid Becky a skeptical glance.

Until this morning when One-Eyed Willie shoved her down beside Eve, they'd been sequestered on opposite sides of the deck. Which was probably because within six hours of their capture she'd not only tried to sabotage the *Serendipity*'s engines but also sneak rat poison into the pirates' food. No doubt the Somalis had thought it best to keep them apart should she attempt to solicit Eve's help in some new escape scheme.

"Uh, I don't…I don't see any surveillance drones," Eve said, the look on her tired face clearly telegraphing her belief that the Indian Ocean sun finally had baked Becky's brain to the rubbery consistency of overcooked shrimp.

Becky could only smile. Poor Eve. The last six days would frighten anyone, but for someone with Eve's pampered and protected upbringing, it had to be truly terrifying.

"It's long gone," she explained calmly, trying to infuse her tone with enough confidence to bolster Eve's waning spirits. "As best as I can figure, it flies by every three or four hours. Only stays in sight for about sixty seconds."

Eve swallowed convulsively and glanced into the sky again. "I haven't noticed anything flying overhead."

"You wouldn't unless you knew what to look for. They fly so high, the only chance you have of seeing one is when the angle of the sun hits its fuselage, causing it to shimmer like a little point of daytime starlight."

"Ah," Eve murmured, once more propping her chin on her raised knees, folding her arms around her legs like she was trying to make herself as small as possible. Like maybe she was trying to disappear completely.

Becky glanced at her sharply. "You don't believe me?"

"It's not that," Eve soothed, looping a comforting arm around her shoulders.

"You *don't* believe me," Becky laughed incredulously, slapping her knee and dislodging Eve's arm in the process.

It was just as well. Neither of them had showered in nearly a week, which meant neither of them was particularly daisy-fresh. What she wouldn't give for a new bar of Dove soap and a smooth stick of deodorant. And while she was wishing for things she couldn't have, she'd take a big, fat burger from Bull and Bear restaurant and a double side of onion rings.

If she never saw another fish for the rest of her life, it would be too soon.

"Well, you must agree it's a bit far-fetched," Eve replied. "If there really were surveillance drones taking our picture, don't you think the little man in charge would know about it and deny you the ability to write your messages?"

"His name is Ghedi, and he can't read," Becky explained. "I convinced him I'm taking notes for the novel I'll write once our families pay for our freedom. He's very excited to be in an American book. I told him I'd call his character One-Eyed Willie." She wiggled her eyebrows, grinning.

Eve stared at her blankly, and Becky could only laugh at her friend's shocking lack of knowledge when it came to pop culture. "Look, Ghedi hasn't a clue we're being watched. The poor guy probably doesn't even know such technology exists."

"Ah yes, well..." Eve let the sentence dangle, and Becky decided it was time to give Eve the truth. The woman was going to find out anyway when the boys of Black Knights Inc. came racing to their rescue. And they *would* come racing to their rescue. Of that she was 100 percent certain.

"What if I told you the *mechanics*," she made the quote signs with her fingers, "working in my chopper shop are more than they seem?"

"What do you mean?"

"What if I told you they're covert government defense contractors who are on their way to save us right this very minute?"

Eve blinked rapidly, shaking her head. "Are you trying to tell me your brother and all those other no-neck, tattoo-covered, leather-clad bikers you employ and run around with are really spies?"

Becky lifted a shoulder. "Sometimes."

Eve took a deep breath, rolling in her lips as she placed a hand on Becky's shoulder. "Becky, I really think you should get out of the sun and—"

The sound of an outboard engine stopped her. Both of them scrambled to their feet and raced toward the railing.

"Oh, thank goodness," Eve choked on a sob when they spotted a motorboat bobbing in the distance. "We're rescued."

Chapter Two

"I HAVE GOOD NEWS AND BAD NEWS," COMMANDER Patterson said as he marched to the middle of the briefing room.

"Let's have the bad news first, then," Frank grumbled as he searched the commander's curiously brown-gray eyes, looking for...he didn't know. A spark of honor, maybe? The shining light of integrity? Something to let him know Patterson was a man capable of keeping a secret, because Patterson, along with Captain Ernesto Garcia, knew the truth about Frank, Bill, and Angel.

And, *damnit*, that just chapped Frank's ass.

Although he took some comfort in the fact that they were the only two aboard the USS *Patton* privy to the truth. The rest of the *Patton*'s crew suffered under the impression that Frank and his men were a trio of K&R—kidnap and ransom—specialists who'd been hired by Eve's ultra-wealthy family to try to negotiate the safe return of the women.

"Last surveillance photos indicate your ladies and their, uh, *escorts*, have been joined by a third party and have changed course," Patterson reported. "They're heading straight for a British oil tanker, the BP *Hamilton*. The *Hamilton* apparently had catastrophic engine failure two days ago. Twenty-four hours ago, her radio became in-op. Reports show she's still got power, her generators are working, but that's about it. She's basically a dead stick. And though various military vessels are scrambling to assist, it appears the ladies and pirates will get there first. In fact," the commander glanced down at his watch, "given the time delay on the intelligence reports, they're probably already there."

Great. So now Becky wasn't only being *held* by pirates, she'd been conscripted into piracy herself.

Frank didn't know whether to laugh or cry. Since he figured neither was really appropriate, he simply asked, "And the good news?"

"Their course change means we'll intercept them within six hours."

"Now that *is* good news." Because the sooner he got Becky to safety, the sooner he could wring her obstinate little neck for putting him and the rest of the Knights in the position of breaking their covers, and the sooner he could paddle her stubborn little ass for putting them through this emotional hell. Because she wasn't just Bill's little sister, she was like a kid sister to all of them...well, not *him* necessarily. He only *wished* his feelings toward her were brotherly. It would make things so much easier.

Yeah, perhaps if all he wanted to do was throw an arm around the girl's, er, *woman's* shoulders and knuckle her head, he wouldn't walk around most days feeling like a skeevy old perv. Feeling like, despite his best efforts, he'd become no different than—

"Six hours," Bill murmured, glancing at his own watch and interrupting Frank's thoughts. "Midafternoon is a terrible time to attempt a rescue."

"Which is why we'll wait until tonight," Frank decided quickly. "Breaching the catamaran would've been a cinch, and we could've done it at high noon. Overtaking the tanker? That's a little different. Not only are we going to need the time to plan, we're also going to need the cover of darkness in order to ensure our safety and the safety of the hostages."

"Ah, this is obviously some strange usage of the word *safe* that I wasn't previously aware of," Bill said.

"*Hitchhiker's Guide to the Galaxy*?" Angel said.

Bill winked, and the two of them bumped fists.

"Jesus Christ," Frank growled. "You guys are killing me."

They both turned to grin at him.

Patterson glanced at the three of them and finally shook his shiny bald head. If there was ever a casting call for a new Mr. Clean, the commander was a shoo-in. "I agree with waiting for nightfall, but there's one thing I don't get."

"What's that?" Frank asked, fighting the smile pulling at his lips at the thought of the staunch military officer sporting a little gold hoop earring and winking at appreciative housewives across the world.

"Why would the pirates, with nothing more than a couple of skiffs and a catamaran, go after a floundering tanker? There's no way for them to get that beast into harbor, no way to tow it, so why are they risking their lives and the ransom they expect to receive for Miss Edens and Miss Reichert?"

"Bill," Frank dipped his chin, "you want to answer that one?"

"They're hoping Becky can fix it," Bill supplied, totally deadpan.

"They're hoping she can fix what?" Commander Patterson asked. "The ship's engines?"

"Yes." Frank grinned, loving the incredulity on the commander's hard face. "That's exactly right. And what a prize it'll be for them if she does. I'm assuming, given the tanker's designation as one of BP's fleet, she's a big one. Probably carrying a typical load, which, if memory serves, comes to about one hundred million dollars worth of crude. Even if BP is only willing to pay three percent, that's still a major victory for the pirates."

"Three percent?" Angel rasped in his scratchy voice, the one he'd received courtesy of a good old-fashioned vocal-cord scouring, which guaranteed no voice recognition software could ever identify him. "After that catastrofuck in the Gulf of Mexico, they'll pay a lot more than that. The last thing they want is another scandal on their hands."

Catasrofuck?

Frank, a self-described connoisseur of creative cursing, quite liked that little combination. Perhaps working with Angel Agassi wasn't going to be so bad after all…

"Do you think it's possible?" Patterson asked. "Can she get those engines up and running? The ship's engineers have been working on the problem for days with no success."

Frank shrugged. "With Rebecca Reichert anything's possible, and I've never seen a more intuitive mechanic in my life. If there's a way to get the engines going, Becky'll find it."

"By the look on your face, Commander Patterson, I'm assuming you've seen the news footage of Becky." Bill chuckled.

Yeah, unfortunately the networks had gone crazy with the story of the American women captured by pirates. Frank hated publicity as a general rule, and when the media stuck its long nose so close to him and his men? Man, it took every ounce of restraint he had not to go all Sean Penn and start punching folks. That was another thing he could punish Becky for once he got his hands on her…

Oh *Jesus*, he was not going to go *there* again. The mental image of bending her over his knees and paddling her sweet bare ass until it turned pink was just too…*erotic*. He'd never been into S&M before, never felt the need to tie a woman down or playfully spank her butt, but Becky was just so…so…independent and…and damned…*confrontational* that she brought out the caveman in him. He'd like nothing better than to take his flex-cuffs, secure her wrists and ankles to his bed posts, and prove his dominance once and for all. Which was weird, disturbing, and so, so wrong.

But there you go. That summed up his feelings for her perfectly. Weird, disturbing, and wrong. Still, just the thought of having her at his mercy made his shorts tight.

He glanced around at Patterson and Bill, hoping the sight of their manly faces would be just the visual cold shower he needed to wash away the raunchy images heating his brain and other parts of his anatomy, because, yeah, talk about a piss-poor time to pop a boner…

"But don't let her looks fool you," Bill continued. "Becky's an absolute wizard when it comes to wielding a wrench."

"But how would the pirates know that?" the commander asked. His puzzled expression screamed his difficulty at melding the image of the pretty, blond woman he'd seen on television with the one they were all describing.

Good luck with that one, man.

When it came to Becky, the old adage, "what you see is what you get," was blown to smithereens. The woman was like a kaleidoscope. Never the same, always changing, and always surprising you with her brilliance.

"They know she's a crackerjack mechanic because piracy is a big, profitable, highly technical business," Frank explained. "Those malnourished guys you see on TV are just the grunts, the expendables. They're the hired guns brought in to do the dangerous dirty work. Behind them are highly intelligent, well-organized, well-*cloaked* entities with as much access to information as you or me. I'm sure within ten minutes of them finding Becky and Eve's passports, whoever was in charge knew everything there was to know about the women, right down to their Social Security numbers and bra sizes."

34B in Becky's case.

And *no*, he hadn't gone rummaging around in the girl's...*damnit!*...*woman's* lingerie drawer. He'd been doing a load of laundry in one of the two washing machines back at the Black Knights' compound when he'd come across a rather titillating, pink peekaboo lace number wrapped around the base of the washer's oscillating drum. He'd just happened to see the size on the tag as he'd unwound the scrap of lace, and yeah, he could admit, for a brief second, he'd thought about shoving it in the pocket of his jeans and keeping it as a sort of perverse souvenir. Thankfully, sanity quickly surfaced, and he simply hung it over the knob of an overhead cabinet.

But dear Lord, that he even considered doing otherwise was disconcerting.

"Dear Lord," Patterson breathed, "that's disconcerting."

Whoa. *What?*

Frank glanced around, afraid he'd been thinking out loud, but no, no one was looking at him like he'd been eating pervert sandwiches for lunch. So uh, what had they been discussing? Oh yes, the pirates' incredibly disturbing ability to gather information.

"And then some," he agreed, brushing aside the memory of that slip of pink lace as the weight of Becky's predicament once more settled heavily on his shoulders. That weight would crush him if he let it. And the thought of losing her...he shuddered. "I'm assuming those are the tanker's schematics in your hand," he gestured with a jerk of his chin toward the long plastic tube in the commander's fist.

"Affirmative." Commander Patterson handed over the documents.

"Were you able to glean anything else from the last fly-over footage?" he asked as he popped the top on the plastic tube and slid the schematics onto the table.

He glanced up when the commander didn't immediately respond. The man was chewing on the side of his cheek in what appeared to be an attempt to keep from grinning.

"What?" he growled. "What's she written this time?"

The commander lifted a fist to his mouth and democratically cleared his throat. "The footage shows she'd written, *For the love of God, would you guys hurry the hell up already?*"

"Well, at least we know this little experience isn't adversely affecting her attitude," Bill chuckled.

That was Becky, all right. Two tons of unpredictable

TNT packed in one small package…and he nearly crum-
pled from the hard rush of relief that flooded through
him at the sound of those terribly Becky-like words.

That-a-girl, he thought and took a deep, steadying
breath before motioning his men closer. "Okay, gentlemen, it looks like we've got a tanker to appropriate."

Pirate was never a position Becky thought to add to
her résumé but, as usual, her life was chockablock full
of surprises.

The man who'd come aboard was *not* their rescuer, as
Eve had foolishly hoped. Oh no. Although he was taller
and older than the other pirates, superbly well-dressed,
impeccably groomed, and spoke excellent English with
the slightly haughty air that came with any British accent, he was still just a pirate. He'd introduced himself
as Sharif—no last name—the interpreter.

"I worked for the United Nations," he explained
shortly after coming aboard, "before I came into this
business. Now I'm an interpreter."

"What business?" she snorted with derision, crossing
her arms over her chest and eyeing his freshly laundered
clothes with a mixture of jealously and contempt. "Last I
checked, piracy is an international crime, not a business.
Which doesn't make you an interpreter, it makes you a
blackmailer at best and an extortionist at worst."

Sharif just laughed, the sound low and rolling.
Cultured was perhaps the right way to describe it. It
made Becky's skin crawl. "I interpret for nine gangs, all
of whom work independently for the same boss. Sounds
quite like a business to me. A very lucrative one at that."

"Whatever." She rolled her eyes and placed a comforting hand on Eve's shoulder. When it became obvious Sharif was not there to rescue them, her poor friend deflated like a popped birthday balloon.

"I don't care what you think of me, Miss Reichert," Sharif replied, dropping the *t* on the end of her name. "All I care about is that you know how to repair engines."

"Yeah, so?"

"So we're putting off your trip to Somalia," he declared, and her heart filled with hope and started floating somewhere above her head. The Knights, many of them ex–Navy SEALs, were straight-up badasses when it came to work in the water. The longer she kept herself off dry land, the easier it would be for her guys to facilitate a rescue.

"Aw, shucks," she feigned dejection, "and I was *so* looking forward to it." Eve shoved a pointy elbow into her rib cage.

Sharif tilted his head and smiled. Unlike Ghedi, his teeth were large and even and brilliantly white against the darkness of his face. "You have a very insolent tongue, Miss Reichert. What is that expression you Americans love so much? Ah, yes, you had better make sure it is not writing checks your ass cannot cash. Such a wonderfully colorful turn of phrase, don't you think?"

"I think I'd feel a lot better if we kept my tongue and my ass out of the conversation completely."

Another sharp elbow crashed into Becky's side, and she turned to glare at her friend. The look Eve gave her clearly stated the woman was seriously questioning her intelligence. And yepper, when she swung her attention back to Sharif, his dark scowl pretty much telegraphed his intention to kill her, slowly, if ever the opportunity arose.

"I have little patience with mouthy women," he growled, his musky smelling cologne sticking in her nose until she wanted to puke. "Breaking every little bone in your body would gratify me greatly, not to mention the fact that your diminished health would likely only expedite your ransom. So you see, it's a win-win situation for me. It would behoove you to remember that."

She could almost hear Billy in her head, *S squared, Becky. S squared.* Which was his way of telling her to sit down and shut up.

With difficulty, she clamped her lips together and satisfied herself by glowering.

Sharif turned his back on her and informed Ghedi of their course change, while two other members of the crew captained the extra skiffs back to the safety of the Somali coast.

Which is how she now found herself stuck on her own catamaran about to become a pirate …

The crew onboard the BP *Hamilton* hadn't a clue they were being attacked until the first volley of bullets burst across the hull.

This was a nightmare. A really, really scary one where Becky held on for dear life to the *Serendipity*'s rail as the pirates threw down the throttle on the catamaran's two big outboard engines until they were blasting across the choppy seas, hurtling like an uneven cannon shot toward the *Hamilton* as waves crashed over the railing.

Four red flares suddenly streaked from the tanker's bridge, turning the bright sky above the football field-sized ship an angry orange. The people on board were no longer under the mistaken impression the *Serendipity* was a simple pleasure cruiser.

Was the spray of bullets your first clue? Becky thought sardonically, using her free hand to grab Eve as the woman's fingers slipped from the rail, and she started sliding across the watery deck. Becky strained to keep them both from bouncing right out of the boat.

Going overboard would be a case of falling out of the frying pan and into the fire. In this instance, the fire was thousands of miles of endless, shark-infested waters where trying to locate them would be akin to locating a needle in a haystack.

On second thought, that analogy didn't quite cut it.

It was more like, if they managed to separate themselves from the boats and wind up adrift, locating them would be like trying to locate a protozoan in a haystack.

So yepper, it was best just to hang on and hope she could keep them both alive long enough for Frank and Billy and the rest of the boys to pull one of their Mighty Mouse maneuvers—as in, "here I come to save the day!"

She absolutely hated finding herself in a situation requiring a Mighty Mouse maneuver. It didn't bode too well for her chances of becoming an operator…

Another set of flares soared over the *Hamilton*'s big deck.

Is that the best you can do? she thought with derision.

Yes, it probably was. Merchant vessels almost always went to sea unarmed.

The Somalis obviously understood that as well as she did. They didn't slow a single knot as they fired a few more warning shots from their AKs.

She gritted her teeth and tried to use her forearm to push her salty, water-logged hair out of her eyes. Not that she necessarily wanted to *see* the moment when she was blown to smithereens. Every time one of those rounds pinged off the tanker's hull, she expected a giant fireball to ensue. What kind of idiots fired at a ship carrying a ton of combustible fuel?

Somali pirates and their trusty interpreter, that's what.

Being set adrift in the Indian Ocean was looking better and better. If she had to choose a way to die, drowning promised to be much less painful than burning. She turned to look behind them at the plume of white water kicked up by the catamaran's outboard engines and the endless panorama of undulating waves beyond. Maybe she and Eve should just let go and—

She didn't get any further along that train of thought because the pirates yanked back on the throttle, throwing the engines into reverse and causing both women to slide across the slick deck. Scrabbling for purchase, they managed to grab the base of the mast and each other. The *Serendipity* slid in sideways… *oh God, we're going to crash!*… and slammed into the *Hamilton*'s port side about mid-ship with a bone-rattling *thud*!

She was amazed the *Serendipity* didn't just disintegrate on impact, but the little sailboat held together.

Thank you, dear sweet Christ!

She struggled to catch her breath, watching in horrified amazement as the pirates immediately threw grappling hooks over the tanker's railings. They swung their AKs with their improvised rope gun straps over their bony shoulders and started climbing like mountain goats.

And it all happened in about two seconds flat.

Jesus, Mary, and Joseph, she hated to admit it, but they were *good*.

Threading an unsteady arm around Eve's trembling shoulders, she used the sturdy mast to pull the two of them upright as the catamaran rocked and bounced against the side of the immense tanker. The smell of diesel from the *Serendipity*'s steaming engines mixed with the metallic scent of the *Hamilton*'s wet steel hull, making her eyes water.

Surely, that was the cause for her tears and not the sheer terror she'd just experienced.

Uh-huh. Right.

"Are you okay?" she asked once they were both standing on the undulating deck, dripping wet and shaking like leaves. When Eve glanced up at her and saw the bright tears in her eyes, the woman's face started to crumple.

Okay, you gotta pull it together for Eve's sake, Reichert. She quickly brushed a hand over her cheeks and pasted on a wicked grin.

"Boy howdy!" she slapped Eve on the back and feigned bravado, "that was one hell of ride, wasn't it?"

Eve swallowed convulsively. "Cheese and rice, they're completely crazy."

"Ya think?" she grunted scornfully as she tried to slow her racing heart. Glancing down, she grimaced and pointed at her friend's bleeding knees, which Eve obviously received courtesy of the stupid pirates' Wild-West boat piloting tactics. "Those look painful. Are you sure you're all right?"

Eve didn't get a chance to respond when Sharif appeared behind them, shoving a menacing black Glock

19 at the back of Becky's head. With a jerk of his chin, he indicated the ropes dangling down the massive gray hull of the *Hamilton* and handed her a shiny, new rock-climbing harness. The thing still had a price tag attached to one strap.

Ol' Sharif obviously planned ahead and came fully equipped for this little endeavor.

"Start climbing," he barked. "You've got work to do."

She craned her head back, *way* back, to squint up at the *Hamilton*'s railing.

Cheese and rice.

Eve certainly had that part right.

Chapter Three

Ten hours later…

"YOU SURE YOU KNOW HOW TO HANDLE THIS EQUIPMENT?" BOSS asked Angel as Bill rechecked the fuel gauges on his DPV—diver propulsion vehicle—and then went back to his book, concentrating on the Joad family and their trek west on Route 66.

The reading helped…

Scratch that. The reading *usually* helped. He stifled a groan, rubbed at his burning belly, and turned his back on Angel and Boss in order to take a quick chug of Pepto-Bismol.

The three of them were alone down on the USS *Patton*'s lowest deck, waiting for Captain Garcia to divert the attention of his crew, so they could open the aft doors without detection. Then they'd plunge down into the deep blue and really get this party started.

"This gear is technical and highly specialized," Boss growled. "The last thing we need once we get out in the water is for you to fuck up."

"It's no problem," Angel reassured him as Bill covertly re-pocketed the bottle of pink medicine and glanced over the top of his worn copy of *The Grapes of Wrath*. He watched Angel flick up the neck on his wet suit and reach behind his head for the cord on the zipper. The Israeli gave it the kind of hard yank that all divers developed over the years.

Well, at least it appears the guy has been in a wet suit before. That's something.

"You're certain?" Boss pressed, his deep voice booming around the cavernous space. "Because you gotta be one-fucking-hundred-percent certain about this, man."

Boss stood with his hands on his hips, scowling at Angel as if his will alone could compel the guy to tell him the unfettered truth.

To be quite honest, Bill figured it could. There was nothing scarier, in his way of thinking, than Boss. And when the guy towered like that, all 6'4" of mammoth shoulders and bulging biceps, it made a man hesitate to utter anything but the truth, the whole truth, and nothing but the truth, so help him God.

"I know what I'm doing." Angel met Boss's hard glare with one of his own. "I will not fail you or Becky. I might not have been around her long before she left for this vacation, but it was long enough. I will give my life for her if needed."

That surprised Boss. His chin jerked back on his neck like someone just popped him a five-finger sandwich.

Bill didn't share the big man's astonishment. His kid sister just had a way about her. All most folks needed was ten minutes in Becky's lively company, and they either wanted to date her, adopt her, or be her new best friend.

He *did*, however, wonder which category Angel fell into...

Boss hesitated for a second, searching for something in the new guy's eyes. Whatever he was looking for, he must've found it, because he grunted his approval and turned toward Bill. "You ready for this?"

Uh, sort of?

But that wasn't the answer Boss was looking for, so he hardened his expression and gave a curt nod instead.

"Of course you are, you sonofabitch," Boss chuckled, the sound reminiscent of the rumbling purr Bill's beloved Harley made once he got the beast out on the open road. "Look at you," Boss shook his shaggy head, "cool as a fucking cucumber."

Cool as a cucumber…

Indeed.

Only that was a complete and total crock of caca. On the outside, he might look calm and collected, because he'd learned to combat the mounting tension by concentrating on the words streaming across the pages of a book.

But on the inside?

Hell, on the *inside* he was a complete disaster. A bundle of jumpy nerves and crushing anxiety, tormented—just like always—by a nearly paralyzing battery of what-ifs.

What if they couldn't get to Becky? Intelligence reports said she'd been sequestered down in the engine room. That huge space was a rabbit's warren of machinery nooks and mechanical crannies. If they didn't play their cards just right, it'd be a cinch for the guys guarding her to use her as a human shield and bring about a standoff that could very easily end in a bloodbath.

What if the pirates refused to be taken alive? Would they turn on the hostages? Images flashed through his brain like a strobe light. Becky getting hit, falling to the ground, bleeding out, her light forever extinguished.

He squeezed his eyes closed and tried to swallow the bile that climbed up the back of his throat, filling his mouth with the burning taste of battery acid. Ever since they'd received the news of Becky's abduction, his ulcer had been chomping away at his stomach lining like the stuff was made of foie gras.

Of course, none of this showed on his tightly controlled face as the red light above the aft doors clicked from red to green.

"Suit up," Boss commanded, and he pulled his Neoprene hood over his head and shoved his mask over his eyes.

The large steel door through which the SWCC—Special Warfare Combatant Crewmen—boys usually deployed their super sweet Mark V Special Operations Craft rolled open with a well-oiled hum. The low glow of nautical twilight bounced off the nearly glassine seas. It was the time of day when the molten sun slipped below the horizon, throwing golden rays skyward and reflecting off the ocean until it was hard to tell up from down.

Boss grinned and winked. "Perfect time of day for a rescue, my man. Time for the barbarians to come out and play. Hoo-ah?"

And even though he knew Boss was worried sick about Becky, that didn't mean the man didn't just *live* for this shit.

"Hoo-ah!" he gave Boss a thumbs up, trying not to grimace when his ulcer started in on a second helping. He pushed all 165 pounds of DPV out the door, watching it splash down into the dark ocean. A second later he jumped after it, falling six feet into the warm embrace of the salty water.

Scrubbing his mask with sea water to keep it from fogging up, he powered his DPV. With the help of the vehicle, he jetted a few yards from the hull of the slowly rocking destroyer before turning back to watch Angel jump from the huge ship.

The guy was the picture of grace as he pointed his toes and sliced through the ocean without creating the tiniest splash.

And the German judge gives him a perfect ten!

When Angel surfaced, he was quick to adjust his mask, fire up his DPV, and motor over to Bill.

"You really do know what you're doing, don't you?" he asked the mysterious new Knight after plucking out his mouthpiece.

"I do." Angel nodded, then made a face when Boss plunged into the ocean, creating a plume of water so huge it looked like a whale just breached. "The question is, does *he*?"

If the German judge would've given Angel a perfect ten, then Boss certainly deserved a perfect *negative* ten for that little exercise.

"Don't let that dive fool you. I've seen him tightrope walk across phone lines over the roofs of Bagdad, watched him HELO jump out of a cargo plane in pitch-black darkness and manage to hit the DZ right on the X while the rest of us were barely able to come within a kilometer of the thing. One time he threaded himself and a string of det cord through a crawl space so small a raccoon would hesitate to enter. He's just no good at illicit water entry if the jump point is more than a few feet from the surface. Goes in like a damn cannonball every single time."

Angel's painted face couldn't camouflage his skepticism as Boss bobbed to the surface beside them.

"Okay, gentlemen," Boss said, glancing at his water-proof titanium wristwatch, "we've got a fifteen minute swim to the *Hamilton*. Everyone clear on their mission?"

"Affirmative." Bill nodded as Angel echoed his response.

"Then let's harden our balls and our resolve and get this fucker done."

Bill chuckled at the look of incredulity that shot across Angel's face. "I surely love your inspirational speeches, Boss."

———

Sharif Garane watched the narrow back of the American woman as she wrestled with a large bolt on some huge machine in the British tanker's sweltering engine room.

Rebecca Reichert was her name, but everyone called her Becky. He liked the sound of that. It suited her all-American looks.

He did *not* like *her*, however.

And had he known, when the directive came down for him to ensure she repaired the damaged engines on the tanker, that her tongue would be so abrasive, he might have passed on the opportunity.

Then again, probably not. This assignment was his ticket to economic freedom. If he could keep from killing her long enough for her to finish her repairs, that is…

"Sonofabitch!" she said as the bolt suddenly broke free and she banged her elbow on an adjacent piece of machinery.

He chuckled at her discomfort until she turned to glare at him, her dark eyes—so disconcerting against her fair coloring—shooting fire in his direction.

"What's so funny?" She wiped her perspiring forehead with a wrist, leaving behind a black streak of grease.

He stopped laughing to curl his lip at her disgusting level of dishabille. She'd been dirty when he'd come aboard the catamaran. No doubt it hadn't crossed the pirates' minds to allow the women to shower. Now, covered in the sweat of nearly a week and the grease of the last ten hours, she was positively obscene.

"Get back to work," he ordered. "Your stalling tactics are trying my patience. If you persist, I might decide to start taking the lost minutes out of your soft hide. Have you ever seen what a strip of wet leather does to human flesh?"

"I'm *not* stalling," she said. "You're the one who sent the ship's engineers up to the bridge. If you'd left them down here to work with me, I'd probably already be finished."

Perhaps. But he hadn't cared for the way the three men ogled her. It'd been…distracting. Plus, they were three very large men, and he hadn't wished to be alone with them down in the steaming engine room where they could easily overwhelm him if they took it into their thick skulls to chance a bullet wound.

He was in this thing for the money, not to risk death or injury. It was disconcerting enough to actually be involved in this particular venture—he was accustomed to sitting in air-conditioned rooms, waiting for the phones to ring so he could wheedle cash from wealthy western pockets—he didn't want to strain his nerves further by locking himself in a room full of vulgar, overgrown sailors.

No. It was better this way.

Just the two of them. Alone.

Reaching for the buckle on his belt for emphasis he said, "I'm going to count to three, and if you haven't returned to your work by then, I'm giving you three strikes for every second you stalled."

"One," he began, hoping her pride wouldn't allow her to back down. He very much thought he'd enjoy beating her, watching her fair skin turn bright red under his blistering blows.

With a snarl she spun back to her work, cursing him beneath her breath as she attacked the loosened bolt with renewed vigor.

Disappointed at her quick capitulation, he took another hasty sip of water and used his handkerchief to wipe at the sweat running down his temples and the back of his neck. It was an absolute oven in the engine room, and the longer he sat waiting for her to complete her repairs, the more irritable he became. His fantasies involving her punishment were growing ever more creative and violent by the hour.

She glanced at him over her shoulder. "Why are you sweating so much? Aren't you *used* to this type of heat?"

He considered ignoring her. The woman hadn't the first clue how to be a docile, compliant hostage, and he didn't want to encourage her audacity in addressing him when he hadn't first addressed her. Then again, there was something about the husky timbre of her voice. It was strangely appealing...

"Even though I was born in Africa, I spent the majority of my youth and early adulthood in London. Five years ago, I came back to what was left of my home country. Alas, I have yet to re-acclimate."

It was no matter, really. Soon there would be no need for re-acclimation. With the cut he'd get from the ransom of the women and the *Hamilton*, he'd finally have enough money to leave Africa. Enough money to live a life of luxury anywhere his heart desired.

Somewhere in Asia, perhaps. Japan? The climate was far more favorable and the women still meek enough to suit a man's tastes. Though the earthquakes and tsunamis lessened the allure…

She glanced over her shoulder again, eyeing the dampness of his shirt. "Maybe you're not cut out for this line of…*work*."

He didn't like the way her lip curled on the last word.

He decided then that he not only disliked her, he hated her. Hated her sharp eyes and even sharper tongue. Hated the fact that when she bent over to wrestle with a bundle of wires, the sight of her tight, firm buttocks made his manhood stir. As disgusting as she was, covered in filth and sweat, something about her still managed to captivate him.

He gulped angrily at the cold bottle of water in his hand, hoping it would cool his unwanted ardor. That his body could want a creature such as her, despite his overwhelming detestation, was a biological insurrection. An anatomical mutiny.

Then his body did him one better, because all that water he'd been drinking let down and he needed to urinate, *urgently*. Unfortunately, since he'd insisted Ghedi and his men guard the *Hamilton*'s crew so he could sequester himself alone with her, there was no one to take over guard duties.

He squirmed against the stool he was sitting on until he could stand it no longer.

"I'm going to relieve myself," he told her and waved his gun when she turned to scowl at him. He could just urinate in front of her, he supposed. She'd probably seen Ghedi and his men doing much worse during her time in captivity. But the thought of such grotesque, classless behavior disgusted him. He was worlds apart from those dirty, ignorant pirates, and he refused to stoop to their level. "You will continue working. And do not think of trying to escape. We're locked in here. The only way out is if I call to my compatriots on deck and they let us out. Do not take it into your head to hide from me either." He could see the wheels turning behind her eyes. "Let me be clear. If I am forced to come searching for you, you will not enjoy what happens once I find you."

Her nostrils flared, but she turned back to her work, grumbling something he couldn't make out.

Oh, he hoped she'd run.

It would give him a reason to give chase, chase would lead to capture, and capture would lead to punishment.

He really, *really* fancied the idea of that last bit.

―∾∾―

"We secure here?" Frank asked Bill as he pulled a ziptie tight around the wrist of a struggling pirate and shoved the man aside to join his trussed up compatriots. He couldn't help himself, he smashed the man's skull into the bulkhead with just a *little* more force than was necessary.

After covertly boarding the tanker, overtaking the untrained men had been laughably easy. Up in the *Hamilton*'s bridge, more than half of the pirates had been asleep, leaving just two guards to watch over the entire crew of hostages. And though those two men had been vigilant—vigilantly keeping their eyes and weapons trained on their prisoners, that is—they hadn't been prepared for a group of silent shadows sneaking in behind them and relieving them of their AKs in the blink of an eye.

"Affirmative," Bill answered, slapping his hand over the mouth of the small, hogtied pirate kneeling in front of him. The guy kept on screaming, "Parley, parley, parley!"

Frank grunted, motioning for Bill to remove his hand. The little pirate—*dude, is that an eye patch?*—relieved of Bill's restraining hand, took a deep breath before he started begging, "Please, sir, please—"

"Shut up," Frank barked. "This isn't *Pirates of the Caribbean*, and you're not Jack Sparrow… or One-Eyed Willie, for that matter. There *is* no parley."

. Bill made a face, then glanced at the gaudy little jewel glued to the center of the pirate's eye patch and burst out laughing.

Frank felt one corner of his mouth twitch before he glanced into the shadowed corner of the *Hamilton*'s big bridge where the pirates had stacked the tanker's crew together like a pile of sweating sardines. Angel murmured reassurances to the wide-eyed hostages as he sliced through their restraints, but when he caught Frank looking at him for verification that Becky was somewhere in there with the rest of the tanker's crew, he shook his head.

Yeah, that would've been too easy. Obviously she was still being held down in the engine room.

"How many are down in the engine room?" he asked One-Eyed Willie, who was still pleading, blubbering, and switching back and forth between English and his native language in such rapid succession that Frank's temples started to pound. "How many!" He grabbed the guy's shoulder, giving it a hard shake.

Oh man, was that a...? *Kee-rist*, it was. An actual tear leaked from the corner of the pirate's one good eye. The guy...kid really—if One-Eyed Willie'd seen his twentieth birthday then Frank was the bleeding Tooth Fairy—was trembling so hard, he feared the little shit's yellow teeth might rattle right out of his head.

Taking a deep breath, praying for patience, he bent until he could peer into the young pirate's tear- and sweat-soaked face. Damn, the guy needed a Kleenex in a bad way, but Frank tried his level best to ignore the giant snot bubble threatening to burst when the One-Eyed Willie sniffled.

"What's your name, son," he said, grinding his back teeth against the burning desire to wrap his hands around the bastard's neck and just wring the truth from him. Every second Becky remained unaccounted for was one second too long.

"G-Ghedi," the young pirate whispered, his eye huge as he took in Frank's size and shrank away like Jack must've after he climbed up the beanstalk.

Yeah yeah, Frank got that a lot.

"Well, Ghedi, I know from surveillance photos that at least two of your number are piloting the skiffs back to Africa, but that leaves one of your group unaccounted for. Is he down in the engine room with Becky? Is he somewhere else?"

"No, no, no," Ghedi shook his head, and Frank warily eyed that snot bubble. The thing was going to burst any minute, and he sure as hell didn't want to be anywhere near it when it did. "She alone. Other men, they all on boats back to Somalia. She alone. She all alone, work on engines."

Narrowing his eyes, Frank got as close to the guy's face as he figured was safe, "If you're lying to me, fuck-wad, I'll kill you."

"No lie. No, no, *no* lie."

Bill nudged his arm and leveled his gun at One-Eyed Willie's leaking nose. "Well Boss, let's go get our girl."

Frank didn't bother with a response or wait to give Bill instructions to stay and guard the pirates, he just turned tail and made like Carl Lewis as he raced toward the engine room.

Chapter Four

"HELLO, REBECCA."

The words, spoken over Becky's left shoulder in that deep, grumbling voice, nearly had her dropping the wrench and sliding to a weepy puddle on the floor.

Thank you, sweet Lord, we're saved.

She'd just spent the last three minutes arguing with herself about whether she should ignore Sharif's warning and attempt an escape. She'd figured she could find a nice little hidey-hole, wait for the right moment, then jump out and bash him over the head with the wrench. She'd really enjoy that part—the bashing him over the head part—and of course, she'd have his Glock. But what then? She'd still be locked in the engine room, and the pirates just might take it into their heads to do something terrible to Eve in retaliation.

All that pondering was for naught, because Frank had arrived. The man she admired, respected, and adored from afar—sincc he made it absolutely clear that's as close as he wanted her—had arrived.

Here I come to save the day!

Mighty Mouse maneuver complete. *Finally*.

She considered throwing her hands in the air and crying hallelujah or maybe bursting into soggy tears of gratitude—have herself a real Oprah moment. But that was so cliché, so very damsel-in-distress. Instead, she pasted on a fierce scowl, swung around, and fisted her greasy hands on her equally greasy hips.

"Well, it's about damn time you got here," she groused, tilting her chin far back and letting her eyes drink in Frank's wonderfully familiar face.

The bright overhead lighting—which didn't do a thing to help with the stifling heat in the engine room—highlighted his frame and reminded her just how big he really was. With shoulders like a stevedore, bowling ball-sized muscles in his upper arms, and thighs like a professional baseball catcher, he was a mountain of a man. But he was so precisely proportioned, every part of him so in harmony with the rest, that unless you were standing next to him, you'd never know he was a behemoth.

A wonderful, beautiful behemoth.

Okay, maybe beautiful was pushing things a bit, especially since he had a thick, gruesome scar that slashed through his left eyebrow and a thin white one that cut up from the right corner of his mouth. According to her brother, Frank received the first in a knife fight with a jihadist outside a café in Karachi, Pakistan. The story behind the second one was a mystery no one had been able to solve.

So no, he wasn't beautiful. But his storm-gray eyes were the fiercest she'd ever seen, and his thick, curly, sable-brown hair was as silky and shiny as mink fur. Add those features to a wide forehead and rather full lips, and you came up with an incongruent face that was…well, breathtaking in a brutal, visceral sort of way.

Not that she could see much of that breathtaking face right at the moment, considering it was covered with an uneven pattern of gray/black face paint, and his thick hair was hidden beneath a tight diver's hood. Still, she was able to make out the mocking twist of his lips.

"I wouldn't let you become an operator, so you decide to try your hand at piracy, is that it?" he asked with feigned exasperation.

She stuck her tongue in her cheek and lifted one brow. "A girl's gotta find excitement where she can."

He snorted and let his gaze wander over her, his hard expression suddenly softening.

Okay, yepper, she must look about as good she felt.

"Are you okay?" His tone was unusually gentle.

"I'm just hunky-dory," she reassured him even as hot tears burned the back of her throat and proceeded to make camp in her nose, stinging like a fresh cut doused in alcohol. It was appalling to realize she wanted nothing more than to throw herself into his capable arms and cry, cry, cry herself dry. Just release all the pent-up fear and anxiety of the last six days.

Boy, wouldn't *that* shock the hell out of him? Tough-as-nails Rebel Reichert letting someone bear witness to any vulnerability? Proving, for once, that yes, she was a woman, prone to tears just like the rest of them? And then there'd be the whole touching him thing.

In the three years they'd worked together, she could count the number of times they'd had actual physical contact on two hands. And in each of those instances, he'd jumped away like she was on fire because, you know, he wouldn't want to give her any ideas or anything. Wouldn't want her to start thinking they could have any sort of relationship beyond employer-employee.

So yeah, if she were to leap into his arms and bury her face in his neck, he'd probably need to be fitted for a body bag, and *then* where would she be?

Armed, that's for sure, she thought as she swallowed down the hovering tears and covetously eyed the waterproof M4 strapped across his broad back.

"Did you bring me a weapon?" She raised a finger toward the matte black barrel of the automatic. The smell of him, the smell of hot male skin and salty seawater invaded her nose and made her dizzy. Or maybe it was just the fumes from the busted diesel engines.

That had to be it, because she was *not* the type of namby-pamby girl to get all gooey over one guy's particular aroma. Although…she could admit she was very partial to the way Frank usually smelled. A strange combination of Zest soap, warm leather, and gun oil.

Oh, who was she kidding? She wasn't just partial to the way Frank *smelled*. She was partial to *Frank*. Which only made it that much more infuriating when he treated her like the inconvenient annoyance he had to suffer to maintain the cover for Black Knights Inc.

He grabbed her hand away from his M4, his big palm hot as it briefly encircled her wrist before he quickly released her.

Yepper. Go figure…

"I can do you one better than a weapon." He grinned that endearing lopsided grin of his, the one that always hit her straight in the heart. Pulling out a watermelon-flavored Dum Dum, he brandished it in front of her face, then snatched it out of her reach when she went to swipe it from his grasp.

"What's the magic word?" he taunted.

"Gimme," she growled, eliciting a low bark of laughter that sounded so wonderful she nearly dissolved into a puddle again.

Geez, she needed to get some sleep, or at least take a moment or two to pull herself together before she wimped out and totally ruined her reputation as a hardass. Or did something equally stupid like grab his ears and finally, *finally* do what she'd been dreaming of for the past three-plus years…just lay a big, wet one on him.

Yeah, that'd go over well…

He solicitously handed her the sucker, and she flashed him a dazzling grin tinged with watery gratitude before ripping off the wrapper and shoving the treat in her mouth. Her eyes drifted closed when the sweetness exploded on her tongue.

Those idiot pirates had raided her stash of suckers the very first day of their arrival, and she'd been going through sugar withdrawal ever since.

"I might just leave you a little something in my will for this," she murmured around the sucker.

He grunted as he grabbed her elbow and started escorting her down the metal gangway toward the exit. Okay, and apparently the no-touching rule only applied outside the realm of heroic rescues. In which case, she should seriously think about getting abducted more often.

"What'd you, uh…what'd you do with Sharif?" she asked.

"Who's Sharif?"

"The *interpreter*," she sneered the word, even as her elbow tingled beneath his callused palm. "The guy who's been waving a Glock 19 at the back of my head for the past ten hours."

He skidded to a halt so fast he nearly gave her whiplash. He raised his M4. His thick neck went on swivel.

"What?" she whispered, the fine hairs on her arms twanging upright. Even though the room was easily over a hundred degrees Fahrenheit, an icy chill snaked down her spine. "You didn't apprehend him on your way in?"

"No," he spoke in a rough whisper. "We were told you were alone." He activated his throat mic, "Bill, you there?"

Billy?

She glanced with longing at Frank's right ear and the clear, plastic cord snaking up from his throat mic. She wished she was wearing that earpiece so she could hear Billy's affirmative. She'd missed her big, stupid, lovable brother like crazy, and she very much wanted to ask Frank how many of the guys he'd brought with him. The knowledge that "her boys" would come to rescue her, if she just held on long enough, was what kept her going this past week.

"One-Eyed Willie lied," Frank related to her brother, and if she hadn't been so scared, she would've laughed. He'd come up with the same nickname for Ghedi as she had. "There's a sixth man on board. He was down here guarding your sister, but he ghosted."

He tilted his head, listening to Billy's reply. "Affirmative," he muttered as he used one hand to keep her at his back, his big body shielding her, his weapon quartering the area as he continued to hustle her through the maze of machines toward the exit door.

"That goddamned Ghedi." She peeked from behind

the expanse of his back, expecting Sharif to appear at any moment and start spraying 9 mm rounds.

"I told the guy I'd kill him if he lied to me."

"Don't kill him," she whispered, sorry for Ghedi and the plight of all men like him. "He's just a stupid kid. He probably thought Sharif would somehow manage to save his ass."

"Which way did he go?"

"Sharif? I uh, I didn't really—Geez, sorry," she whispered, tripping over a loose hose. His big palm snapping out was the only thing that kept her from face planting. "He said he was going to pee. I didn't see exactly which direction he headed, but somewhere toward the bow I think."

"How many rounds?"

"Fifteen," she related, delighted to be able to answer his question, hoping she impressed him with her knowledge. "The standard clip size."

"Extra mags?"

"Not that I saw."

"Okay, here's what we're gonna do, we're gonna—"

"You're going to drop your weapon and kick it away," Sharif said, stepping out from behind a large instrument panel and moving behind Becky, snaking a sweaty arm around her throat and pressing the barrel of his Glock tight against her right temple.

She was getting really sick and tired of having guns shoved against her head, not to mention the smell of Sharif's overpowering cologne had mixed with his sweat and body odor over the last ten hours to create a sickly aroma that triggered her gag reflex.

As fastidious as the guy appeared to be, upchucking

all over his arm might be just the thing to get him to release her.

She was considering doing just that when she suddenly sensed a...*readiness* in Frank. At the sound of Sharif's command, he'd frozen in front of her. Her fingers, where she was holding on to his gear belt, felt every hard muscle in his wide back tense into living stone. He didn't turn around, didn't so much as twitch, but she held her breath, waiting for his next move.

Sharif must have sensed it as well, the crackle of electricity in the air. "Whatever you are considering doing, you should dismiss it right this instant. I have a gun to Miss Reichert's head, and I will blow her brains all over your back before you so much as have the chance to turn around. Now drop your weapon and kick it away!"

"Don't do it—"

She winced when she heard the hard clank of the M4 hitting the metal decking. It made a terrible screeching sound as Frank booted it across the floor.

"Now your reserve weapon," Sharif demanded. When Frank bent quickly, Sharif's Glock jabbed harder into her temple as he barked, "Slowly!"

Frank complied, carefully bending to remove the Springfield Armory XD-45 from his ankle holster. He flung it over to join his M4 before straightening.

She once more grabbed on to his gear belt, taking comfort in the feel of his hard muscles against the backs of her fingers and the more lethal hardness of...

Oh, Frank, you wonderful, lovely man.

Okay, so Sharif now had them at a distinct disadvantage, considering he was the only one with a gun. Fortunately, he wasn't the only one with a *weapon*, because it wasn't just Frank's taut muscles brushing against her fingers. The deadly length of his seven-inch KA-BAR was right there, too.

Who brought a knife to a gunfight?

Frank Knight, that's who.

Frank figured he was going to need a body bag—triple XL—when Becky's fingers covertly reached into the back of his gear belt, silently withdrawing the deadly length of his KA-BAR. With the three of them crowded up against each other, front to back, Sharif couldn't see that she was in the process of stealthily removing his knife from its sheath at his back and transferring it into the front pocket of her shorts.

Oh man, Rebecca. That's a supremely bad idea!

But there was nothing he could do or say as Sharif commanded, "Hands over your head!"

Yeah, yeah. You're in charge, you fucking fancy-talking pirate.

He gritted his teeth as he reached for the ceiling. His trick shoulder had been whimpering ever since he'd Spider-Manned it up the side of the ship in order to reach their access point. Now that he was holding it above his head? Man, it was flat out shrieking.

Of course, that was the least of his worries considering ol' Sharif was equipped with fifteen rounds of lead death while Rebel Reichert had just armed herself with seven inches of carbon steel.

"Now move to the right, over into that corner," Sharif demanded, and Frank had no choice but to obey. He took six steps to his right, wedging himself into a tight space between the bulkhead and a piece of machinery with about a zillion switches that gouged into his side like sharp, bony fingers.

"Don't turn around!" Sharif screeched when he started to do just that. "Keep facing the wall."

Becky yelped at something Sharif did to her and Frank growled, the sound low and menacing as he rhythmically clenched his hands above his head. The muscles in his arms coiled and uncoiled, coiled and uncoiled.

Grinding his jaw hard enough to pulverize his teeth to dust, he listened intently as the two of them shuffled over to where he'd kicked the M4 and his reserve. The automatic made a familiar *clacking* sound as Sharif swung it over his shoulder and the .45 shushed as the fancy pirate shoved it into the waistband of his shorts.

"Now I'm going to count to ten," Sharif explained quickly, panting slightly.

The guy was panicking.

Not good. Not fucking good at all.

Panic could easily make a man forget just how much pressure he was applying with his trigger finger.

And the thought of losing Becky like that—

No. He couldn't even contemplate it without having to suppress the urge to throw up. And right now he didn't have that luxury. He needed all his senses and wits about him if he was going to get them both out of this clusterfuck of a situation alive.

"If you so much as twitch before I finish," Sharif sneered, "I'll splatter her brains all over this engine room!"

And there you go. His worst nightmare put into words. He screwed his eyes shut and prayed to God Becky wouldn't do anything stupid. The woman had more guts than most men twice her size, and he respected the shit out of her for it, but she didn't have the reflexes or the training needed to get out of this situation unscathed. Sharif had three weapons to her one, which meant the guy had all the advantages. He only hoped she realized this and acted accordingly.

"One, two..." As Sharif started his countdown, Frank's heart double-timed it, pounding in his ears so loudly it was difficult to hear the man's voice as he moved Becky toward the exit. "...five, six..." The sound echoed dully, and he slowed his breathing, visualized his next move. "...eight..." His muscles coiled one last time. "...nine..." The Pentagon Elite II blade strapped to his chest was a comforting weight. "...ten."

In a lightning-fast series of fluid movements, he burst from the cramped corner, reached under his web gear, unfolded the knife from its Kevlar-reinforced handle with a satisfying *snick*, caught sight of Sharif's dark head above Becky's blond one, and sent the stainless steel blade zinging through the air.

A split second before the knife would have embedded itself between Sharif's villainous eyes, the guy slammed shut the airlock door. The blade bounced off the reinforced glass porthole at the top of the hatchway with a loud *clink*, but inside the engine room the sound was drowned out by his enraged roar.

Becky...no!

—◦◦◦—

"Everybody back to the bridge!"

Eve was milling around the deck with the rest of the *Hamilton*'s thirty-some-odd crew members, still trying to absorb the astonishing fact that less than ten minutes ago she'd been liberated by a group of three dripping-wet, black-clad men who'd suddenly appeared like phantoms from out of the darkness of the night. They'd managed to disarm or otherwise incapacitate each and every one of the pirates.

And all in about six seconds.

It'd been a sight to see, that was for sure. Catlike reflexes and precisely choreographed movements. The pirates hadn't known what hit them.

Eve didn't know what'd hit *her*.

Because Becky hadn't been suffering from insanity brought on by heatstroke. He was here...

Billy Reichert was right in front of her, and he certainly wasn't a mere motorcycle mechanic. Heavens, no. He looked more like the real-life version of Jason Bourne or Ethan Hunt. And he was yelling for everyone to return to the stifling bridge where the pirates had been holding them, shoving those people who didn't move quickly enough to suit him. He was...well, he was not what she remembered at all.

"You too, Eve." He barely looked at her, but even his brief glance was enough show his eyes, those chocolaty brown eyes she'd fallen in love with as a girl, were no longer soft and warm. The light shining through them was fierce, almost feral, like a wild animal.

Geez Louise.

A shiver raced down her spine despite the heat of the night. She'd never been afraid of Billy, not all those years ago when he'd been a bad boy from the wrong side of town. But looking at the hard set of his jaw, at the barely leashed power in the bulging muscles of his shoulders, it occurred to her that the tender boy she'd known was gone, replaced by this hard, callous man... this *dangerous* man.

"Why?" she asked as she tried to still the pounding of her heart. "What's happening?"

"Becky's in trouble," he said, hustling her across the deck. "The guy who was guarding her is missing."

Eve opened her mouth but didn't manage to utter a word as Becky's terrified voice broke through the confusion on deck. "Billy!"

Eve turned, along with the rest of the crowd shoving to get in the door leading to the *Hamilton*'s bridge, and her stomach sunk to her toes. The muttering of the group sputtered to a halt as everyone slowly realized what was happening.

Sharif stood in the center of the deck with one arm around Becky's throat, keeping her in front of him as a living shield while he pressed the hard barrel of his handgun to her temple.

"Stay back!" he yelled when Billy coiled like a spring, ready to pounce.

"Just let her go!" Billy demanded. But Sharif paid him no mind as he dragged Becky toward the *Hamilton*'s portside railing. The harsh lights shining onto the deck from the top of the bridge spotlighted the two of them like a movie set.

It was totally surreal...and totally terrifying.

"Boss?" Billy said, pressing his thumb and forefinger against the strange black band he wore around his throat while he tracked Becky and Sharif's movements with deadly end of his big, intimidating gun. "You copy? Our sixth target is topside with Becky in tow." He paused, listening, then cursed viciously before finishing with a grumbled, "Roger that."

"Stay back! Stay back! I'll shoot her!" Sharif screeched, his black eyes darting between the crowd of the *Hamilton*'s crew bunched at the door and the right side of the bridge house. One of the men who'd arrived with Billy stopped dead in his tracks. He'd been slinking around the bridge house, trying to outflank Sharif.

"Eve," Billy whispered, never taking his eyes off his sister.

"Yes?" she rasped, noting he was beginning to inch to the side, making Sharif split his attention between him and the other guy with a monstrous black machine gun.

"When he's not looking, I need you to slip back through the crowd, make your way down to the engine room, and unlock the door."

Gulp.

"O-okay," she said, even though the very last thing she wanted to do was go crawling around, *alone*, in the bowels of the tanker.

You can do this, Eve Edens. You can do it for Becky.

Her legs were trembling as she waited until Sharif was distracted by the man near the bridge house, then she inched backward and began pushing her way very carefully and very quietly through the *Hamilton*'s gawking crew. "Move, move, *move!*" she muttered beneath her breath as she slithered between the crush of sweaty bodies.

Finally, she made her way to the interior of the ship, ignoring the gloomy corners and dark stairwells as she used her years of yachting to direct her toward the engine room. Racing along the metal gangways, she didn't make one wrong turn. Of course, she was helped by the fact that once she got close, she heard an unholy clambering and what sounded like a lion's roar.

The clambering turned out to be the third man who'd arrived with Billy, the *giant* one. He was bashing a huge wrench against the glass porthole on the airlock door to the engine room. And the lion's roar was coming from him, as well.

Holy moley!

She swallowed past the dry knot of fear clogging her throat, licked her parched lips, and reminded herself that this wasn't a monstrous creature but a man. A guy. One of the *good* guys even.

On three, she told herself, then did a quick countdown before turning the wheel. No sooner had the lock released than the door burst open, slamming against the bulkhead. She instinctively jumped back, but the giant didn't spare her a glance. He just barged past her, his soft Neoprene wet suit boots pounding up the metal stairs.

Chapter Five

SHARIF—*THAT ASSHOLE*—WAS A DEAD MAN.

No one put a loaded gun to Becky's head and lived to tell about it.

"Are you in position?" Bill's low voice rumbled through Frank's earpiece.

"Affirmative." He crouched behind a small shipping container located about twenty yards from where Sharif stood with Becky against the *Hamilton*'s portside railing.

When Sharif attempted to step over the top rung, he and his guys would make their moves. He only hoped Becky didn't try to "help out" before then. If…no, when, *when* he got her out of this, he was going to take her home, lock her inside the Knights' compound, and throw away the goddamned key.

It was just too dangerous letting Rebel Reichert wander about. And after this night, he figured he'd need, oh, about two years of absolute peace and quiet before his blood pressure dropped back down to levels his doctor wouldn't blow a gasket over.

"He's going to do it," Angel's ragged voice whispered in his ear. "He's going to jump."

"He'll have to let go of her to step over that railing. When he does, you take him out," he ordered, his heart thundering in nervous anticipation.

Angel was in the best position to put a bullet in Sharif's brainpan, and Frank hoped like hell the guy was as good as he promised. It made his balls turn to raisins having to put that much faith in the abilities of an unknown, but what other option did he have? Bill wasn't in a position to take the shot, and he was without the *means* to take the shot.

Of course, that didn't mean he was totally unarmed.

He had a pair of French-made throwing knives held loosely in each fist. They had little, hidden vials of liquid mercury that would keep the blades oriented forward when he hurled them at his target.

Now, as a rule, he wasn't too partial to the French. They tended to be too effeminate for his tastes, and he could not listen to them speak English without thinking of Pepé Le Pew. "I am zee peanut butter; you are zee jelly. Come, cherie, let us make a sandwich of luuuv."

That being said, he had to give credit where credit was due. They made one helluva set of throwing knives, and if Angel's shot missed its mark, he was right there ready to replace a lead round with a steel blade.

"Wait for it," he whispered as Sharif swung one leg over the railing. "Wait until she's clear…Ah, goddamnit!"

Becky whirled on Sharif like a dervish as soon as he lowered his weapon to balance himself, whipping out Frank's razor sharp KA-BAR from where she'd hidden it in her shorts and driving all seven inches into the guy's gun hand. Sharif squealed like the pig he was, dropping his Glock over the side as Becky lunged at him.

Sonofa—

Frank burst from his hiding spot, "Take the shot! Take the shot!" he yelled as he freight-trained it toward the struggling pair.

"She's not clear!" Angel's voice blasted into his ear.

Motherfucker! He didn't have a shot either. Becky's blond head kept bopping in the way as she played conquering heroine and valiantly struggled with the guy.

Frank threw every ounce of strength he had into making it those last fifteen yards. Becky managed to land a hard elbow to Sharif's nose—*that-a-girl*—causing blood to spray in a wide arc that glistened in the bright illumination of the bridge's spotlights.

Dazed, Sharif stumbled backward, and with one foot already on the ocean side of the railing, it was all the impetus needed to have him slipping right over the edge. He scrambled to grab onto the top rung, but with the KA-BAR skewering his right hand like a shrimp on the barbie, his fingers refused to work.

His left hand found its grip, however…in Becky's long ponytail.

Frank saw it all happen in slow motion. Sharif windmilling backward over the railing with one arm while he used the other to jerk Becky headfirst after him.

Good Lord! Frank couldn't get his legs to work right.

It felt like he was running through sticky molasses, and no matter how hard he pumped his arms and pleaded with his legs to turn faster, he seemed to be humping it at one-quarter speed. His terrified heart threatened to explode. *Boom!* Lights out!

No, no, *no!*

This couldn't be happening. Not to Becky.

And then, like a hiccup in a stop-motion film, he was suddenly there, at the railing, just as her feet slipped over the top rung.

He had only one chance.

Dropping his knife, he plunged one arm through the space between the top rail and the one below it, managing to snag her slender ankle. He was instantly jerked forward by the combined momentum of her and Sharif's falling bodies, and his head slammed into the top rung. *Bam!* A bright burst of stars circled in front of his eyes as, with a hard thump, Becky and Sharif simultaneously crashed against the *Hamilton*'s hull.

That's when it happened.

He felt it.

His shoulder just...wow, it just...gave way. Bone and muscle and tendons tearing away and snapping. The sharp blast of agonizing pain was quickly followed by burning numbness, and then the weight pulling against him suddenly disappeared.

Oh sweet lovin' Lord, no!

He'd dropped her! She'd slipped through his numb fingers and...

With a roar of gut-wrenching fury, he managed to blink away the happy stars giddily swirling in front of his vision to peek over the side and—

Oh, thank God.

He still had her. She was flailing and cursing and trying to grab onto the hull, but he still had her. Sharif—*that asshole*—wasn't so lucky. He'd lost his hold on her hair and was falling, screaming, into the sea below.

Good riddance.

With a mighty heave, his wet suit boots scrabbling for purchase on the deck, Frank started reeling her in. And then his feet slipped, jerking him hard against the railing until all he could do was grit his teeth and hang on. Just when he thought he might lose her for real, Bill

and Angel were there beside him, reaching over the top
rung and grabbing her legs.

*Thank you, thank you, thank you, dear sweet Lord...
and Bill and Angel.*

Only when Becky was safely in her brother's arms,
Bill crooning, "You're okay. We gotcha," did Frank
manage to uncurl his fingers from their death grip
around her slim ankle.

Interesting. He had absolutely no feeling in that hand.

Staggering back, he glanced up to see Angel quartering
the sea below with his M4. After a few moments, the guy
turned with a shrug, "I don't know. Maybe the fall stunned
him, and he drowned. I can't see...oh, um, Boss?"

"Yeah?" Frank frowned at Angel's strangely appre-
hensive face.

"That, um, that does not look too good." He pointed
at Frank's right arm.

Frank glanced down and noticed, with a sort of odd
detachment, that his hand was dangling at an unnatural
angle against his thigh.

"Dislocated," he said, not giving a rat's ass about his
arm. All that mattered was Becky. That she was safe...

"I think it's more than that," Angel murmured, then
suddenly spun on his heel, racing back to the railing.

A grumbling roar managed to split through the loud
ringing in Frank's ears, then Angel was discharging
his weapon. The harsh *thump, thump, thump* of the M4
sounded curiously muted, and no matter how hard he
tried, he couldn't seem to remember what the guy was
shooting at.

Angel swung around a few moments later, his face
fixed in hard lines. "So he didn't drown. He's on the

catamaran, and I managed to take out one engine, but"—he shook his head—"he's too far out of range now."

Ah, yes. Sharif—that asshole. That's what Angel was shooting at. Now he remembered…

"Call it in," he instructed, wondering why it sounded like he was talking through a tunnel.

"That's a pretty bad bump on your head, Boss," Bill said, and when Frank turned to glance at him, the guy's face looked all wonky. "You're bleeding like a stuck pig."

I am?

"Frank?" Becky stepped toward him, her gorgeous brown eyes dark with worry inside a face that was as funky-looking as Bill's.

He didn't care. She was still beautiful and, more importantly, she was safe. And when she said his name, *Frank*, in that dusky voice, he wanted to whoop with joy. Oh, how he'd missed the sound of her—

Whoa.

Why the hell was the deck suddenly rushing up to meet him?

———

Wowza. Whoever came up with the expression, "falling like a ton of bricks," must've seen something very similar to Frank's nose dive into the *Hamilton*'s deck. Becky dropped to her knees beside him, calling his name, but he was out cold. Stone cold. The gash along his hairline leaked thick rivulets of dark blood all over his pale face and onto the deck.

This was bad. This was real bad.

Losing consciousness after a head injury was a sure

sign of concussion, and she knew from the elementary medical training she'd received from Steady, a concussion could sometimes turn deadly. You could just slip into a sleep from which there was no return...

"Frank," she whispered his name, gently shaking his good shoulder as anguish burned up the back of her throat like nitric acid. "Wake up now, Frank. You're too tough to let something like a bump on the head bring you down."

Nothing. Not so much as a twitch.

Oh God. If he died while saving her, she'd never forgive herself. She'd never—

No. No way. He wasn't going out like that. Not the legendary Boss Knight.

"Frank," she nudged him harder, pressing the gauze pad Angel handed her against the deep cut on his forehead. The tears she'd been holding at bay for nearly a week finally burst through the emotional barriers she'd erected, flowing hot and salty down her cheeks as her racing heart threatened to shatter into a thousand little pieces.

Looking at him lying there, so still and pale without the bright vigor that usually animated him, made her more scared than she'd ever been in her life—which was saying something considering mere moments before she took a header off the side of an oil tanker.

Just when she was about to press a finger to his carotid to check for a pulse, his gray eyes fluttered open and lasered in on her. He lifted his good hand to rub at the swelling lump on the side of her cheek where her face had introduced itself to the *Hamilton*'s steel hull.

"Are you okay?" he rasped.

Are you okay…

He was bleeding profusely, undoubtedly concussed, and that arm was certainly dislocated if not broken, and he was asking *her* if *she* was okay.

God love the man. She certainly did…

Hiccupping on the tears clogging her throat and running down her cheeks, she managed, "Thanks to you I am."

He blinked at her, then frowned.

"You're crying." He said it like one might say, *I believe in unicorns*, with a heavy dose of incredulity.

"Yep." She wiped her runny nose on her forearm—gross, but she was without another option. "I do that sometimes." Way more often than she'd ever admit to anyone, especially him.

"Don't."

"You can't tell me whether I can or can't cry, Frank. Geez." Although, she was so glad to see him awake and talking, she couldn't quite imbibe the comment with her usual level of sarcasm.

"Nothing to shed tears over, woman," he told her, wincing when she lifted the gauze to check on his cut. The bleeding had slowed. Angel handed her another pad, and she pressed the fresh gauze to his forehead. "You lived, didn't you?"

"I'm not crying over my near face-plant into the ocean, you big, dumb dill-hole. I'm crying because you scared me to death when you fainted."

His lips twisted. "Men don't faint. I just…I…uh… lost consciousness."

"God, whatever," she huffed, but inwardly she was smiling.

It didn't matter that he was determined to keep their relationship on a strictly professional level. It didn't matter that most times she irritated the ever-lovin' hell out of him and he had no qualms about letting her know it. It didn't even matter that he kept a girlfriend up in Lincoln Park. What mattered, *all* that mattered, was that he was alive. Because she couldn't stand the thought of a world without him…

"My point is," she continued, smoothing some hair back from his forehead, reveling in the fact that she was able to touch him like she'd always dreamed of doing, even if it was only because he'd been knocked silly and didn't have all his faculties about him, "you went nose first into the deck and were out for nearly thirty seconds. That combined with the fact that you look like a piece of meat that's been through the garbage disposal frightened me. And *yes*, when I get really frightened, sometimes I cry. Just deal with it."

He blinked at her for several seconds like he was having trouble focusing. "No need to be scared for me. Imokay." He crushed the last two words together as he struggled to sit up.

Testosterone. God save her.

"No, no." She laid a palm on his uninjured shoulder. "Just be still."

"Can't," he said, pushing past her restraining hand and into a sitting position. "Hafta finish the mission. Hafta get going."

"It's finished," she assured him. "You saved us."

"Yeah." He shook his head like a dog shakes off water, dislodging the gauze pad and causing little drops of blood to splash across her tank top. "Sorry 'bout that," he said as he pushed to a wobbly stand—as if a little blood on top of all the grease and grime was anything to worry about. No amount of washing was ever going to get her tank top and shorts clean again. The only logical future for the garments was an up close and personal introduction to an incinerator. "But now we've got to ghost it out of here," he finished, swaying slightly.

"What?" she swung toward her brother. "What's he talking about?"

Billy's lips curled in as his hard jaw sawed back and forth. It was his classic you're-not-going-to-like-what-I-have-to-tell-you expression. He'd donned it fairly regularly since they were kids, and it never boded well.

"Out with it," she demanded, hands on hips.

"He's right. It's the only way to maintain our cover," Billy explained. "Besides you and Eve, no one on board the *Hamilton* knows who we are. It'll be hard to keep it that way if we don't get out of here now."

"Okay, but...but where will you go?" They were all certifiably nuts. Frank was in no condition to—

"Back to the USS *Patton*, the destroyer we arrived on. She's anchored a few miles out. Once on board, we'll sail over here and pick up you and Eve and any of the *Hamilton*'s crew that needs medical attention."

"*He* needs medical attention!" she yelled, pointing at Frank's freaky-looking arm.

"Just need to pop it back into place," Frank said, his tone similar to the one he might use for *pass the potatoes*. She spun to glare at him, letting him read in the her face exactly what she was thinking in her head—which was that they were all frickin' frackin' crazy.

That arm was...well, it was not right. He should

be medevacked to the nearest hospital, raced into surgery and—

"Will you do the honors?" he asked, turning to Angel and completely ignoring the fact that her head was threatening to explode.

"No, he most certainly will n—"

That's all she got out before Angel grabbed his arm and with a twist and a shove snapped the appendage back into place.

Oh, sweet Jesus, the sound it made. She figured she'd hear it in her nightmares.

"Once on board the *Patton*," Billy told her, drawing her attention away from the makeshift sling Angel started fastening out of bungee cords, "you can't let on that you know us, or that we're the ones who facilitated the rescue. Except for the captain and the commander, the entire crew thinks we're simple K&R specialists hired by Eve's father to secure your ransoms."

"Okay," she said absently, sneaking a peek over at the slapdash field dressing that was going on, "but I still think—"

"Let's do it," Frank said, wiping the blood out of his eyes with the hand that wasn't secured in the temporary sling.

"You can't possibly think to—" she began, but none of them were listening to her. They all started jogging across the deck, making their way toward the aft of the drifting ship.

She raced after them. "Stop!" She tried pulling on Billy's arm, but with the disparity in their weights, it was like trying to halt an elephant. "Billy," she pleaded, "he can't make—"

Her brother spun and slapped a hard palm over her mouth, his eyes bright with fury. He nodded for Boss and Angel to continue when they stopped to glance at him over their shoulders.

"I'm right behind you," he assured them and once they were out of earshot growled, "This is how it's done, sis. You wanna be an operator? Well, an operator protects his cover, through injury, through torture...hell, he'll even die to protect it. So you go on back to Eve, impress upon her just how important it is that she keep her damn mouth shut, and I'll see you on board the *Patton*. Do you understand me? Nod if you understand me."

What could she do? She nodded.

Billy gave her one last probing look before he raced to catch the others, and she could only watch helplessly as, one by one, they disappeared over the side of the tanker and into the starlit night.

"*Aahhhh!*" Sharif screamed as he pulled the big knife from the center of his right palm, biting his cheek against the mind-bending pain until the bright coppery taste of blood filled his mouth.

He threw the blade over the railing with a vicious curse and ripped off his wet shirt, clumsily trying to secure it around his useless hand.

"That bitch," he whispered, managing to use his left hand and his teeth to tighten the makeshift bandage. The maneuver ignited a flame of hot agony that exploded up the length of his arm and detonated at the base of his skull.

That bitch...

Staggering, swallowing down the urge to vomit, he grabbed the smooth wooden steering wheel and squeezed his eyes closed, sucking in ragged breaths and praying for the weakness to pass.

When it finally did, *finally*, he blinked open his eyes and turned to glance behind him. The smoke from the ruined engine parted for a brief moment and in the blackness of the nighttime ocean, he saw the bright lights of the *Hamilton* on the far horizon. It was a shining, taunting beacon heralding the position of the prize that would have allowed him to leave this distasteful business once and for all.

"That bitch! That bitch! That *bitch!*" he yelled over and over, pounding his fist against the wheel and imagining it was her pretty American face.

If she had not stalled, if she had not had the audacity to ignore his repeated threats to blister her soft hide for every minute she dawdled at tasks he knew she could have accomplished in moments, she would have had those big diesel engines repaired, and *he* would have been sailing back toward the Somali coast aboard a multimillion dollar trophy instead of this ridiculous sailboat.

"I will kill her," he vowed, grinding his teeth as he tucked his ruined right hand up into his armpit. With a shriek of vitriolic agony, he applied, what he hoped, was enough pressure to stop the bleeding. "I will find her," he panted through the pain. "I will find her and show her what a woman's true place is in this world…and then I will kill her."

"So does this pass muster?" Becky asked Billy and

Angel as she held out her arms and pirouetted. "Am I allowed to go see Frank now?"

The wait for the USS *Patton*'s arrival after the guys disappeared over the side of the tanker had seemed interminable, and she knew her pacing made everybody onboard the *Hamilton*, especially Eve, nervous, but she wasn't able to help it. All manner of horrific scenarios had flashed through her brain, not the least of which being Frank eaten by a huge great white shark because he'd been bleeding into the water.

She kept seeing that mammoth shark from *Jaws*, and that creepy *da-da…da-da…da-da-da-da* music circled endlessly through her brain. Add in the horrific picture show of those last seconds with Sharif at the rail, the certainty she'd felt that they were her final moments, and it was an understatement to say she was going nuts. Just when she was on the verge of screaming and pulling out her hair, the big destroyer arrived on the black horizon, its sparkling lights like a lodestar in the night.

She and Eve were the first to transfer aboard where they were met by Billy and Angel. Both men looked rather guileless in their civilian clothes and anyone seeing their innocent, freshly scrubbed faces wouldn't believe they'd just frogmanned a pretty spectacular rescue.

Oh, but they had.

"Hello, Miss Reichert, Miss Edens," Billy shook their hands. "I'm Vinnie, and this is Bruce," he said as he nodded to Angel. "We're here to negotiate your ransom, but uh," he shuffled his feet and grinned—he stopped just short of *aw shucks-ing* it, and she fought the urge to roll her eyes—"I guess that's a moot point now, isn't it? Still, your father is paying us hourly, Miss Edens, so we'll do our best to see to your comfort until we can get you both home."

Under the watchful eyes of the destroyer's crew, she and Eve carefully played their parts, shaking hands with the men and feigning unfamiliarity. But as soon as the four of them were alone, trudging down a metal gangway, she snorted, "Vinnie and Bruce, is it? And is Mark down in sick bay?"

Billy glanced at her over his shoulder, his eyes widening in feigned surprise. "As a matter of fact, he is. How in the world did you know?"

She shook her head and chuckled. Leave it to her big brother to come up with aliases that all just happened to be the names of the transient band members of KISS.

"How is he?"

"He's fine," Billy answered.

"He's fine," Angel echoed from behind.

Pfft. "Well, then, when can I go and see *Mark*?"

"After you shower, my dear girl," her brother told her, stopping before a metal door labeled *women*. "Not to be rude, but you two smell like something that recently crawled out from under a rock…at the dump… one that was sitting in the Porta-Potty section."

From the corner of her eye, Becky saw Eve's tired face glow crimson in the artificial overhead light.

Poor Eve. She'd always been particularly vulnerable to Billy's bad manners.

"Geez, Billy," she growled, "tell us how you really feel, why dontcha?"

"I just did," he grinned as he held the door wide, handing her and Eve each a towel and a stack of clean, folded clothes.

The shower was heaven, and she heard Eve's deep groan of pleasure from the stall next door, but she didn't dilly-dally. She wanted to see Frank. She *needed* to see Frank in order to assess his situation for herself. Angel and Billy were obviously complete crap at accurately diagnosing a man's injuries, evidenced by their quick assurances that he was absolutely fine.

He was not. How could he be? His arm was nearly ripped off!

After quickly scrubbing away the grease and grime of nearly a week, she put on the warm-up suit someone— one of the female crew members, she suspected—had loaned her. Slipping on the pair of blue hospital booties, she opened the door to find both men waiting.

Which was why she was twirling, arms held out, in order to give Billy and Angel a good gander at the racy, red, über-chic, cotton warm-up. Someone shopped at *Victoria's Secret*. She made a mental note to find her mysterious benefactor and thank the woman.

"Angel's going to take you down to sick bay," her brother informed her. "I'll wait here for Eve."

She folded her arms and scowled up at him. "You be nice to her."

Billy's jaw locked, and she tried not to roll her eyes. That hard-ass expression of his might work on some. Not her.

"I was never anything *but* nice to her," he grumbled.

"Pfft," she punched him in the shoulder and gave up on not rolling her eyes. "I'm serious. She's been through a lot. The last thing she needs is you rehashing the past."

"Since when do I ever rehash?" He planted his fists on his hips. She called it his Superman pose. It made the little sister in her want to hold her finger an inch from his nose while chanting, "I'm not touching you, I'm not touching you…"

She resisted the urge, saying instead, "Just don't mention—"

"Becky," he growled, "I swear, after all you've put me through this week, I'm going to wring your neck if you don't turn tail and run."

It was his favorite threat, one he'd once made good on when she was five and he was ten. Although at the time, he hadn't understood what the expression actually meant, so he'd taken a big black permanent marker, held her down, and drawn fat circles around her neck.

As punishment, their father forbade him to play Nintendo until the evidence disappeared completely. And she—never having been one for vanity—had delighted in "forgetting" to wash her neck. The humiliation of wearing the black smudges was nothing compared to the sheer joy of watching Billy gaze longingly at his Super Mario Bros. cartridge.

It'd taken weeks for the marks to vanish and to this day, she couldn't help but grin every time he repeated that particular threat.

Ow!

Damn, that hurt. Her injured cheek wasn't quite ready for grinning yet.

Note to self. No overly demonstrative facial expressions.

Billy patted at his pockets. "I know I've got a marker around here somewhere…"

"All right, all right," she capitulated. "I'm going. But you're a greasy, grimy monkey turd," she called over her shoulder as she darted down the gangway, Angel following behind her.

"Grow up!" her brother hollered back.

"A greasy, grimy monkey turd with fish lips and bird legs and the brain power of an amoeba!" she yelled, joy and relief at finally, *finally* being back where she belonged making her voice bright.

"Oh yeah?" Billy just couldn't let her have the last word. It would've gone against twenty-six years of tradition. "Well, you look like a can of smashed buttholes, and your breath smells like you eat used kitty litter!"

Her laughter echoed through the ship.

Man, it's good to be back.

Chapter Six

"I FEEL LIKE A NEW WOMAN," EVE SAID AS SHE EMERGED from the women's shower room, and Bill's laughter at his little sister's crazy antics died like a grease fire doused in baking soda.

Eve was dressed in a royal blue version of the cotton warm-up Becky'd worn—Angel had wheedled the clothes out of some starry-eyed female sailor—only on Eve's 5'10" frame, the hems of the legs hit her mid-calf.

Still, she managed to pull it off. Oh hell, who was he trying to kid? She made the damn things look like they were supposed to be those short little island pants women donned when the weather turned warm. The kind of pants she'd worn that summer they dated. The kind of pants she'd paired with a super sexy set of wedge heel thingamabobs that'd made her mile-long legs look even longer.

Some things never changed. Just his goddamned luck.

"You don't look like a new woman," he told her. "You look exactly the same way you did eleven years ago."

Without a week's worth of grime and grit covering her face, she was just as drop-dead gorgeous as he remembered...unfortunately.

"Where's Becky?" she asked, ignoring his last statement even though a blush climbed up her throat to stain her cheeks.

"She went to check on our boss."

"Good, I'll go join her." She nibbled on her lower lip like she always did when she was nervous. The gesture was so familiar, reminding him of everything that happened between them, and he couldn't stop the sudden fury that raced through his veins. "I want to tell her that I…Hey! What are you doing?"

What was he doing?

He was frog-marching her toward the briefing room Captain Garcia had allocated for the Knights' personal use, that's what he was doing.

It was amazing how the years just…fell away. Leaving room for all the old hurts to come rushing in.

"You can go see Becky later. For now, you and I need to talk."

"I…I don't know what we have to say to one another," she stammered, her big eyes wide. "It's been over a decade. S-surely we can just let bygones b-be bygones."

"If it was up to me, I'd take you up on that, sweetheart. But it's not up to me."

She sucked in a stunned breath before she ripped her arm out of his grasp. "Don't call me sweetheart, and *don't* touch me! You lost that right eleven years ago!"

"Lost the right!" he bellowed at her. It was as if he was a twenty-year-old kid again, with the same twenty-year-old temper. "You obviously have a very selective memory, *sweetheart*."

"Oh!" she stomped her foot, and *there* was the pampered little princess who'd broken his heart. He unceremoniously shoved her into the briefing room and kicked out a chair. Motioning for her to sit with a hard point of his finger.

She threw her nose in the air and crossed her arms over her chest.

God*damn*it!

He wasn't handling this well, but she always did that to him. Made him act out of character.

Whenever she was around, he felt the need to beat his chest and knock heads together, and the whole thing was as disconcerting as it was ridiculous. "Eve," he growled. "Just take a damn seat. I promise you I'm not here to rehash the past. Whether you believe it or not, there are more important things to discuss."

"Like what?" she asked, still refusing to sit.

Fine. Let her stand. He, for one, was beat.

He plopped down in a chair on the opposite side of the conference table and scrubbed a hand over his face. Sighing heavily, he said, "Like the fact that you can't tell anyone, I mean *no one*, not even beloved Daddy, about me or my partners' involvement in this little endeavor."

"But…why?" She obviously chose to ignore his slur against her father.

"Because one of the things that makes us so effective is the simple fact that no one knows the true nature of our work—besides the President and his Joint Chiefs, of course." And now the two commanding officers of this naval ship. *Damn it!*

"You're kidding me," she shook her head, eyes darting around the room as if trying to find the hidden cameras. Only no one was going to jump out from behind the door and yell, *You've been punk'd!*

Nope. Not this time.

"Becky said you guys were private government

defense contractors. There are tons of those, so I don't know why—"

"We're more than that," he told her. "Much more."

"But…but," she shook her head again.

Yeah, a lot of folks had trouble believing the reality of 007 when they were faced with it. Probably because the real-life version was so much less sexy. Blood and guts and days spent wallowing in your own smelly sweat certainly weren't "martinis, shaken not stirred."

"But the captain and his first mate know who you really are. Becky told me so."

"Yeah, they do, and don't think for one minute it didn't burn our asses to blow our covers." He didn't bother to correct her terminology in reference to the commander.

"But Dad is going to wonder what happened to me. He's going to ask…" She started chewing on her lower lip again.

"So tell him the truth. A group of spec-ops guys rescued you and then disappeared. End of story."

"But that's *not* the end of the story, and I've never lied to him."

"It's not a lie, Eve," he grumbled, frustrated. "It's an omission."

"Lie, omission, they're the same thing, and I don't understand why I'd need to compromise my relationship with my father just so—"

He growled, slamming a palm on the table and causing her to flinch.

Good. Great. She needed to be scared. She had no idea the power of the powder keg of information parked beneath her oh-so-fine ass.

"Let me rephrase," he enunciated slowly, "you *will* keep this to yourself."

She searched his face for a brief second, her rapid breath causing her chest to heave, before she cautiously lowered herself into the seat he'd kicked out.

Finally.

He was getting a damn crick in his neck looking up at her.

"The things we do, the things we're *tasked* to do, don't necessarily fall under the guidelines of international law. This mission included. And given that, there are quite a few really, really bad guys out there who'd love to know our true identities."

"But I don't know any bad guys," she murmured.

"Maybe not. But you of all people know how quickly rumors fly." Being the daughter of one of the richest men in America, she'd graced the cover of more than one tabloid.

"So you're telling me…*What* are you telling me? That our government sanctions illegal activity? That you guys are the ones they call to conduct it?"

"Which is harder to believe? The fact that our government skirts the boundaries of global bureaucracy or the fact that they trust me, a gearhead from the projects, to do the honors?"

She stared at him for a long moment, her eyes filling with tears that she tried to blink away. His damn ulcer lifted its head at the sight and started gnawing away at his stomach again.

Good going, Bill. Way to put the "ass" in class.

"I never cared where you were from, Billy," she whispered. "You were the one who had a problem with it."

"Fine. Whatever." He shook his head, feeling like someone should probably kick his ass for the way he was treating her, but he just couldn't help it. "My point is every major power on the planet does the exact same thing as our government. Only the really good ones, the really smart ones—which I like to believe Uncle Sam falls into both categories—do so without any *real* evidence of direct meddling left behind. In order to do that, there have to be men like me, men like the Black Knights, who can be trusted to work autonomously, completely off-the-grid. Men who can be depended on to go in, get it done, and get the hell out of Dodge. Men who can be counted on to take the terrible secrets they carry in their heads all the way to the grave. So you see, it's really very simple." He raked in a calming breath. "If you tell anyone who I really am, what I really do, it could get me and the men I work with killed."

Her narrow throat worked as her eyes widened to the size of saucers. "Holy moley, Billy," she said.

"Yeah." One corner of his mouth twitched at the familiar G-rated profanity. "You said it."

"You look very pretty in red," Angel said in that deep, husky voice of his after they'd gone some distance down the gangway from the women's shower room.

"Whatever," Becky rolled her eyes. "With this cheek, I look like I should be staring in a Lifetime movie."

"If I say you are beautiful, then you are. I don't make a habit of lying to my friends."

She angled her head over her shoulder, eyeing the mysterious ex-Mossad agent's dazzlingly beautiful face. "Are we friends, Angel?"

"I think you are my *only* friend, Becky."

She shook her head as she descended a set of stairs. Angel's big boots echoed hollowly on the metal risers behind her, drowning out the quiet shushing of her hospital slippers and reminding her that every step she took was bringing her closer to Frank. She denied the urge to take off running because, geez, she couldn't be *that* obvious.

"That's not true," she reassured Angel. "You have all the other Knights. They're your friends now."

"Nonsense," he snorted before instructing her to hang a right. "They tolerate me. That is not the same thing as actually liking me." They both turned sideways and nodded at the *Patton* crewman who passed them on the narrow walkway.

"They'll come around," she assured him. "Just give them time."

"You did not need any time. You accepted me right away."

Yepper, she sure had. But only because she'd felt so darned sorry for him.

He'd been forced from his country, his culture, his family, his job. He'd been made to undergo extensive surgery in order to completely change his appearance.

Man, she still had trouble imagining what it must be like for him to wake up every morning and stare at a reflection that wasn't his own...

Disorienting at best, she figured. Downright spooky at worst.

And having always had a soft spot for the underdog— which he definitely was, coming into the tight-knit group of the Black Knights the way he had—she'd immediately decided to take him under her wing.

"I was just trying to make the transition easier on you," she admitted. "I know what it's like to be the outsider." After all, since Patti's death—Patti had been the Knights' secretary extraordinaire and Dan "The Man's" wife—Becky was the only one in the Knights' employ who wasn't actually part of the team. She was just the face of the "public" operation. The wunderkind motorcycle designer who made sure all their covers as simple mechanics remained in place. But when it came to their missions, to the actual work they all did? She was kept smack-double-dab in the D-A-R-K, which, yep, pissed her off…big time. And was just one more reason why'd she'd started studying to be an operator.

Angel stopped her with a hand on her shoulder. She turned, glancing curiously into his dark eyes. They were the only part of him that hadn't changed from the man he'd been before. Oh, the plastic surgeon had no doubt altered the shape, but the eyes themselves were likely the same. And if the eyes were the windows to a man's soul, then Angel's soul was lost…lost and hurting…

"I never really thanked you for your hospitality that first night," he said, squeezing her shoulder. "For making me feel welcome by cooking that, um…meal."

She swallowed down the deep sorrow that stuck in her throat like a load of peanut butter every time she really allowed herself to stare into Angel's sad eyes and forced a playful snort. "That's because you were too busy trying not to throw up."

"The matzo ball soup was not so bad," he assured her.

"It was barely palatable, and you know it."

He shrugged. "Okay, but the kugel—"

"Was downright inedible," she finished for him.

"I thought the rugelachs were very tasty."

"Uh-huh, once you got past the fact that chewing them was tantamount to chewing rocks."

"Becky," he grabbed her other shoulder so she was forced to continue facing him. His eyes were bright with sincerity. Too bright. Her cheeks heated. She'd never been very good at accepting gratitude. Even the head-knuckling "thanks" she usually got from the guys after doing them some favor usually made heat wash like water from the top of her head down over her shoulders. "It was wonderful of you to go to such trouble. I want you to know how much it meant to me."

"Stop," she waved her hands in front of her eyes, trying to divert the conversation away from the uncomfortable road it was heading down, "you're making me all *faklempt*."

He shook his head, his lips twisting. "You know the real pronunciation is *verklempt*."

"Well, that's what I get from learning all my Yiddish from *Saturday Night Live*, isn't it?" She made a face and he laughed.

Thank God. Joking, palling around, now *this* was footing she was comfortable with.

"Now," she said, once more turning to head toward sick bay, "give me the scoop on the story everyone's being told about the *Hamilton*'s liberation."

"They are saying the pirates surrendered without a fight once a specialized group of spec-ops guys boarded the ship."

"And these spec-ops guys? Where'd they supposedly disappear to?"

"It is a mystery." She could hear the smile in his voice. "You know how those spec-ops guys are."

"Do I ever…"

They stopped and nodded to another crewman who squeezed by them. Angel waited until the man was out of earshot, before continuing, "They're telling everyone there was another ship, a NATO vessel—whose identity will remain secret—from which the group of men operated. Of course, that vessel has since quit the area."

Of course.

"And the media?" she asked.

"Will be fed the same story."

Sleight of hand built upon lies layered on top of deceit. Welcome to the Wonderful World of Clandestine Missions.

Rounding a final turn, they finally came to sick bay. Anxiously stepping inside, she quickly took in the half dozen crisp, white hospital beds spaced three feet apart and lining opposite walls until her hungry gaze lighted on Frank at the far end of the long room. Every bed had its own blue-and-white striped curtain attached to an overhead, semi-circular bar. Its purpose was to give the patients a modicum of privacy. Lucky for Frank, since he was currently the only resident of sick bay, privacy was not much of an issue.

The size of the hospital bed, however? Now *that* was an issue.

She could see his big, bare feet dangling off the end of the mattress.

He didn't seem to mind, however, considering he was fast asleep, his heavy chest rising rhythmically in time to the gently fluctuating hum of the *Patton*'s big engines.

She took a hasty step forward before Angel wrapped a restraining hand around her elbow, giving her a nearly negligible shake of his head before smiling winningly as the ship's surgeon strolled toward them.

"Sorry to interrupt," Angel rasped as the doctor shoved thick, black-rimmed glasses up a rather short nose while tucking a clipboard under his uniformed arm. "But Miss Reichert wanted to personally thank the man who spearheaded the negotiations for her ransom, even if all our work on her behalf turned out to be unneeded," he added quickly. "Is now a bad time?"

Geez, Becky. Use your head.

Frank was supposed to be a perfect stranger, so she couldn't very well run to his bedside and start crooning over him. But that's exactly what she'd have done had Angel not held her back.

And you think you're ready to be an operator? Pfft.

The doctor ran a critical eye over both of them before glancing at his watch. "No. It's time for me to wake Mr. Smith anyway," he used Frank's alias, "and test his cognitive abilities. Come with me."

"And how is the patient?" Angel asked as they followed the doctor toward the back of the room.

"He has three problems," the ship's surgeon said, referring to his clipboard. "The first is the laceration near his scalp. I stitched that up and, as long as he keeps it dry and clean, it should heal rather nicely with barely a scar."

Not that another scar would make that much difference, she thought lovingly, her eyes glued to Frank's battle-ravaged face as they approached his hospital bed.

"His second problem is that he's concussed. His CT

scan shows some bruising but no bleeding, so as long as he takes it easy, he should be back to form in a couple of days. His third problem, however, isn't such an easy fix." The doctor stopped, and Becky wanted to howl *No, damnit! Keep walking!* But she was forced to peel her eyes away from Frank to fix her attention on the doctor. "You said he came by this injury after falling from the second story railing outside the mess hall?"

"Yes." Angel shuddered for effect. "I think I'll hear that bone-rattling *thud* in my dreams tonight."

The doctor cringed in sympathy. "Yes, well, when I first examined his shoulder, Mr. Smith explained how he's had a rotator cuff tear that has gone untreated for years. Unfortunately, this latest injury makes the option of forgoing treatment impossible. He'll require surgery once he's back stateside."

"Mmm," Angel shook his head, "he won't be too happy to hear that."

Um, yeah. That might be putting things a *tad* mildly since, as Billy liked to say, Frank was a 100 percent tear-off-your-head-and-shit-down-your-throat warrior. Being out of commission for whatever length of time it was going to take to rehabilitate himself was going to make him mad as hell.

The doctor escorted them the final feet to Frank's bedside, and Becky had to lace her hands behind her back to keep from reaching out to touch him.

"Mr. Smith?" The doctor gently shook Frank's un-injured shoulder. "I need you to wake up for me. Can you do that?"

Frank's eyes instantly snapped open, but they were dull and glassy, unfocused.

"Mr. Smith," the doctor began but was cut off when Frank lazily glanced over at her.

"So beautiful," he murmured dreamily. "Beautiful Rebecca Reichert."

Alarm slammed through her like a sledgehammer blow. "What's wrong with him? Is it the concussion?" Because Frank didn't say things like that to her. *Ever.'*

"No, no" the doctor assured her. "He's had an...um, unexpected reaction to the pain meds. I used the correct dosage for a man of his size, but he's been flying high as a kite ever since. It happens sometimes. Has something to do with a quirk in a person's metabolic rate, but he'll come down soon enough."

"Ooohhh," Frank pursed his lips, making a pouty face that astounded her as much as it disconcerted her, "that poor, poor li'l cheek." He raised a big, calloused hand toward her cheek. "Come lemme kiss it better."

She laughed uncomfortably—after all, the man was supposed to be a total stranger, and he was talking about kissing her—but a little part of her heart broke off. She'd waited years for him to make a move, and now that he had, it didn't count—considering he was blitzed out of his gourd on happy pills. He'd probably be just as excited to kiss a potato.

That was confirmed when the doctor cleared his throat. "Please don't pay him any attention, Miss Reichert. He doesn't know what he's talking about. Mr. Smith?" Frank slowly turned his head on the pillow, lowering his hand and blinking owlishly as if trying to bring the doctor into focus. "Do you know where you are?"

"Navy Destroyer USS *Patton*," Frank replied, dragging the final *s* out like a hissing snake.

"Good." The doctor nodded. "And do you know why you're here?"

"To save the girl and win the day." Frank giggled, actually giggled. Becky didn't know whether to giggle right along with him or fall down dead from a heart attack.

"Yes," the doctor assured him, "that's right. But you needn't worry about that now. As you can see, Miss Reichert is safe and sound. She's come down here to meet you."

With an awkward swivel of his neck that made his head look like it weighed about ten thousand pounds, Frank turned back to her. "Hello, Rebecca," he murmured warmly, his expression certainly *not* that of a man meeting a complete stranger.

Heat flooded up her neck into her face, making her injured cheek pound like a second heartbeat.

"Hello, Mr. Smith," she whispered, hoping the look on her face wasn't all but screaming her fear that Frank was about to let slip something he shouldn't.

"Mr. Smith," the doctor said again, and Frank growled in inebriated annoyance, once more turning his head on the pillow, this time to glare at the doctor. "Do you remember how you got hurt?"

Becky held her breath, which caused Angel to surreptitiously pinch her elbow. She realized then that her eyes were wide as pie plates, and she was disgusted to discover she was actually wringing her hands. Calling herself ten kinds of stupid, she fisted her hands at her sides and pasted on what she hoped was a look of mild indifference.

Frank's broad forehead wrinkled as he considered the doctor's question. Then he ran his tongue over his lips as if they were numb, which, considering how blasted he was, was probably true. "Weight was too much," he said, only the last word sounded more like *mush*. "The shoulder went."

"Yes, that's right." The doctor marked something in his chart, and Becky covertly blew out a relieved breath. Turning from his patient, the doctor addressed Angel. "His cognitive abilities appear to be fine. It's the pain meds making him loopy, not the concussion. I'll continue to wake him every hour, but I'm confident he'll—"

"M'feet'r'cold," Frank mumbled, causing all of them to glance down at the size sixteens protruding off the end of the bed.

"We didn't have booties big enough to fit him." The doctor frowned. "I'll get another blanket."

"He needs socks," Becky declared, then bit her tongue when she realized how inappropriate it was for her—a supposed stranger—to make any sort of suggestion about Frank's well-being.

"I'll go search through his gear and find a pair," Angel offered, sliding her a look that clearly stated she should stay exactly where she was. It was obvious he wasn't comfortable leaving Frank alone with the doctor given his current level of incoherence.

She had to agree.

"I'll stay with Mr. Smith until you get back," she offered just as the telephone over in the corner rang.

The doctor absently handed her the extra blanket, which she immediately tucked around Frank's bare feet, before scurrying to answer it.

"Just try to keep him from saying or doing anything stupid," Angel whispered, keeping a wary eye on the doctor. "I'll tell the others we'll take bedside shifts until these pain medications wear off and we're assured he's not going to open a can of worms or spill the beans or whatever other quaint little phrase you Americans like to use."

"I've never seen him like this before." Even to her own ears her voice sounded tight with concern.

"He'll be fine just as soon as—"

"I'll go out with you," the doctor interrupted Angel, snatching a first-aid kit. "I've got a midshipman with his finger caught in a gear shaft."

Angel nodded and followed the doctor toward the door. And after they disappeared down the corridor, Becky blew out a shaky breath and turned toward the man of her dreams.

Chapter Seven

"FRANK?" SHE MOVED TO THE EDGE OF THE HOSPITAL BED and smoothed a lock of soft dark hair away from his bandaged brow.

He sucked in a ragged breath, and Becky jerked her hand back. "Sorry. Sorry, geez, I didn't think that'd hurt."

"It didn't." He opened his eyes again, his expression warm and bemused.

"It didn't?"

"No." He shook his head, smiling drunkenly. "I just like th'sound of that."

"Of what?"

"My name."

She fought a grin, relaxing now that the doctor was no longer in the room avidly listening to Frank's confused ramblings. "You like the sound of your own name? Man, Frank, that's a bit egomaniacal, even for you."

"No." He shook his head on the pillow. The action caused his thick hair to fill with static and stand on end. That combined with the softness of his expression made him appear almost boyish. Okay, not boyish, but perhaps a bit more…approachable. "I like the sound of my name when *you* say it."

She swallowed and blinked down at him, shakily smoothing his hair back into place—God, it was so cool and silky she figured she could run her fingers through it for days and never tire of the sensation.

Don't get your hopes up, girl. He's delusional.

Of course, not getting her hopes up was easier said than done. Her heart was suddenly a ninety-pound weight throbbing in her chest.

"You don't like it when I call you Boss?" she asked, holding her breath, knowing she probably shouldn't be having this conversation with him now, while his faculties were compromised. But having his faculties compromised might just be the only way she'd ever really get the truth out of him.

He was always so guarded around her...

"Hmm-mmm," he closed his eyes, grabbing the hand she was using on his hair, threading his thick fingers through her thin ones. He pulled her palm down to his chest, flattening it firmly over his beating heart. "You should always call me Frank."

The tingling in her hand, clasped so warm and tight between his calloused palm and hard chest, spread up her arm and branched across her chest until her nipples pebbled.

"I don't know," she gulped and tried to ignore the storm of strange sensations flashing across her nerve endings. "Are you going to stop calling me Rebecca and start calling me Becky?"

Besides her father, Frank was the only one to refer to her as *Rebecca*, and it always made her feel like a child awaiting admonishment. Initially, she thought he'd done so to drive home the difference in their ages because, okay, so...she'd sort of suffered from a case of hero worship from the very beginning. But later she'd come to realize he called her Rebecca because he didn't care to encourage her familiarity. He called her Rebecca because he was her boss and she was nothing more than the irritating woman whose company he was forced to endure since she happened to supply his cover...

Or was she? The way he was acting now she wasn't so sure.

"What's wrong with Rebecca?" he asked, rubbing his rough thumb along the back of her hand until she thought she'd go crazy. The way her body was reacting, you'd think he was rubbing something far more intimate. "It suits you."

"It does not," she rasped, trying with all her might to focus on the conversation instead of letting her eyes cross in pleasure. "It makes me sound like I should be Angel's grandmother."

He chuckled, the sound low and rolling and strangely... *intimate*. Her insides turned to mush. "It really sticks in your craw to be called Rebecca, doesn't it?"

She swallowed again and tried to moderate her breathing. Her whole body was on fire. "If I—" she licked her suddenly dry lips, "if I say yes, will that just encourage you to keep doing it?"

"Maybe." He chuckled again, and her knees started wobbling.

"You are the most impossible man," she whispered hoarsely, because at some point she'd inadvertently swallowed the *Titanic*.

"I've been called worse."

"Whatever," she tried to growl with her usual level of sarcasm, but the word just came out all low and husky.

"You know," he said, opening his eyes, the color was dark and turbulent, like Lake Michigan after a nor'easter, "I've missed your sharp little tongue."

The way he said the word *tongue* made her own feel as if it was weighed down by an anvil.

And the way he was staring at her? Man, she was either dreaming or imagining things, because this just couldn't be real.

"You've missed my sharp tongue?" she managed, panting as he brought her hand to his whisker-covered cheek. He rubbed his face on her palm like a cat seeking comfort. "Now why is that, Frank? Is nobody stepping up to the plate and poking holes in your ego on a..." she licked her lips again, "on a regular basis? Is your swelled head st...starting to hurt?"

"Mmm," he grinned, his big square teeth blazing as white as the bandage on his head, "maybe." He lazily snaked his hand around the back of her neck and slowly started pulling her down.

If she'd been the fainting type, she'd have gone lights-out right then and there, but she was *not* that type of girl. And thank God she wasn't, or she'd have missed the feel of his hot breath brushing across her tingling lips.

"Frank," she whispered his name, her heart threatening to come crashing through her breastbone.

He groaned, the sound intoxicatingly fierce and darkly yearning, and then he was kissing her.

Frank Knight was kissing her.

Her. Rebecca Reichert, the thorn in his side, the professed bane of his existence, and his full male lips were so warm and surprisingly smooth as they brushed over hers.

She was instantly caught in a storm of his making when he angled her head with the gentle pressure of his thumb along her jaw, licking lazily at the seam of her lips.

Opening to him wasn't an option; it was automatic. And when he dove inside, she melted against his chest. That wasn't an option either since her knees folded under her like wet noodles.

Oh, she finally understood what it meant to be tempest-tossed. But what she couldn't understand was whether Frank was the storm or the shelter *from* the storm. She only knew that she wanted it to go on forever. The devouring plunge of his tongue into her mouth, the smell of him so warm and male, the feeling of his heavy chest cushioning the sensitive weight of her breasts, the deep sounds of hunger and triumph he made at the back of his throat, and the answering groans of desire and surrender at the back of her own.

This is wrong. This is so wrong!

She recognized that voice. It was reason, and it occasionally screeched at her, but she chose to ignore it because what they were doing felt so, *so* right.

She thought perhaps she'd have crawled on top of him, damn the impropriety of having full-out monkey sex in the middle of sick bay and the certain moral contemptuousness of taking advantage of a man who was obviously out of his mind, if the sound of a throat being cleared hadn't had her jumping away like a teenager caught necking in the park.

She lifted a hand to her trembling lips and tried to still the thundering of her heart as she glanced at Angel standing in the doorway.

Embarrassment or contempt.

She'd have easily expected to see either of those emotions in his handsome face…but the pity caught her off guard.

"I—"

He lifted a hand to halt whatever explanations or excuses she was going to sputter. "Do not, Becky."

She swallowed and lowered her eyes, embarrassed, ashamed. Not at having kissed Frank—she'd wanted to do that for what seemed like a zillion years and boy-oh-boy, her fantasies hadn't held a candle to the real thing—but she was horrified at having allowed the moment to happen when Frank didn't have a clue what in the hell he was doing.

Dear God, Becky, you're a complete reprobate.

Angel advanced into the room, his quiet steps and still tongue were so much more terrible than if he'd harshly admonished her or made a joke of the whole thing. She was used to both from Billy and the rest of the boys...from Frank even. She could've fallen back on her usual quick temper or come back with a quip of her own, something about having a weakness for semi-conscious men. But she had nothing to handle or combat Angel's silent...*judgment.* It was as if St. Peter himself was measuring her worth and finding her lacking.

When he reached her side, she dared a quick peek at his ethereally beautiful face, but surprisingly, she didn't find any judgment there, only a sort of sad sympathy.

So the judgment had been all in her head. *Dang.* For some reason that was worse, and she suddenly felt the urge to bawl her heart out.

"You're...what is it you call it?...playing with fire. You realize that, yes?" he asked quietly.

"It's not what you think," she assured him, then realized how ridiculous that sounded.

"It's not?" He tilted his head, lifting one sleek, black brow. "So you're not in love with him?"

Sucking in a horrified breath, she glanced at Frank only to discover, to her utter humiliation, he was dead asleep, his carpenter's square of a jaw slack, his thick chest rising and falling like the tide.

Scorching heat burned across her face like she'd stepped too close to an open fire.

"I...I..." She shook her head, unable to give voice to her feelings for Frank. Respect, longing, lust, frustration...she experienced all of that and so, so much more. Love? Yes, she certainly felt that, too.

Angel's mouth twisted. "He's involved with someone else."

"I know he is," she gulped, the tears that'd steadily been climbing up the back of her throat now threatened behind her eyes.

"You'll get hurt."

Yeah, she knew that, too.

He sighed heavily and shook his head before moving to slide the socks he'd brought onto Frank's big, square feet. "You should go and take a nap. Your brother has arranged a transport for us at oh-nine-hundred."

"Angel—"

"Just be careful," he interrupted her.

Careful. Not a word she usually put into practice, but this time, she figured she'd be smart to heed his advice.

"I will," she promised, fighting the hot tears pooling in her eyes as she turned away and made herself walk, not run like her legs were begging her to do, out of sick bay.

Exactly which portion of your anatomy were you just thinking with, Becky?

If she'd been a dude, she figured the answer would be her dick. But since she was woman? What was the equivalent body part?

She very much feared it might be her stupid, reckless, hopeful heart…

Port of Haifa, Israel
Eighteen hours later…

"What *is* that smell?" Eve asked Becky irritably as they waited for the transport vehicle that would take them on their next leg of the journey. "I think I can taste it."

It took every ounce of willpower she possessed not to reach up and pinch her nose closed or risk enjoying the spaghetti dinner she'd eaten aboard the *Patton* for the second time.

All she wanted at this point was to curl up in the first-class cabin of a big Boeing 747 with a cold mimosa in one hand and a sleep mask in the other. Unfortunately, given how the last several hours had gone, she figured that was pretty much out of the question.

She'd only gotten a few hours of sleep in the "rack" she'd been assigned aboard the *Patton* before she'd been none too gently shaken awake by Billy and gruffly told they were heading out.

"Heading out" turned out to be a six-hour helicopter ride from the deck of the destroyer to a tiny, desolate, dusty landing strip out in the middle of nowhere, Egypt, where they boarded what could barely be called a plane for a hellacious flight to some farmer's seaside field in Israel. From there, they'd hopped on a speedboat and roared through the choppy Mediterranean for what seemed like hours.

Their journey finally landed them here, at the huge docks that ran the length of the colorful Port of Haifa. And even though darkness had descended a few hours previous, the docks still bustled with noise and activity.

"That smell," Becky answered, reaching into the pocket of her borrowed warm-ups to pull out two Dum Dums, "is fuel mixed with dead fish combined with a little excrement and tinged with God only knows what else."

She handed Eve one of the lollipops, and Eve gratefully popped it into her mouth. Squeezing her eyes closed, she tried to concentrate on the burst of sugary sweetness. It helped. But only marginally. Probably because her sense of smell was still reeling from shock.

Deciding the only way to avoid the rancid air would be to stop breathing entirely, she reluctantly opened her eyes, only to find the huge man once more eyeing her friend like a hawk eyes a field mouse. Even injured, with a bandage on his forehead and his arm in a sling, he was still the most dangerous-looking individual she'd ever laid eyes on.

Geez Louise.

"Uh, that man is staring at you again," she whispered, shivering at the hardness of the guy's face and the fierce heat reflected in his eyes.

"I know," Becky said, refusing to look, using her tongue to shift her sucker to her opposite cheek. It clacked loudly against her teeth, a strange sort of expletive. "I'm trying to ignore him."

"I can't tell if he wants to kiss you or kill you."

"He's already done the first, so I'm thinking it's the second he's after now."

"*What?*" When Becky pinched her arm in warning, she lowered her voice. "He *kissed* you?" she whispered incredulously, snatching the sucker out of her mouth so she could gape with appropriate horror at her friend.

Which was a big mistake, because then she really *could* taste the fetid air.

She shoved the lollipop back in her mouth and tried to breathe shallowly.

"More like I kissed him…or maybe I allowed him to kiss me when I shouldn't have, or…hell, I don't know." Becky bit down on her lollipop, the crunch so loud Eve wondered if her friend had lost a tooth. Apparently not, because Becky started chewing angrily, taking out whatever frustration she was suffering on the poor piece of candy. "I'll tell you all about it when we get home," she promised.

Eve watched as Becky finally snatched a glance over at the big man and saw the moment their eyes met and clashed. She fancied even *she* could feel the shocking jolt of electricity in the visual exchange.

"Cheese and rice, Becky." The tiny hairs on her arms stood up as in warning of a potential lightning strike.

"I know," Becky moaned, jerking her gaze away. "It's a disaster. Please talk to me about something else."

"Okay," she said, racking her brain for a change of topic as she shivered in response to the charged atmosphere. She grabbed at the concern foremost on her mind. "Please tell me this is the last leg of the trip. I just want to be home."

Becky shook her head and fished around in her pocket for another sucker. "I wish I could. But you'll be glad to learn there are only two more transfers in our future. We're catching a military transport from here to Andrews Air Force Base in Maryland. From there, you and I will hop on a commercial flight back to O'Hare."

"Just you and me? What about the others?"

"They'll be taking another military transport from Andrews to Great Lakes Naval Base."

"But why aren't we all going together?"

Becky sighed and laid a gentle hand on her shoulder. In response, Eve's intestines tied themselves in big, loopy bows because that was Becky's habitual forerunner to the words, *you're not going to like this*.

"You're not going to like this…"

Sometimes she hated being right.

"*What* am I not going to like?"

"The press is meeting us there."

"Oh crap."

She absolutely *hated* the press. They'd dogged her her entire life, reporting on every humiliation she'd ever suffered…and she'd suffered more than a few.

"Must we talk to them?" she asked.

"*Yes*," Becky stressed, "we must. Apparently we're one of the top stories, so we're going to have to withstand our time in the limelight. I say we just tell our tale—pun intended—and get it the hell over with so our lives can go back to normal. The sooner the better. My guys can't afford to have their faces splashed all over the front page. Hell, you've seen the lengths they've gone to to ensure our travel itinerary is so convoluted no one will ever be able to trace our movements. Can you imagine them cheesing it for the reporters? No way." She shook her head. "I need you to help me do everything humanly possible to make sure this story dies a quick and painless death."

"Fine by me. I'd just as soon it never breathed life in the first place, but...uh, your guys?" She raised a brow, wondering if Becky even realized how proprietary she sounded.

"Huh?"

"You called them *your guys*." She stressed the last two words.

"Yeah. That's kinda how I think of them...as mine, you know?"

No, she didn't know. She couldn't imagine living day in and day out with a bunch of brutes the likes of Frank Knight and Billy Reichert.

"They're like my brothers," Becky added.

Uh-huh. "And Frank, er, Boss? Is he one of your brothers?"

Becky swallowed and started studying her dirty hospital booties as if they were made from the most fascinating weave on the planet. "I feel a lot of things when it comes to Frank Knight," she finally admitted. "*Sisterly* certainly isn't one of them."

Yup, just as she Eve suspected.

Glancing again at the big man, she grimaced before wrapping a comforting arm around her friend's shoulders.

She very much feared Becky was headed for deep, deep trouble where Frank Knight was concerned.

—⁂—

Frank glanced at Angel and Bill pacing along the far end of the dock, and tried like hell to remember just exactly what'd happened down in the *Patton*'s cold, sterile sick bay.

It was all a blur.

All of it except for that kiss.

He remembered that kiss very, *very* clearly.

Even blitzed out of his ever-lovin' mind on some heavy duty narcotics, he'd still realized the dead last thing he should do was pull her sweet lips down to his.

He knew that, but he hadn't been able to help himself.

And then she kissed him back, and she was so much more...*mind-boggling* than he ever imagined. Her cool fingers had been on his face, her soft breasts had been on his chest, her silky, hot tongue had tangled with his, and he knew he was doing the exact thing he always swore he'd never do, but...he just hadn't been able to help himself.

Then she'd pulled away, and the room suddenly closed in on him. The next thing he remembered was the doctor leaning over him, shaking him awake, and asking him all manner of inane questions.

After the drugs wore off, he initially thought it was all a dream, but then she was barely able to look at him as the chopper lifted them from the destroyer's big deck and he knew it was more than just another one of his very, *very* real fantasies starring him and her and the nearest horizontal surface.

Shit. He was such an *asshole*!

He stole another glance at her as Angel sauntered up behind him.

"She is not as tough as she would have everyone believe," the former Mossad agent rasped quietly.

"I know."

"You are not the right man for her."

He swung around to glare at the Israeli's calm, inscrutable face. Had he been that obvious? "What would you know about it?"

"I know the look of a man in lust, and I know the object of a man's lust very rarely meets a…shall we say, *happy* end."

"Fuck you, Angel," he growled, unaccountably mad.

Of course, he had to admit, despite appearances, his anger wasn't aimed at Angel. Nope. That would've been too easy, and he was *not* an easy man. What he *was* was truthful. And the truth of the matter was he was pissed as hell at himself, because every word out of Angel's mouth was spot-on.

"Just mind your own damn business," he finished with a weary sigh.

"Do you deny it?"

"Deny *what?*" He really considered picking the guy up and chucking him over the docks and into the ocean.

"That you're not the right man for her."

"No, goddamnit! I know I'm not!" And that's what made the thing that happened between them in sick bay so fantastically terrible. Then a horrible thought occurred to him. "Do you think *you're* the right man for her?"

Angel lifted that annoying brow of his, and Frank barely resisted the urge to rip the sucker clean off. "I might be."

Like hell…

He opened his mouth to tell Angel exactly what he'd do to him if he so much as *looked* at Becky sideways, then snapped his jaws closed with an audible *clack*.

Maybe Angel was right. Maybe he *was* the right man for Becky. Lord knew he had to better for her than Frank. At least Angel was born in the same decade as Becky, which was more than he could claim.

Shit.

He lifted his good hand to rub at the sudden pain shooting through his chest and marched toward the transport vehicle that pulled up to the end of the dock.

Never in his entire life had he wanted to be home as badly as he did at this very moment. And that was saying a lot since he'd spent endless amounts of time in quite a few less-than-hospitable environments.

He just wanted to get back to Chicago, back to the compound, back to normal.

Unfortunately, he couldn't help but wonder if things would ever be normal again, because right at that moment he caught Becky watching him, and the look in her eyes was one he easily recognized. He easily recognized it because it was the same look reflected in his own.

Abject longing.

That about summed it up.

And how was he ever going to resist her now that he knew she wanted him as much as he wanted her? How was he ever going to resist her now that he knew the sensation of her in his arms? The taste of her on his lips?

Sweet Christ, help me.

Chapter Eight

Northern Indian Ocean
Six hours later…

"Sonofabitch!" Sharif howled in frustrated impotence as the catamaran's last working outboard motor sputtered to a hiccupping halt.

Ominous silence settled over the little sailboat.

He was out of petrol, minus a satellite phone, running low on food and fresh water, and without a breath of wind to fill the sails…

He had not signed on for this…for *any* of this. He was supposed to answer the bloody phones, not find himself wounded and afloat out in the middle of the goddamned Indian Ocean. And it was all the fault of that little blond American *bitch*!

He threw his head back and shrieked his rage over and over into the endless expanse of the cloudless sky, then fell to his knees and convulsed in a long series of bone-cracking shudders that made his back teeth ache.

"I'm dead," he whispered into the lonely silence, lifting eyes that were as red and swollen from his vitriolic outburst as they were from the fever that wracked him.

I'm dead.

Strangely, the thought didn't frighten him. Not in the usual sense, in the *fear of the unknown* sense. In truth, he didn't much care what happened. He'd never been particularly religious, had always considered himself of a scientific mind, so he figured chances were pretty good that nothing happened. One second you're here, having thoughts, making plans, eating, working, fucking. The next second you're gone. End of story.

So no, the thought of death held no fear. But that didn't mean he wasn't royally miffed by the idea. Because he was going to die, and Rebecca Reichert—that bitch—was going to go right on living her entitled little American life and that was just so incredibly unfair he could barely stand it.

He glanced around, looking for something, anything, on which to take out his frustrations. But there was nothing. Just him and kilometer after kilometer of placid, turquoise water.

For the first time in his life, he lamented the fact that he wasn't surrounded by the dirty, seething mass of humanity. With his hand swollen to the size of a cricket glove, and the infection ravaging his system, what he wouldn't give to see the face of one skinny, ignorant pirate or one snide British football fan—or *soccer* as the Americans liked to call it. Leave it to them to filch the name of a four-hundred-year-old sport and apply it to a totally new endeavor, then condescend to call the original sport something entirely new.

He hated American audacity. Scratch that. He just hated Americans. One small, blond American in particular…

Listlessly, he let his gaze roam around the sailboat, cataloging what would soon become his floating coffin.

Something sparkled over by the aft railing.

Struggling to his feet, he shuffled over to investigate. What he found was a long, thin fillet knife, its tip wedged under the metal lip that secured the railing to the deck. Bending, ignoring the thick blood that pounded through his head and hand at the maneuver, he picked up the blade and studied it with a sort of abstract fascination.

Ah, yes. And so the solution presents itself.

He almost smiled.

He'd just end it. Right here. Right now. On his own terms. Put a period on his life that had been tragically condensed to this lonely little world of infinite glassy seas and relentless agony.

He'd heard there wasn't much pain in slitting one's wrists. And bleeding to death promised to be much quicker and so much less horrific than dying from dehydration coupled with starvation and infection.

He tested the blade with his thumb.

Sharp.

Sharp enough to do the job with very little effort.

That was good. He was never very brave when it came to facing pain.

Gripping the handle with his uninjured hand, he laid the thin edge of the knife against his swollen left wrist. Holding his breath, girding himself against the sharp bite of agony to follow, he smiled when a warm gust of wind cooled the sweat on his fevered brow.

Mmm, it felt wonderful. Like a sweet benediction at the end.

He'd just begun to press the blade into his skin, watching with a sort of detached delirium as a tiny drop of blood welled at the tip, when another breath of wind whipped by him, chilling him, causing gooseflesh to rise over his skin.

He dropped the blade. The loud *thunk* it made when

it hit the deck echoed like a cannon explosion in his pounding head, but he ignored it as he eagerly glanced out at the softly rolling seas. The deck beneath him bucked gently, a physical lullaby, but the very last thing he was going to do was sleep.

I'm saved!

With a cry of triumph, he stumbled to the main mast and began the arduous task of unfurling the sails.

He was a two-day sail from the Somali coast, and with the infection multiplying in his body every minute, the odds were stacked against him. But he'd been bucking odds his entire life.

"Here I come, Becky!" he yelled, laughing hysterically as the sails caught the wind and snapped tight. "Here I come!"

———

Outside the gates of Black Knights Inc.
Goose Island, Chicago, Illinois

"We're here." Patrick Edens's cultured voice roused Becky from what she realized must have been a dead sleep. There was a giant smear left by her cheek on the limousine's rear driver's side window, and was that...?

Yepper, she'd been drooling. A big slobbery glob slowly cut a path down the tinted glass.

Perfect. Just perfect.

Of course, when she looked over and found Eve on the opposite side of the swank leather seat as dead to the world as she'd been, she didn't feel quite so bad. Although at least Eve had had the decorum to simply tilt her head into the corner with her mouth closed and her hands tucked daintily between her knees.

Go figure.

Eve did everything with grace and panache, and Becky loved the woman to distraction, but sometimes she felt like a complete clod by comparison.

Wiping the wetness from her chin, she glanced out the window toward the high, wrought-iron gate that was the only public entrance into the compound and gazed lovingly at the warm, brick buildings beyond. It was quite a sight, especially when compared to where she'd started in that little pre-fab building. The main structure on the compound, the old factory they'd turned into lofts, office space, and her chopper shop, glowed dark red in the late afternoon sun. Yellow light glinted off the leaded glass windows on the upper floors. It was beautiful. It was her pride and glory…it was *home*.

And she couldn't wait to get inside.

"Thanks for the ride, Mr. Edens," she whispered quietly so as not to wake Eve. "Tell Eve I'll call her tomorrow."

Patrick nodded regally, and she took that as her cue to depart.

Fine by her. Eve's father had a way of sneering at her down the length of his patrician nose that tended to make her fingers itch to close themselves in a fist and plant one right in his puss.

Eve always claimed she was imagining things, but Becky knew the score. Patrick Edens didn't think she was good enough to lick the bottom of his daughter's couture pumps, much less be her best friend.

Asshole.

But right now even the slightly condescending tilt to his chin couldn't bank her enthusiasm. Because she was home.

Finally.

Hastily, she pushed open the limousine door before the driver had a chance to do it for her. Stepping onto the curb, she watched the long, black car pull onto Cherry Street and disappear around the corner.

She took a deep breath, dragging in the damp, fishy odor of the Chicago River mingled with the sweet smell of cocoa drifting on the wind from Blommer Chocolate Company. The tension inside her ebbed like the retreating tide.

She knew exactly how Dorothy felt, because no truer words had ever been spoken than "there's no place like home."

Grinning, she turned toward the gatehouse and the big, red-headed beast of a man working inside.

"Hey there, Rebel!" he called, hauling himself out of his chair and ducking under the door frame as he exited the little building. He'd been seriously wounded in the same incident that resulted in Patti's death, but, by the looks of him, he was making a full recovery.

The sight did her heart good.

"Manus!" she squealed, running and stopping herself from jumping into his burly arms at the last second. Gingerly, she wrapped her arms as far around his barrel chest as they would stretch and hugged him softly.

"Well now, that's no kind of hello." He pulled back, his round, freckled face wreathed in smiles below his shock of unruly Irish hair. "Since when do you handle me like a piece of Venetian glass?"

"Since you had a bullet cut out of your chest a couple of months ago."

"Bah," he waved a baseball-glove-sized hand through

the air. "I'm fit as a fiddle." To prove it, he tilted his head back, beat his heavy chest, and did a pretty terrible Tarzan impression.

She wrinkled her nose. "I'm not sure, but I think you just insulted every self-respecting ape on the planet."

He chuckled and caught her up in a bear hug that lifted her completely off the sidewalk and had her ribs protesting.

She didn't care. She hugged him back with equal fervor.

"I'm sure glad you're back in one piece," he told her gruffly. "You had us all scared half to death."

"I'm glad to be back," she managed to wheeze.

"Yo, Tarzan," Rock's cheerful drawl sounded behind her. "Let go of Jane before you squeeze the life outta her."

"Rock!" she whooped and ran through the gates once Manus set her back on her feet. This time she didn't refrain from jumping into the set of strong arms stretched toward her.

"Oomph," Rock staggered exaggeratedly, the heels of his alligator cowboy boots clacking against the sidewalk. "What did those pirates feedya? Cheeseburgers and apple pie?"

"Can it, you big Cajun," she growled even as she planted a smacking kiss on his ear.

"You know, *ma petite*, I'm used to comin' home to find you've stirred up a hornet's nest, but this last episode beats all. Pirates? Really, Becky?"

"It's not like I do it on purpose. Trouble just seems to find me."

"Hmm," he murmured noncommittally, turning his sweat-stained John Deere baseball cap around backward so he could get a good look at her. A frown had the corners of his dark goatee drooping.

"I'm so sorry I couldn't be there, *chère*." He softly touched her injured cheek. "I couldn't get back in time to make the transport outta here."

"Don't sweat it. Frank, Billy, and Angel pulled off the rescue without a hitch." She took his arm and started pulling him toward the shop. She just wanted to get inside.

Funny, when she left to go on vacation almost a month before, after Patti's death and Frank's promise to do everything in his power to impede her becoming an operator, she thought she couldn't escape this place fast enough.

Now? Well, now all she wanted to do was lock herself inside the old factory's thick, warm walls until the memory of Sharif's brutal pistol carving a place into her temple and her flying over the *Patton*'s railing didn't leave her weak and shaky.

"So I heard and saw," Rock said. "Ya looked very brave, *très vaillant*, givin' your story to the reporters." He used his key to unlock the shop's big double doors. They popped open with a muted hiss as the airlock released. He gestured for her to precede him, and she gratefully stepped over the threshold and into her safe, welcoming, ofttimes chaotic world. "Very tragic and heroic at the same time what with your cheek and tremblin' lips. The newspapers and networks are eatin' it up."

Ugh. She hadn't realized her lips trembled. Her knees? Yepper, they'd been knocking together like wind chimes in a hurricane, but she thought she'd managed to keep her lips under control.

Apparently not.

Great. Just...frickin' great.

She and Eve had arrived at O'Hare International Airport only to be hustled by airport staff into a tight, windowless room packed to the brim with reporters shoving microphones in their faces. The flash of camera bulbs had been blinding and disorienting but, together with Eve, she'd recounted the tale of their capture, captivity, and eventual liberation by a heroic and mysterious team of men.

They'd stuck to the script and Becky, with her knocking knees and dripping palms, envied Eve's ability to remain cool and unruffled—of course, she comforted herself with the thought that Eve had had a lot more practice dealing with the press.

And she especially wished she'd had just an ounce of Eve's unflappable poise when Samantha Tate, one of the *Chicago Tribune*'s newest and most ambitious young investigative reporters, called out, "Miss Reichert, do you think your life is jinxed given that this most recent incident is coming so soon on the heels of the supposedly gang-related shooting outside the front gates of your business, which resulted in the brutal death of one of your employees?"

There were so many offensive things in the question, that she'd opened her mouth only to have nothing come out but an insulted sputter.

First of all, her life wasn't jinxed. It was just that trouble tended to run hand-in-hand with danger, and she happened to pal around with a very dangerous crowd. Second, Miss Tate's emphasis on the word supposedly in reference to the drive-by shooting slipped under her skin until the image of wrapping her hands around the woman's thin white neck burned very bright in her mind's eye. They'd all worked incredibly hard to make sure that story was fed to the press, and General Fuller had had to pull—er, *yank*—a lot of strings to ensure the truth of that incident stayed buried in the bottom of some file in some safe room in some forgotten, bombproof basement at the Pentagon.

Not to be all Jack Nicholson-y, but the world couldn't handle the truth of what'd really happened that day. The truth that one of their own senators had hired a group of thugs out of Las Vegas to end the lives of a sanctioned government operator and the woman with him who happened to be holding the evidence that proved the senator's culpability in treason.

And lastly, *yes*, she thought it was beyond tragic that the whole world thought Patti Currington had died in gang crossfire when the truth of the matter was she'd been taken down by a careless assassin who didn't give a good goddamn which innocent people he caught with one of his stray bullets, but that's just how it was in their business. And the fact that some nosy reporter smelled something bigger and was trying like hell to force a few jumbled pieces into some sort of order scared the life right of her, but she'd *finally* managed to find her voice.

"No, I don't think my life is jinxed. Perhaps plagued by a string of bad luck recently, but that's only one way to look at it. Another way to look at it is I'm extremely lucky. I'm alive and well, aren't I?"

Miss Tate had smiled knowingly, the look in her eye enough to curdle Becky's innards, but the woman thankfully refrained from asking any more probing questions.

"Well, if the press is eating it up," she told Rock now, "I can only hope that means they'll soon be full. I just want it to all go away." She dragged in a deep breath and smiled at the familiar scents of motor oil, bad coffee, and the slightly minty, alcohol aroma that lingered in the brick walls from the building's previous life as a menthol cigarette factory. "Oh, it's good to be home."

Rock smiled as they made their way down the long hall that ended with an entrance to the huge expanse of the shop. "It's good to have ya home, *chère*."

"Where are the others?" she asked as they pushed into the strange silence of the shop. She craned her head back to scan the open second floor where the offices and conference room were located, frowning when she found everything to be ghostly quiet.

Then a muted *thump, thump, thump* had her gaze focusing on the metal stairway, and she clapped her delight. "Peanut!" she squealed at the giant, gray cat lumbering down the staircase. "Aren't you a sight for sore eyes, you fat, mangy furball?"

The tomcat landed with a hard *thud* on the shop floor and meowed a loud welcome before winding his substantial self around and between her legs. He gazed up at her with soulful, yellow eyes in a scarred face only a mother could love.

Bending, she hefted him into her arms and chuckled with happiness when he fired up his motor, purring so loudly it felt like a jet engine rumbled inside his chest.

"He's missed ya somethin' fierce," Rock said,

crossing his arms and cocking his head to the side, eyes twinkling at the sight of the two of them.

"Oh, I've missed him." She buried her nose in the cat's patchy fur and grimaced when he afforded her the rather dubious honor of his kneading nails.

"From what I hear, he walked around here for two days after you left, meowin' incessantly and refusin' to eat."

She joggled Peanut, testing his rather *ample* weight. "It doesn't appear to have had much of an impact."

"Oh, I think he quickly realized extra helpings of Fancy Feast worked wonders on his depression."

She chuckled, scratching Peanut under his furry chin until his yellow eyes rolled back in ecstasy. "So where is everybody?"

"Steady, Mac, and Christian are all still on assignment. Ozzie's at some hacker-fest or geek-fest or somethin'. Ghost just got back from a mission, and when he learned you were safe and sound, he headed down to North Carolina to play househusband—if you can imagine that. Vanessa's in DC finishin' up a consulting job for the Agency. God only knows what dingy, disgustin' rock Dan Man is hidin' under. And your three heroes aren't on site yet. They had a delay and landed at Great Lakes about an hour after you touched down at O'Hare. Their ETA is approximately..." He looked at his watch and smiled when a muffled whistle pierced the thick brick of the shop's west wall, "right now."

He ambled over to the large, red button mounted high up between her Craftsman ten-drawer rolling tool chest and the metal staircase leading to the second floor. After smashing it with his palm, an alarm briefly sounded, and the west wall began its laborious slide to the right.

No matter how long she worked at Black Knights Inc., she doubted she'd ever get accustomed to the eerie sight. Shades of the House of Usher.

"Why'd they come via the Bat Tunnel?" she asked, referring to the secret bolt-hole that extended from the chopper shop down under the Chicago River. It terminated in a parking garage two blocks away.

"After I saw Miss Tate grill you, I figured it best if our guys didn't arrive home right after you'd told the story of a group of mysterious men racin' to your rescue. Ya know, just in case the lovely Miss Tate is keepin' her eagle eye on things, waitin' for a juicy story to land in her lap."

Becky shuddered. "She's a shark. We're gonna have to watch out for her."

"Indeed," Rock agreed, walking over to the lathe in order to snag the sandwich lying atop the expensive tool's flat surface. He took a mammoth bite.

"What've I told you about keeping your dang sandwiches off my equipment?" she demanded, lowering Peanut to the floor so she could plant her hands on her hips.

Rock shot her a wide-eyed, innocent look that didn't fool her for a second. She was just about lay into him for the one-hundred-and-first time concerning that particular offense when the west wall opened just enough to admit Frank's extra-wide shoulders. She swallowed her words as she watched the Black Knights' fearless leader slowly shuffle into the shop.

Wonderful and terrible. That's how he looked.

Wonderful because...come on...he was *Frank*. Terrible because the bandage across his forehead was smudged with dirt, his hastily wrapped shoulder and sling were all askew and looked more like a Rube Goldberg machine than a medical device, his hair was a mess, his beard was coming in thick and black, not to mention the fact that he was pasty pale and carrying enough luggage beneath his eyes for a European vacation.

"Goddamn, *mon frere,* just look at you." Rock grimaced and then grinned from ear to ear. Wait for it… "You look like warmed-over, day-old dogshit."

Aaaannnddd, there it was. The first salvo. Some things just never changed.

Nor would she want them to.

"I feel worse," Frank grumbled, shaking the hand Rock extended to him. "So what have you heard about Sharif? Have they found him?"

Just the sound of the man's name sent a chill streaking down her spine, and she had to remind herself she was safe. She was *home.*

"Negative," Rock shook his head. "The ships in the area have reported no sign of the *Serendipity*, nor have they picked up anything on radar. Surveillance drones are doin' fly-overs, but it's a little ship out in the middle of a big ocean. It was just plain ol' luck we were able to locate it the first time around."

"What about Interpol?" Frank asked.

"They've put out an APB and sent a description of the *Serendipity* to all major ports up and down Africa's western seaboard. Of course, if he makes it to Somalia…"

Rock didn't need to go any further. If Sharif made the Somali coast, it was game over. They'd probably never find him. She swallowed the hard lump of fear that lodged in her throat at the thought of that man being out there…somewhere.

It doesn't matter, she reminded herself. *You're home, now. You're safe.* And the Knights' compound was more secure than most nuclear missile sites.

Then all thought of Sharif vanished when Frank focused his exhausted but still fierce attention on her.

"So how'd it go with the reporters?" he asked.

And that was Frank. Always on the job.

Just once she wished he'd ask her something benign, like, oh say, "Hi, Becky. How was your flight?"

But then he wouldn't be Frank…

"It went fine," she said, finding it incredibly difficult to hold his gaze when images of the two of them down in the *Patton*'s sick bay kept flashing before her eyes. She still thought maybe she could taste him, feel him, and she *so* longed to throw her arms around his neck and repeat the entire sordid experience. But the shuttered expression he wore all but screamed he wasn't of a similar mind. Like Eve said, he looked less like he wanted a peek at Becky Reichert, Girl On Top Part Deux, and more like he wanted to kill her.

Could she really blame him? She'd taken advantage of him when he was hopped-up on happy pills. What kind of person did that?

Her apparently.

God, she was such an asshole, and she needed to apologize; but she couldn't rightly do it there, in front of her colleagues and her older brother…

"Now don't you be humble." Rock hooked an arm around her neck and knuckled her head until she turned to glare at him. "She did great, Boss. Stuck to the script and didn't bat a lash, despite some rather probin' questions from Samantha Tate, I might add. We'll make an operator outta our little Rebel yet."

"Rock," Frank warned, his left eye twitching, "I'm not in the mood to get into that with you right now."

"You're not?" Rock did a pretty convincing impression of being crushed. "And after I sat up, night after night, longin' for the sight of your boyish puss so we could continue the discussion? Well, of all the ungrateful…"

Rock harrumphed, Frank growled, and Becky marked shot number two on the invisible scoreboard of quips she liked to keep in her head.

"Gentlemen, not that I haven't missed your lively repartee, but I'm in desperate need of a cherry Dum Dum." She'd run out of the suckers on the transatlantic flight, and her blood sugar had to be dropping to near critical levels. "And a long, hot shower."

She ducked out from under Rock's arm to stretch on tiptoe and lay a kiss on her brother's cheek. "Thank you for coming for me," she whispered, squeezing his shoulder and flashing him the same smile she'd flashed the day he punched that lying snake Curtis Mitchell for telling the whole school she'd gone down on him in the back of his Ford pickup truck.

"Oh sister mine," Billy grinned, "like there was really any other option?"

No, she supposed there wasn't. They'd been coming to each other's rescue in one way or another their whole lives.

She hugged him tightly, and he kissed her forehead before she moved on to Angel.

"We barely know each other, and yet you risked your

life to save mine. I'll never be able to thank you enough."
She pressed one of his hands between both of hers.

"Like I said back on the destroyer, you are my friend.
Aristotle once said, 'the antidote to a thousand enemies
is one good friend.' I would do it again in a heartbeat."

Blinking back sudden tears, she went with impulse
and reached up to kiss his whisker-roughened cheek
before she turned to Frank. Forcing herself not to flinch
as she met his intense stare, she cleared her throat before
whispering. "I'm sorry I caused such trouble. Thank you
for coming for me."

A heavy muscle ticked in his jaw, but he managed a
terse nod.

"I uh, I need to talk to you after I get out of the
shower," she told him, resisting the urge to lower her
head and shuffle her feet. Instead, she forced herself to
hold his gaze, hoping he'd see the regret in her eyes.

Another brusque nod was all the response she received.

Okay. So, obviously he was biting his tongue lest he
give her the verbal lashing she so richly deserved.

She felt miserable about her part in that whole scene
down in the *Patton*'s sick bay but...geez, the least he
could do was say *something* so she'd know how much
groveling was required. Because right now all she could
come up with was, *Uh, sorry I was on the verge of rap-
ing you, man*. And no matter how many times she turned
that sentence over in her head, it just didn't have quite
the right ring.

Chapter Nine

FRANK STOOD OUTSIDE THE CHEERY RED DOOR OF THE RE-stored brownstone on North Sedgwick and experienced none of the comfort he usually gained from being there.

But God knew he couldn't stay back at the compound…

When Becky said she wanted to talk to him after her shower, the only word that registered was *shower*, and his brain had conjured a quick slideshow of erotic images. All of which had included her, gloriously naked, sweet breasts lifted as she raised her slender arms above her head to sluice the water from her long hair. The mental picture of warm, glistening droplets running over her taut belly and sleek hips was so clear that his mouth had watered like one of Pavlov's damn dogs, and he'd known he was too exhausted to resist the temptation she embodied.

So he'd done the cowardly thing and run here.

He rested his forehead against the cool, wooden surface of the door—the door he painstakingly painted three springs before—and called himself one hundred kinds of prick for what he allowed to happen on the *Patton* and what he wanted to happen over and over again. It went against every fiber of his being, against the very nature of the man he was always convinced he was.

And, worst of all, it was a…*betrayal*—there was just no other word for it—of the woman who lived behind this door.

A cool October wind whistled in off Lake Michigan. Its icy fingers slipped under the collar of his motorcycle jacket, pulling him from his futile thoughts.

Yeah, no matter how many times he turned it over in his mind, there was no way for him to shift the blame for what happened to somebody else.

The fault was all his, which was just fan-fucking-tastic.

Allowing himself one last florid string of curses, he pushed away from the door, pressed the little brass bell, and listened to the happy chime. Its tinkling peal was quickly followed by the squeal of a toddler.

The door swung open to reveal the cherubic face of the three-year old boy who was Frank's most precious treasure.

"You's back!" little Franklin declared gleefully, clapping his dimpled hands together even as he tried to clamber up Frank's leg.

Frank managed to secure the wiggling little bundle of energy in his good arm, hoisting him up against his chest. The smell of peanut butter, crayons, and warm little boy filled his nose and made his heart ache.

"Franklin," Shell admonished as she came through the kitchen door, wiping her hands on her apron and looking so beautiful Frank's aching heart swelled with pride, "the correct words to use are *you're* back, not *you's* back. And how many times have I told you not to open the door without me?"

Franklin ignored her as he pushed back in Frank's arm, his storm-cloud gray eyes scanning Frank's scarred face.

"He's back," he told his mother seriously, "and he's got boo-boos."

Franklin tried to pull the bandage away from Frank's forehead to get a peek underneath and must've been somewhat successful because he quickly followed that up with, "Ooooh, he's got bwud."

Franklin placed a sticky hand on each of Frank's cheeks and regarded him intently. "Does it hurt?" he asked, his eyes wide with worry.

"It did when it happened, but not now," Frank assured him.

Franklin nodded sagely before wriggling to be let down. Since the initial excitement of his arrival wore off and the mystery of his injuries had been thoroughly examined, the little boy was anxious to get back to whatever he was doing, which, by the looks of the colorful balls of clay on the coffee table, was the construction of a Play-Doh menagerie.

Frank lowered him to the floor and swallowed the sudden lump in his throat as he watched the little guy run back to his play on short, sturdy, denim-clad legs.

"How's it possible he's grown an inch since I saw him a week ago?" he asked.

"Because he takes after you," Shell said as she walked over and placed a cool hand on each of his cheeks— like mother, like son. She quickly scanned his face, the worry in her own obvious.

"Well, I'm glad you're home in *mostly* one piece," she observed, and he suddenly wanted to cry. She started pulling him toward the warm, delicious-smelling kitchen. "As it happens, I'm making your favorite."

Of course, she was…"How'd you know I was coming?"

"I saw the news coverage. The interview of that cute motorcycle designer you have working for you."

Dear, sweet kee-rist, talk about a dagger through the heart.

"So I figured it wouldn't be long before you'd come looking for a little peace and quiet. Such as it is." She made a face and glanced back at Franklin who was in the middle of facilitating a war between a lion and monkey, if the sounds he was making were anything to go by. "I also figured a nice, home-cooked meal wouldn't go unappreciated."

He squeezed her with his good arm. "You know me too well."

"After all these years?" She threw her head back and laughed. "I guess I'd better, huh?"

"Where's Frank?" Becky asked anxiously, standing behind the overstuffed sofa in the media room.

Angel turned down the volume on the big-screen plasma television and twisted off the cap on an extra bottle of Honker's Ale as he patted the cushion beside him.

Oh gosh. That didn't bode well. A sick feeling settled in the bottom of her stomach as she rounded the sofa to stand in front of him, hands on hips.

"Rock and your brother have gone to bed," he said, his dark eyes soft on her face. The fire crackling in the corner grate filled the air with the smoky sweetness of burning pine logs and cast dancing shadows around the room. Still, there was enough light to make out his expression, and was that…?

Yep, that was pity plastered all over his handsome face.

Okay, and now she really felt ill. "That's not what I asked."

"I know." He patted the seat next to him again.

Swallowing down the sudden urge to yank out her hair and scream, she blew out a frustrated breath and plopped down beside him, absently accepting the beer he handed her.

"He's gone," he murmured quietly.

"Where'd he go?" She tried to make her tone sound casual but realized she missed the mark when Angel wrapped a comforting arm around her shoulders and gave her a gentle squeeze.

"Where do you think?"

"Well…crap." She heaved a weary sigh, her shoulders sagging. "I guess that's about perfect, huh?"

Angel didn't answer. He just pulled her closer, laying his cheek on the top of her head.

Peanut strolled into the room. And after two failed attempts, he managed to jump onto the sofa, curling up next to her and purring loud enough to drown out the crackle and hiss of the logs burning in the fireplace.

Oh great. Everyone felt the need to comfort poor, foolish Becky.

Inexplicably, tears clogged her throat. She took a hasty sip of beer to try to wash them down.

"It's kinda funny when you think about it," she mused after a while, although the last thing she felt like doing was laughing.

"What is?"

"Well, here I was, determined to apologize for what happened, and Frank's probably up in Lincoln Park doing the same. No doubt trying his best to explain the whole sordid affair to his girlfriend without making me look like a…like a…frickin' *predator*." She tilted the bottle back and took another healthy swig.

Maybe the best thing to do would be to get drunk. Just get good and wasted…

Of course, her troubles would be waiting for her in the morning. *And* they'd be compounded by a hangover.

"I don't understand." Angel pulled back to look at her. "What have *you* got to apologize for?"

She wiped her mouth with the back of her hand and slanted him what Ozzie liked to refer to as her patented *well, duh* expression. "Uh, for forcing myself on a nearly unconscious man? Does that ring any bells?"

"Yes, the scene is still very fresh in my mind's eye." She felt her cheeks heat. "But believe me when I tell you he knew exactly what he was doing. All those painkillers did was lessen his inhibitions."

"Uh-huh," she curled her upper lip, "that's what all the college boys claim when the girl wakes up in the fraternity house the next morning and starts yelling rape. *She wanted it at the time, your honor. I swear it.*"

He shook his head. "What happened between you and Boss was not like that."

"Just how do you figure?" she demanded. "You were there. One minute he's sticking his tongue down my throat, the very next he's sawing logs like a dadgummed lumberjack. I think that pretty much establishes me as the culprit. After all, *I* was still in my right mind."

Angel took a slow sip of beer, regarding her through narrowed eyes. "Let me ask you this. Who instigated the kiss?"

"Um…"

"Was it you?"

She screwed up her mouth, replaying the scene in her mind for what had to be the thousandth time. *Frank, looking at her so sweetly, rubbing his face against her hand, reaching up to pull her down…*

"No." She shook her head. "I wasn't the instigator. I specifically remember him pulling me down, but—"

"So there you go."

"What?" she sputtered. "That doesn't change anything. He. Was. Out. Of. His. Head. I should've stopped him."

"*That* we can agree on."

She made a face and sank back against the cushions.

"What I'm saying is you shouldn't take on the blame for this. I can assure you, Boss has wanted to kiss you for a long time, and he used the excuse of his inebriated state to do just that."

"He's wanted to kiss me? How do you know that? Did he tell you?"

Okay. And that didn't sound desperate or anything. Geez…

"I know it the same way I know every time you look at him you see him stomping on a wineglass while you stand under the chuppah."

Huh?

"Um, Angel? I don't know what a chuppah is, but I get the wineglass reference, and I don't see him doing that…mainly because we're not Jewish." She mumbled the last bit.

"Fine, then you see white doves and orange blossoms. My point is you have happily-ever-after written all over your face."

She swallowed, sinking farther into the sofa, wanting to just…disappear. "Do you think he knows?" she asked, not really wanting to hear the answer.

"He'd be a blind man not to."

"Aw, geez." She threw a hand over her eyes, the beer she'd swallowed threatening to reverse directions. "This is a disaster."

"Only if you let it become one." He grabbed her hand, forcing her to face him. "You want my advice?"

Advice?

Hell, yeah. She needed all the advice she could get.

"Forget about it," he told her. When she frowned, he added. "Forget about the kiss, forget about your girlish dreams, forget about *him*."

"Yeah, well," she blew out a breath of frustration, "that's a little hard to do considering I work with the guy."

"Okay, so use that."

She lifted a brow.

"He's your coworker, yes? It's always bad luck to get involved with a coworker. Believe me, I know. And if that's not enough to dissuade you, then simply remember he's already in a relationship. Are you prepared to be the other woman? Because I wouldn't have thought you were the type."

"Of *course* I'm not. But it can't be that serious, can it? This thing he's got going with this woman up in Lincoln Park? I mean, he's been seeing her for as long as I've known him. If it was something serious, he'd have proposed marriage by now, don't you think?"

"Are you really that naive?"

She groaned and closed her eyes.

"I know how hard it is," he squeezed her against his side, "to want someone you can't have."

She stared at the stark emotion on his face. "Who was she?" she asked quietly.

In answer, he simply shook his head. "It doesn't matter."

Like hell. But Becky knew that was guy-speak for, "I don't want to talk about it." And she decided it was best not to press him on the issue.

Laying her head on his shoulder, they sat and drank in companionable silence for a long while before she finally snorted. "We're a pair, aren't we? A couple of lovesick fools..."

———∿∿∿———

"So what's up with the shoulder this time?" Shell asked him as they sat on the sofa in the living room, enjoying a second glass of Chardonnay and the little fire he'd lit in the fireplace—the fireplace he'd personally restored tile by tile.

Franklin had been bathed and put to bed, his little belly full of Frank's favorite beef stroganoff.

It was all so very familiar, so very homey, his earlier tension began to dissolve. And with the anxiety of the past week melting away, the pain in his shoulder took center stage.

"Two words," he told her, adjusting himself to try and relieve some of the ache, "it's fucked."

"Surgery?" she asked, oblivious to his potty mouth after all these years.

"Uh-huh. No way around it if I want to keep doing my job."

"It'll be different this time," she told him, patting his arm. "Now that you know you have an adverse reaction to general anesthesia, your anesthesiologist can keep a sharp eye on your levels."

He grunted in reply. The thought of being put under after what'd happened last time scared the holy hell out of him. Give him RPG-toting terrorists or tweaked-out drug lords any day of the week over a masked man with a shiny needle.

"You *will* be okay," she assured him, leaning over to smack a kiss on his cheek. "You haven't survived everything you've been through just to have your lights blink out during a miniscule shoulder surgery."

Lord, let her be right.

The last time he felt this scared was when he'd woken up after the surgery to have his tonsils removed to find out One: that he'd died on the table only to be revived, and Two: that the strain of almost losing a son had been too much for his father, who'd subsequently decided he wasn't cut out to be a family man.

Robert Knight had left, bags in hand, that very afternoon.

"So who are you seeing?" she asked and, for a moment, he froze. Then he realized she was asking about his surgeon. Shell was in pharmaceutical sales and knew most of the doctors in the city.

"I have an appointment with Dr. Keller in the morning."

"Good." She nodded. "He's the best. He'll have you back in fighting form in no time."

"Shit," he laughed, "I wish that was true. I think my fighting form days are long gone. I'm getting old, Shell. Too old for this line of work."

"You shut your mouth," she harrumphed. "If you say you're getting old, that means I'm getting old, and I absolutely refuse to believe it."

He grinned and wrapped his good arm around her shoulders, planting a kiss in her hair—*mmm, vanilla.*

The smell would always remind him of home, and she always knew just what to say to make him feel better.

"I love you, you know," he told her.

"Yeah," she sighed, leaning into him, "I know."

———

Bill paced back and forth in his loft bedroom on the third floor of the shop, his worn copy of *Moby Dick* open on his bed, his cellular phone gripped tightly in his hand.

Should he call her or shouldn't he?

He'd seen the news coverage and the interview she and his sister had given. To anyone who didn't really know her, Eve'd looked poised and unflappable.

To him? Man, she'd been a wreck.

She hated the press, hated the spotlight, hated having her life flayed open for public perusal, and then there'd no doubt been the cross-examination by her father...

Why do you even care?

Yes, that was the question of the day, wasn't it? Why *did* he care? "Goddamnit!" he cursed and rubbed at his complaining stomach before jerking open the door and sticking his head into the hall.

He was hoping to see a light on under his sister's door, but...

No luck.

He went to pull his head back in when he caught the soft murmur of voices and the warm flicker of firelight coming from the media room.

Padding on bare feet down the hall's warmly polished wood floors, he jerked to a shocked halt at the doorway to the media room. He had a crystal clear view of the back of the extra-long couch and two heads tilted very close together. The smoky-sweet scent of burning pine logs filled the large space, tinged with the earthier aroma of hops and barley.

What's this? His sister and the mysterious Mossad agent sharing a beer and cuddling on the couch in front of the fire?

Not if he had anything to do with it!

Oh sure, Angel had handled himself like a pro out in the field, had been quick and agile and rock steady. The guy appeared to be well-educated and well-read—unlike a lot of meat-headed, spec-ops bozos. And, on top that, Angel had been willing to risk his life to save Becky's, but all that didn't add up to the kind of man Bill wanted dating his sister.

Not by a long shot.

Because Angel and his past were still a huge question mark, and if there was one thing he didn't like when it came to his baby sister, it was question marks.

Before he could take a step into the room and demand to know just what the hell was going on, Angel called out, "Come on in and join us, Bill."

The dude hadn't turned his head, hadn't flinched, hadn't so much as missed a beat in the conversation he was having with Becky.

Whoa. Can you say spooky, boys and girls?

Of course, Bill was used to working with spooky men. In fact, some might even consider *him* a bit spooky...

Coming to stand in front of them, he narrowed his eyes at the hand resting on Becky's shoulder. But instead of doing the smart thing and removing the offending appendage after accurately reading Bill's blatant get-your-goddamned-hands-off-my-sister expression, Angel simply allowed one corner of his mouth to quirk.

Oh, you've got balls. Huge, suicidal balls.

Bill experienced a pressing need to jerk the guy up by his collar and demand to be told just exactly what his intentions were toward Becky. Unfortunately, he'd already tried that on one or two of Becky's suitors and had paid the price for it.

His kid sister was diabolically devious and frighteningly inventive when it came to retribution, and his meddling in her affairs—especially her love life—always called for retribution, at least in her mind.

Stubborn, prideful, vengeful woman.

He swallowed back the words perched on the tip of his tongue, and he shoved his cell phone at his sister. "Call her."

"Huh?" She wrinkled her nose, blinking up at him.

"Call Eve. Make sure she's okay."

"Billy," she rolled her eyes, "Eve's *probably* fast asleep."

"Nope," he shook his head, waving the phone at her until she huffed and snatched it out of his hand. "She's *probably* rehashing the interview with the reporters and the interrogation by her father and gnawing the living shit out of her thumb. She needs someone to reassure her that she did the right thing today, lying to the press and Daddy Dearest."

"You're nuts."

"Yeah, and I'm also right."

She scanned his face for a brief moment before grumbling something unkind about his lineage, which was kind of funny considering she happened to share those same ancestors.

"Fine. I'll call her. But when I rouse her from a dead sleep, I'm letting you make the apologies."

"Fine." He crossed his arms over his chest, watching her punch in the numbers and trying to ignore his burning ulcer. He'd be damned glad when he could wash his hands of this entire situation. Maybe then he'd be able to lay off the Pepto.

"Eve," Becky said into the phone, "I'm sorry to wake you, but—oh, you were awake?" Bill smiled triumphantly, but she ignored him. "Well, I just wanted to check on you and see how you're doing and—"

She listened intently for a while then shot him an astonished look. "Well, put a Band-Aid on it so you won't be tempted to self-mutilate."

Angel, listening quietly and still with his cursed arm around Becky's shoulders, lifted one sleek brow. Bill chose to ignore him. It was either that or give in to the nearly overwhelming urge to chop that damned arm right off.

The machete he kept in his room would do the job quite nicely…

"No, no," his sister said, her tone reassuring. "You did great. And it *was* the right thing to do. Don't think of it as lying so much as simply omitting a few details… Yepper, okay, I will. Call you tomorrow, okay?"

She ended the call and handed his phone back to him, pursing her lips. "Don't say it," she said, referring to the I-told-you-so hovering on his tongue.

"I don't have to say it. You know it's the truth."

"Whatever." Her favorite word to end an argument she had no chance of winning.

"All right, well I'm beat, so I'm gonna hit the sack.

You should do the same." He held out his hand to her while simultaneously shooting Angel a meaningful look.

"I'll head to bed," she said, ignoring his hand, "just as soon as I finish my beer."

Sometimes her stubborn streak drove him nuts. Oh, who was he kidding? It *always* drove him nuts.

And he couldn't very well take a seat beside them after he'd made the statement about being beat. It'd be too obvious, and she'd never let him hear the end of it.

It's fine, he assured himself. *She's a big girl.*

Still, he couldn't help but cast one last concerned look over his shoulder before exiting the room.

This didn't bode well.

His stomach made a rough sound of agreement and, as he made his way back to his room, he reached into the front pocket of his jeans for the travel sized bottle of Pepto-Bismol he'd taken to carrying there.

So much for laying off the stuff...

Chapter Ten

IT WAS GOING ON OH-TWO-HUNDRED WHEN FRANK finally schlepped his tired ass up the metal stairs leading to the lofts and the living spaces on the third floor of the shop.

The murmur of the big screen and the crackle of the fire indicated someone was still awake in the media room, which wasn't unusual given the off-the-wall schedules of the men living there. So he wasn't quite sure what made him turn right once he topped the stairs, toward the media room, instead of hanging a left toward the row of loft-style bedrooms.

A sixth sense, maybe?

A higher power?

Probably.

Because the scene that met his eyes when he rounded the end of the sofa was pretty much the universal kick-in-the-teeth he needed to help him get his head screwed on straight.

It all made perfect sense now.

Angel's death-ray stare back on the *Patton* when he said he'd give his life for Becky. The guy's growled assertion that Frank wasn't the right man for her. The man's proprietary arm around her shoulders on that last leg of the flight from Israel to the states…

That same arm was around her shoulders now, his hand dangling dangerously close the gentle curve of her softly rounded left breast.

The sight went through Frank like a bolt of lightning. He didn't know if he was simply stunned or on fire with jealously.

The first, he assured himself, but the heat climbing up the back of his neck and burning the tips of his ears was a clear physical call of liar-liar-pants-on-fire.

Great. So now, on top of being a total A-hole for… well, a variety of reasons, he could add *jealous bastard* into the mix.

A growl built in his chest, but he suppressed it because it would've woken the two sweet little lovebirds— *barf!*—from their beauty sleep. Angel's dark head was thrown back on the cushions of the sofa while Becky tucked hers under the guy's freshly shaved chin. Peanut curled next to them, purring quietly.

It all looked so very idyllic, so very…*right*, what with them both being so young and so exceedingly pretty.

Holy hell, when Frank had kissed her, it probably looked like a classic case of beauty and the beast. So… yeah, this made a whole lot more sense.

Man, he was a fool, and a *blind* fool at that. Because he hadn't seen it coming.

Sure, he'd seen the pair of them with their heads together a time or two since Angel's arrival. But Becky was always joking around with the guys, treating them all like family, so he hadn't thought much of it.

Or maybe he'd just been so sure of her continued adoration of *him*, he'd missed the signs of her transferred affections.

Sonofabitch! That was it. It had to be.

And it hadn't been desire he'd seen burning hot and bright in her eyes after what'd happened between them down in sick bay. It'd been humiliation, and probably a little guilt because... yeah, she'd kissed him back.

He remembered that part very clearly.

So...why had she kissed him back?

Out of curiosity. Out of a need to prove to herself once and for all that he really wasn't the one she wanted.

Well, fuck-fuck-fuckety-fuck. There you go.

And as he stood there, looking down on the picture-perfect little tableau, his shoulder started aching like a month of Mondays, and he suddenly felt every single one of his thirty-nine years.

This is how it should be, he told himself, absently rubbing at the bandage around his shoulder. After all, he couldn't offer her all the things she wanted or needed. To do so would be to betray Shell, and he'd sooner cut off his stupid, injured arm than do that.

So...okay, this was good. This was right.

Uh-huh, so then why does it feel so wrong?

"Is there something I can help you with, Boss?" Angel's voice startled him, particularly because the guy hadn't opened his eyes or changed the modulated rhythm of his breathing. He appeared to be as fast asleep as when Frank first walked into the room.

Spooky.

"No," he answered, wishing like hell he could scream, *Yeah, you can get your goddamned hands off my woman!* But that was the thing, wasn't it? The fact that Becky could never be his woman? "I was just checking to see who was still awake."

"It appears it's just you and me," Angel said as he raised his head from the sofa cushions to glance down at Becky who, God love her, was drooling down the front of the guy's T-shirt. After smiling softly at the sight, Angel lifted his dark eyes and pinned Frank with a challenging stare.

Oooh, that's ballsy. "She's been through a lot," Frank said, fisting his hands to keep from using them to not-so-gently help Angel wipe that smug look right off his face. "She should be in bed."

"I'll make sure she gets there," Angel promised, his tone insinuating.

"Great," Frank managed to grind out before he turned and stomped from the room.

Yeah, great. Just…great!

Slamming the door to his bedroom, he went to wrench his shirt over his head before he remembered the damned sling and the wrapping and—

Sonofa—

He sank down on the bed and pummeled the mattress as the pain and frustration and…jealousy—yes, that was definitely jealousy—raged through him like a runaway forest fire. The walls would've been a preferable outlet for his temper, but they were three feet thick and made of brick, so there was really no doubt as to who'd be the victor of that little duel.

The repeated jarring of his shoulder soon had pain lancing through him like a hot knife. Only then did he stop Muhammad Ali-ing his bed and raise his head to stare blankly at the warm brick wall in front of him and the beautiful painting of the nighttime Chicago skyline.

The woman was so damned talented.

Although Becky usually didn't paint landscapes—she tended toward portraits and abstracts—she'd managed to capture the vibrancy and life of the city until he fancied he could actually hear the resonating *boom* of the fireworks bursting over Navy Pier. Feel the cool breeze blowing off Lake Michigan. Taste the salty sweetness of Garrett's popcorn.

He had no idea she'd seen him studying a photographer's snapshot of the Chicago skyline that day when the group took a break and ventured out to the Old Town Art Fair. He had no idea, that is, until two months later when she presented him with this canvas precisely reproducing the photograph.

It was his thirty-seventh birthday, and he'd realized then that what she felt for him went beyond the employer/employee relationship and, God help him, he'd simultaneously loathed and loved the fact. Loathed it because there was absolutely no way he could ever act on the longing he sometimes saw in her eyes. Loved it because she was so damned beautiful and bright and just so flippin'…*wonderful* it was impossible not to feel honored by her sweet affection.

And now that sweet affection had turned from him to another man and—

Sonofabitch!

Well, it'd been bound to happen, hadn't it?

He couldn't expect her to continually sow the seeds of love in inhospitable soil, could he? No. It was inevitable she'd move on to more enthusiastic pastures.

And Angel, that prick, appeared to be enthusiastic as hell.

He punched the mattress one last time before throwing himself back on it, staring in bleary-eyed oblivion at the silver ductwork snaking its way across the timberwood ceiling.

There were only two rules he considered ironclad, fucking-A unbreakable. One was you never leave a man behind; the other was you never steal another man's woman.

Well, by all accounts, rule number two was now in full effect.

Somehow, when he least expected it and when he wasn't looking, Becky became Angel's woman.

So that's it, he thought, throwing his good arm over his eyes. *It's finally over*.

And holy hell, it hurt so much more than he ever thought it would.

—◊◊◊—

Who is she?

That was the question on Becky's mind when she awoke alone on the sofa in the media room, Peanut snuggled next to her, the fire reduced to bright, orange coals in the grate.

Who is the woman Frank sneaks out to see?

She couldn't be his wife, because all Navy SEALs were required to list their spouses and significant others with JSOC—Joint Special Operations Command. It was a way for the government to keep eyes on their agents and their agents' families, but it was also a way to keep those same families safe.

And Becky had seen Frank's SEAL file.

No wife. No fiancée. Not even a serious girlfriend had been listed.

And *yes,* she'd probably be in deep doo-doo if anyone ever found out she'd taken a good long gander at those highly classified files, but thanks to Ozzie—who'd taught her the back door into JSOC's network in exchange for a lesson on designing and hand-rolling a gas tank—she'd been able to sneak in and sneak back out without anyone being any the wiser.

She briefly considered the possibility that the woman up in Lincoln Park—she preferred to think of her as Chesty McGivesItUp—was a recent installation, but she quickly disposed of that idea because, as memory served, no sooner did Frank and the boys purchase the rat-infested, decaying compound they'd eventually turned into Black Knights Inc., than Frank started making his stealthy trips up north. Which meant the woman had been firmly ensconced in his life *pre*-Black Knights Inc. and she should have been listed in his file. Unless, of course, she was just a girlfriend. A girlfriend that he had for over four years…

So why didn't he propose? Why didn't he talk about her? Was it possible she was simply a friend with benefits?

That's what made the most sense.

Yeah, now that she thought about it, Ms. McGivesItUp had to be Frank's go-to gal when the ol' libido started acting up. But, *damnit*, why did the big dill-hole have to go all the way up to Lincoln Park when *she*, Becky Reichert, was right there, ready and willing to fill that particular position in his life?

If all he wanted was a little in-and-out, she had a slot A that would be more than willing to accommodate his tab B on occasion and then, maybe, they could—

"Oh good. You're awake." Frank came to stand in front of the sofa, a steaming cup of coffee in one hand and a watermelon-flavored Dum Dum in the other. He handed over both.

"Thanks." She accepted them gratefully, noting the fact that he brought in her usual breakfast, in bed no less…er, perhaps it was more accurate to say he brought her breakfast in sofa?

Whatever. Regardless, it was clear that although he might not like to entangle himself in messy, personal *relationships*, he sure as heck knew her personal *habits*. So, like it or not—and she was very sure he would prefer *or not*—the two of them were entangled.

Just not as entangled as she wanted them to be.

"What's up?" She took a sip of the scalding coffee and unwrapped the sucker.

"Just got a new order in from one of the Blackhawks players. He wants a custom-made Black Knights chopper to auction off for a charity he's sponsoring." He handed her a memo with the details, and just like that, it was business as usual.

Frickin' frackin' *great*.

But really, did she expect anything else?

"But uh…you don't…what I mean to say is that if you're n-not ready…" He took a deep breath, scratched his chin, and muttered a curse as he stared at the scuffed toes of his biker boots like they might hold the secrets to the universe.

Okay, so maybe it *wasn't* business as usual, because that halting, stuttering man in no way resembled the never-hesitate, suck-it-up, get-back-to-work Frank Knight she'd come to know over the past three-plus years.

Glancing at him curiously, watching the muscle tick in his square jaw, she scratched a crusty glob of sleep from the corner of her eye in order to get a better look at the man standing before her. "What?" she asked around the sucker. "If I'm not ready for what?"

"For work," he ground out, searching her face. "If you need time to see doctors or specialists or…fuck, I don't know. But if you need time to—"

"Doctors for *what?*"

"For…for." He swallowed, his Adam's apple bouncing in the thick, tanned column of his throat. "For all the things that happened while you were held hostage by those goddamned pirates."

Her chin jerked back as her eyebrows climbed toward her hairline. She popped the sucker from her mouth. "And just what do you think happened while I was held hostage by those goddamned pirates?"

"I don't know," he groaned, rubbing at his chest as if his heart hurt. "And not knowing is *killing* me, but I'm afraid knowing is going to be worse, because the thought of—"

"Frank." She lifted a hand, stopping him. The concern in his fierce eyes made her chest warm with pleasure. "Nothing happened. I wasn't beaten. I wasn't raped." His eyelids squeezed closed as he drew in a deep breath. "The worst thing I suffered while on board the *Serendipity* for those six days was a moderate sunburn and a little mental anguish."

His eyes flew open as he regarded her intently. "Do you need to talk to someone about that, uh, mental anguish? Someone professional," he was quick to add.

"No. At least I don't think so," she said when he gave her a disbelieving look. "I feel okay about the whole hostage situation. Really, I do. I knew if I could just keep the boat in the water that you and the guys would come for me eventually. I *knew* that. And that knowing helped keep the terror at bay. So I don't think I'm suffering from PTSD or anything. Nothing that serious. In fact, I feel pretty good. I'd feel better if Sharif was in custody, but…" She shrugged.

"Don't worry about that. Interpol will catch him. And if they don't…well let's just say me and the boys will make sure this is one loose end that gets tied up in a pretty little bow. Even if it means we have to scour the wastelands of Somalia in order to do it, we *will* find him and bring him to justice."

"Oh Frank," she replied softly, "I know you will." If there was one thing the Black Knights were good at, it was protecting their own. Her boys wouldn't sleep until they knew she was safe, until they knew Sharif no longer posed a threat. That support system, that knowing there was always someone there who had her back, was more precious to her than she could ever express. It gave her the courage and the strength to continue, "And while we're on the subject of things that happened out on the Indian Ocean, I think we should discuss that little incident down in sick b—"

"Let it go," he growled with a raised hand and a terse jerk of his stubbled chin.

"But—"

"And since you're feeling up to getting back to work, the date of the Blackhawk's charity auction is two months away. That should be plenty of time for you to design, fabricate, and get the bike out to the powder-coater and chromer."

Okay, so obviously talk of what happened on the *Patton* was strictly prohibited.

Duly noted. And totally frustrating.

Two days later…

Sharif crested a shallow wave and caught a long glimpse of golden coastline dotted by multiple graduated lines of tall, white structures. The skeletal framework of cranes looked wispy thin in the distant harbor, dwarfed by the steel gray hulls of numerous freighters.

It was a port of some sort. A large one by the looks of it, and the city snuggling next to the bustling port appeared to be larger still.

A sane man would've cried with joy, but Sharif felt no elation. Because he feared he was no longer sane. Because he could no longer believe his own eyes. What he was seeing might very well turn out to be a mirage.

A hallucination.

After all, this morning he'd been carrying on a conversation with his dead mother…

Only, she hadn't been dead. This morning she'd been standing at the wheel, dressed in a beautiful *guntino* and staring at the taut white sails.

"You've been led astray, my son," she said softly.

He'd been in the process of explaining how things had changed since her death, how he'd been forced into his current situation, when she suddenly dissolved, simply faded into nothingness, much like Alice's Cheshire Cat. Except there'd been no lingering smile hanging on the warm wind, only the quiet words of her gentle condemnation…

So no, he set no store in the vision before his eyes,

only licked dry, cracked lips and steered toward the horizon, waiting for it to all just disappear.

Only…it didn't.

A motorboat sped by him, kicking up hot salt spray and churning bright green algae in its wake.

This was no hallucination. Even his fevered brain couldn't conjure those details.

Still, it felt like years passed as he gradually inched closer and closer, closing in on a giant freighter slowly lumbering into dock. A man standing on the deck of the freighter waved his arms and angrily yelled something.

Sharif didn't speak Swahili, but he understood enough to know the man was telling him he shouldn't sail here. Something about merchant vessels only.

Sharif tried calling out, but a dull croak was all he could manage from his parched throat. So he held up his injured hand, now dark and bloated with infection and managed to whisper one word in English, "Hospital," before his whole world faded to black.

—⁓—

"Interpol needs a sketch of Sharif's face."

That name, and the memories it evoked, made Becky shiver like she'd been sitting in a bucket of ice water. Swinging away from the computer and the CAD software she was using to design the bike for the Blackhawk's player, she stared at Frank's concerned expression.

"Do you think you can do that?" he asked softly.

She made a face and waved her hand at the fifteen-foot tall caricatures she'd painted of the Knights all along the shop's impregnable walls, each one was detailed and specific, not to mention a spitting image of the man it was modeled after. "What do you think?"

"I'm not talking about can you accurately *draw* the guy." He frowned and went to cross his arms before wincing and remembering he had one in a sling. The man should've gone in for surgery days ago, but for some reason, she had no idea why, he appeared to be putting off the inevitable. *The big, stubborn oaf.* "I'm asking if you're emotionally ready to see that face again?"

Emotionally ready? Uh, no. She could happily go the rest of her life without setting eyes on that ugly mug. But she wasn't the type to throw up her hands and play the wounded victim when there was something she could do to help put the bastard securely behind bars where he belonged. "What about the surveillance photos you have of us on the sailboat? Don't some of them show his face?"

"Nope. They only caught glimpses of his profile and the back of his head. Not enough to run against facial recognition software. And of the million or so Sharifs in the world, about one hundred have worked as interpreters for the U.N., if you can believe that statistic. The guys and gals at Interpol would very much like to find out just which Sharif they're after."

"Yeah, okay." She nodded, bracing herself to not only *see* that evil face again, but to personally *construct* it. Somehow that was worse, more...*personal.* "I guess there's been no word at the ports?"

He shook his head, regret and frustration clear in his expression.

Yeah well, she was pretty regretful and frustrated herself. Regretful that she hadn't driven that KA-BAR straight into Sharif's blackened heart when she had the chance, and frustrated that he was still roaming around out there…somewhere.

The thought sent a shiver of trepidation racing down her spine, but she ignored it. With the U.S. government's resources and those of the international community, he'd be caught eventually. Of course, it had taken nearly ten years to get Osama bin Laden, so maybe she was playing the part of the cockeyed optimist.

Whatever.

She wasn't going to think about that. Not now. Especially when she had something she'd been needing to get off her chest and, what do you know? Here he was. Here she was. And, for the first time in two long days, they were alone together.

"Frank," she murmured, "I know you said to let it go, but I can't help but notice there's this…*tension* between us, and I…I just wanted to say—"

"Are you going to do the damned sketch or not?"

Every single hackle she had stood up and started shaking an angry fist. "Yes!" she hissed, thrusting out her chin. "I'll do the damned sketch!" *You big, stupid dill-hole!*

"Good." He nodded, then turned and stomped back to his office.

Oooh, the insufferable…

How she could continue to *want* him, to *love* him after the way he'd been treating her the past few days was a complete and utter mystery.

She was a glutton for punishment.

That was the only answer.

Chapter Eleven

A DOOR OPENED DOWN THE HALL. FRANK KNEW THAT squeaky hinge. Becky was up.

He snatched his diver's watch from the bedside table and glanced at the softly glowing dial. Oh-three-hundred.

What the hell was she doing awake at this hour?

He very much feared he knew the answer to that one. And his name started with an A and ended with an L and—

Sonofabitch!

He threw an arm over his gritty eyes and tried not to picture Angel and Becky together.

It was impossible.

Ever since the night he'd caught them doing the cute and cuddly bit on the couch, all he could see when he closed his eyes was Becky in that damn Mossad agent's arms. It was enough to have him needing some of the Pepto-Bismol Bill had taken to toting around.

And yeah, so Angel hadn't taken her to bed then, evidenced by the fact that she'd still been on the sofa the next morning—a miracle for which Frank had nearly dropped to his knees and thanked the good Lord—but that didn't mean they weren't currently giving each other the ol' slap and tickle.

Ugh. Just the thought made him want to vomit.

On the verge of plugging his ears so he wouldn't have to hear the sound of Angel's door opening, he sat bolt upright when the muted *chic-chic* of a round being chambered met his ears instead.

What the hell?

He tossed back the covers and raced to the door, jerking it open only to be greeted by Becky's wide, panicked gaze and the business end of Springfield XD-9 Subcompact pistol.

"Whoa!" He threw his hands in the air, wincing when his injured shoulder shrieked in protest of the movement.

"He's here," she whispered hoarsely, turning to aim the pistol down the long, dark hall. "Somehow he broke in and—"

"Who's here, Becky?"

"Sharif!" she hissed. "He killed Toran out at the gatehouse and now he's here and—"

She swung around and nearly blew Peanut to hell when the cat had the bad sense to plod out of her room and into the hall.

"Oh, God, Peanut! I nearly sent you to kitty heaven!" She cried even as she spun back and once more quartered the dimly lit hall, slowly moving in the direction of the stairs.

"Becky, I need you to—"

"Where's your weapon, Frank? You need to get a weapon!" Her voice cracked on the hard edge of hysteria, and he realized what was happening.

He'd seen it all before. Men, fresh in from the field, seemingly fine, go to sleep one night only to wake from a nightmare so vivid they're unable to tell what's real and what's simply a figment of their over-stimulated brains.

"Becky," he told her calmly, "you had a nightmare.

Sharif isn't here. He didn't get in. Toran is fine and still—"

He could tell by the wild look on her face, she didn't believe him.

"Come with me." He laid a gentle hand on her shoulder and slowly led her down the stairs to the bank of computers on the office level. She didn't relax her grip on the pistol the entire way and continued to quarter the area like a well-trained commando.

"Look," he pointed to the screen showing Toran in the gatehouse. The guy was eating a jelly donut and sipping coffee from the cap of his drab-green thermos. Very much still alive.

"But I…I saw him. I mean…I think I…oh, God." She shook her head slowly, then swallowed and carefully placed her pistol on the conference table.

He saw it coming. Her shoulders hitched up around her ears, her lower lip quivered.

And then his fucking heart shattered, because tough-as-nails Rebel Reichert broke down in tears. No. Not tears. They were hard, heaving, gut-wrenching sobs.

"I must be going crazy," she wailed into the hands she'd thrown over her eyes. "I was so sure…" She didn't finish. She didn't need to. He knew exactly what she was going through.

"I know you were," he murmured as he gathered her into his arms—damn the bum shoulder and the protest it lodged. Damn his promise to himself to keep his hands off of her. "I know you were," he repeated as he half carried/half dragged her up the stairs and into the media room.

He sat on the couch, pulling her into his lap as he smoothed her hair and let her cry herself dry.

It took everything he had not to kiss away each and every one of those tears, but he satisfied himself with simply burying his nose in her hair and breathing in her clean, sweet scent.

"I thought I was stronger than this," she whispered against his throat sometime later. He tried to ignore her hot breath against his skin.

It wasn't working.

Especially with her oh-so-fine, boxer-covered ass planted directly over his dick which, in response, was sounding a rousing chorus of, "happy, happy, joy, joys."

Goddamn, he was a total reprobate. Here she was in pieces, and all he could think about was getting her naked and driving himself into the wet haven of her female warmth.

"You are strong," he told her, adjusting her in his lap so she wouldn't feel his always-optimistic cock pounding in rhythm to his too-fast heartbeat. "Having nightmares after going through a situation like that is normal. Especially since you don't have any closure. *Yet*," he quickly added.

"I think it was sketching him this afternoon. Seeing his face again. It brought it all back, you know?" She sniffled and pushed from his chest to look at him.

Her hair was a mess, her eyes were puffy and bloodshot, her cheek was still discolored, and she was the most beautiful woman he'd ever seen.

"I do know. But you need to remember that you're home now. You're safe." And he'd make damned sure she stayed that way.

After a deep, shuddering breath, she nodded and gingerly crawled from his lap.

Instantly, he missed her warmth.

Curling into a ball at the end of the sofa, she shoved her cold, bare feet under his thigh and sighed as he covered her with the afghan draped over the back of the couch.

"Stay with me until I fall asleep, okay?" she asked around a huge yawn. Now that she'd come down from the adrenaline rush, it was going to be lights-out in a hurry.

"I will," he told her and grabbed her foot, chafing some warmth back into it.

Becky had the most elegant feet he'd ever seen. Long and slim and always with some crazy polish on her toes thanks to her weekly "pedi" as she liked to call it.

The woman was a damned paradox. So tough and tomboyish one minute and then he'd turn around, catch her in a different light, and she was the softest, sweetest, most feminine thing he'd ever laid eyes on.

Her gentle snore had one corner of his mouth lifting before the thought of what needed to be done had him scowling into the darkness.

There was no more putting it off. The surgery...

He'd thought maybe...but, no. If he had any hope of being able to protect her, of being able to continue his job, he had to have the use of both arms.

Ever since he'd left Dr. Keller's office with assurances that he'd be just fine, that they'd be careful with the dosage of the general anesthesia and monitor him closely, he couldn't shake the feeling that the surgery would end with his shaking the bony hand of the Reaper.

He wanted to chalk it all up to paranoia, but a growing part of him was beginning to believe it was something a lot closer to premonition.

Still, Shell assured him he was being silly and, yeah,

when he stepped outside himself and looked at the situation rationally, he couldn't help but agree with her.

So...it was time he quit acting like a pussy and started acting like the steel-balled warrior he was. His men needed him. Becky needed him. And if there was a chance he could be made whole again...

He'd call Dr. Keller's office in the morning.

———

The pain in his hand was back, sharp and piercing as the moment that stupid bitch had shoved the length of her big knife into it.

"Unnngh," he moaned, not wanting to wake fully, afraid when he opened his eyes all he'd see was cloudless blue sky and kilometer after kilometer of bright, rolling ocean.

"Wake up," a deep voice commanded in heavily accented English.

Sharif blinked in confusion at the dark face of the strange man leaning over him. He grimaced when something tightened painfully around his arm, then swallowed a cry of relief when he realized it was a blood-pressure cuff.

"What's your name?" the man asked, a doctor by the looks of him. The stethoscope, the white lab coat, the stern expression all fit the bill.

Sharif turned his head and the room around him shimmered into focus. White walls, white tile floors, and a blue door with a file holder attached to its metal surface.

It was a hospital. He was in a *hospital*. He made it! He was alive!

He wanted to whoop with the joy of it, but a sudden

shaft of pain lanced through his hand, making him grimace instead.

"What's your name?" the doctor repeated the question in Somali, but Sharif just shook his head, biting his bottom lip against the fiery agony shooting up his arm. Despite the coolness of the air-conditioned room, sweat broke out on his forehead and beaded on his upper lip.

"All right," the doctor said, "don't strain yourself. We will answer all of these questions later. Like who you are and what you were doing piloting a boat that was reported hijacked almost two weeks ago."

Sharif's eyes snapped open as he scanned the doctor's hard expression. An icy chill washed over him, momentarily freezing the sweat on his skin and the rhythm of his heart.

The doctor knew what he was, or more appropriately, what he'd become. A pirate. And that meant he was in deep, *deep* trouble.

"Where am I?" he managed to rasp.

"Ah," the doctor smiled narrowly, unwinding the stethoscope from around his neck. "So you do understand what I am saying."

He swallowed. His throat was excruciatingly dry, like he'd been ingesting wads of cotton for a week.

"You are in Mombasa, Kenya," the doctor explained, plugging the earbuds of his stethoscope into his ears and placing the cool, round diaphragm above Sharif's pounding heart. "And it is a good thing, too. Had you made the Somali coast, you would have been lucky to find anyone who could save that hand."

Sharif glanced down to his wounded hand but could

see nothing past the thick white bandages wrapped around the throbbing appendage.

"We've rehydrated you and cleaned out the infection. The last finger had to be amputated. There was no saving it; the infection had reached the bone."

Hot bile climbed up his parched throat at the thought of being permanently maimed, disfigured. And the burning rage that quickly followed scorched away the ice that'd briefly filled his veins when the doctor mentioned the hijacked catamaran.

"We will have to wait and see how much nerve damage was done before we can determine how much mobility you will retain," the doctor continued, completely oblivious to the dark thoughts of death and retribution flashing through Sharif's fevered brain.

When the doctor finally left the room, he raked in a deep, steadying breath and pushed up on the narrow hospital bed. The walls slanted in on him as the floor bucked. It was like walking through a funhouse—only not nearly as fun. Taking slow, measured breaths through his nose, he managed to breathe away the dizziness. And when his head finally quit spinning, he surveyed his condition.

With his good hand, he grabbed one of the bags of fluid hanging from a metal pole beside his bed and read, "saline." Gritting his teeth, he yanked the needle administering the fluid out of his arm. After flinging it aside, he grabbed the other bag. Nafcillin. An antibiotic. That one he unhooked from its metal pole in order to secure the cool plastic bag under his perspiring armpit.

He wasn't taking any chances with the infection in his hand. Slipping his feet over the side of the bed, he tested his strength, found it pathetically lacking but firmed his jaw and took a step anyway. He couldn't afford to waste one minute.

Pleased when he didn't collapse on the floor, he shuffled to the little plywood wardrobe shoved in the corner. Empty—save for an extra blanket and pillow. Frustrated, he stumbled toward the door, carefully pulling it open. The hall was quiet and wonderfully vacant.

With a small smile of victory, he slipped from his room and padded to the next blue door. Knocking softly, he listened for a response and, hearing none, swept inside.

There was a man lying on the bed, hooked up to a great number of beeping, shushing, monitoring machines. The man's dark skin hung over his face like a brown shroud, and the room reeked of astringent cleaning products, old urine, and the lingering putrescence of imminent death.

Sharif swallowed the overwhelming desire to gag, breathed through his mouth, and opened the small wardrobe.

Ah-ha!

He was pleased to discover the familiar red-and-white checkered cloth of a *shemagh*. A circular black *igal* lay on top of the carefully folded Arabic head scarf.

Most Kenyans, especially those living on the coast, tended to don western-style clothing, but Sharif was happy to see this man, whoever the poor dying sod was, did not. Hiding his injury and his bag of antibiotics in the billowing folds of traditional Arabic dress would be so much easier.

He couldn't have picked a more perfect or comfortable disguise if he tried.

"Thank you," he whispered to the dying man after

donning the clothes. He shuffled to the door, once more peeking into the hallway. Still empty.

Stepping out, he wiped the cold sweat from his brow, lengthened his stride to conceal his weakness, and made his way quickly down the corridor.

It wasn't until he pushed through the hospital's wide front doors and out into the scorching African sun, that he dragged in a shaky breath.

His knees wobbled like they were made of spaghetti, his head pounded like a jackhammer, and his whole arm was ready to fall off, but he'd made it.

It was time to find a phone and get far, far away from the international police force that was sure to be hot on his trail.

—◊◊◊—

Frank stood at the second-story railing and glanced down at the grease-stained shop floor below.

Dan "The Man" Currington had managed to crawl out of the bottle this morning and was diligently working on a production bike—the standard model of chopper the Black Knights built for purchase by the general public, as opposed to the one-off, custom-theme bikes they designed for corporations or the ultra-wealthy.

The assembly of a production bike was probably about all Dan, who'd been steadily trying to kill himself with Jack Daniels since his wife's brutal death, could handle. And given that Dan had built so many of the damn things, he could probably do the deed ten sheets to the wind, half-asleep, and blindfolded.

This morning, gaunt and pasty pale, Dan appeared to be batting three out of three.

He was still drunk. He was certainly dead on his feet, stopping occasionally to rest his palms on the bike lift and let his head hang limply between his skinny shoulders. And even though the poor guy wasn't blindfolded, he might as well have been. It didn't take a genius of Ozzie's caliber to see Dan was on cruise control, his motions smooth and mindless, his glassy eyes vacant.

It broke Frank's heart to see one of his men sunk so low, but nothing any of them did seemed to make any difference.

So, all that was left was to watch and wait. Give the guy more time to mourn. And hope like hell Dan was able to pull himself together before his liver went tits-up.

What a goatfuck…

The sound of playful bantering drew his attention to the other side of the shop, where Becky and Angel hunched over a large drawing board shoved against the east wall. Their heads were bent close together, their shoulders touching. Something Angel said had Becky throwing her head back, laughing that dark, husky laugh of hers that always hit Frank like a thousand licking tongues, making each and every one of his nerve endings stand up and salute.

He growled as his dick started stiffening with a little homage of its own. The stupid thing had yet to get the memo that Rebecca Reichert was no longer interested.

So what else is new?

His cock was always the first to respond and the last to clue in, which right about now was just *grrreat.* Men of nearly forty years weren't supposed to spring boners at the mere sound of a woman's laughter, were they?

No, definitely not. Though once again, his little head

chose to ignore logic, and he was forced to furtively arrange himself into a more comfortable position as he scowled down at the oh-so-happy pair.

For the last couple of days, he'd covertly watched the progress as Becky and Angel finalized the design of Angel's chopper, alternating between the radioactive version of jealously and a dull, aching acceptance. Right then, he was somewhere between the two, though when Angel slung a muscular arm around her shoulders, he quickly starting leaning more toward radioactive jealously again.

He'd very much like to march down there and rip the offending appendage right off the smooth-talking pretty boy…and yessir, it was official. His spent fuel rods were no longer being properly cooled and a meltdown seemed imminent. It probably had something to do with the fact that he'd known her for over three years and the night before he'd held her in his arms while she cried out her fear, and somehow both of those things made him feel like he had some sort of claim over her.

Which was ridiculous.

"So." Bill came to lean a hip against the railing, crossing his arms over his chest, causing the back of his T-shirt to stretch tight across his shoulders. "Tomorrow's the big day, huh? You're going under the knife."

The fiery venom that'd been heating Frank's blood instantly banked as a chill raced down his spine, like a ghost slipped an icy finger over the length of his vertebrae—or maybe that was simply Death giving him a glimpse of what was to come?

Well, at least that takes care of my jealousy and the little problem behind my fly, he thought. *Thank goodness for small miracles.*

Or not.

Perhaps he should be rejoicing in the exhilaration of boiling jealousy and the pleasure of an untimely erection. After all, it might very well be the last time he experienced either.

No, goddamnit!

He was not going to give in to his bone-tingling sense of…*certainty*.

If he had a chance, just one small chance of making it out alive, of being able to protect Becky and continue to do his job, it was worth it.

And despite what his gut kept telling him, one thing he could be certain of was that nothing was ever certain.

"Yeah." He nodded, trying to push the dismaying sensation away. It was fairly easy, especially when Angel— that prick—leaned in to whisper something in Becky's ear. He had no hope of hearing what Angel said, what with Poison pounding out of the array of computer speakers behind him and Ozzie—the kid had arrived back from his meeting with his super-geek buddies this morning— noisily crooning, "Every Rose Has Its Thorn." The kid really needed to branch out musically, but the overabundance of 80's music continually blasting inside the shop's brick walls was the very least of Frank's current problems. "Tomorrow's the day," he confirmed. "Do or die."

He very much feared it might well be the latter, but it was a chance he had to take.

"Well, it's about time you took care of that shoulder," Bill proclaimed, nodding, oblivious to the turmoil churning inside of Frank. "You've been popping ibuprofen so long it's a wonder your stomach lining isn't torn to shreds."

"Stomach trouble has never been my problem," he murmured, thankful for that small bit of luck because he *had* been downing pain meds for years instead of taking his chances with surgery.

Bill patted the bottle of Pepto-Bismol in his hip pocket and grimaced. "Wish I could say the same."

"I've seen you swilling that stuff. Is there, uh, is there something you want to talk about?"

"Lord, no," Bill replied. Which was guy-speak for *as long as I don't say it out loud, there isn't really a problem*.

Frank understood. He wasn't much for the touchy-feely, tell-me-all-your-woes-so-I-can-commiserate kind of thing himself. Sometimes a man just needed to work through his own shit in his own time. He just hoped Wild Bill worked through his before he needed a stomach transplant.

Ah...perfect. So now Dan Man was going to need a liver transplant, Bill was going to need a stomach transplant, and he couldn't miss the irony that the downfall of both men wasn't a case of terminal ballistics or capture by enemy forces. Hell no. The direct cause of both men's maladies was a woman, or more accurately the *absence* of a woman.

Jesus H. Christ, wasn't that always the way of it? The toughest, meanest men on the planet turned into whiskey-guzzling, Pepto-chugging, shit for brains when someone with a round ass and sweet-smelling hair minced her precious self into the picture.

It was almost enough to make a smart man want to avoid the fairer sex all together...*almost*.

A burst of laughter cut through Ozzie's Bret Michaels

impression, and Frank once more focused on the couple down below, grinding his jaw so hard his eye sockets ached when Becky stuffed a sucker in Angel's breast pocket.

His vision actually hazed with red as he wondered if the lollipop was root beer flavored.

Becky had taken to eating Dum Dums years ago as a way to help herself quit smoking. She liked all the flavors except root beer, which she'd pitched in the trash until the day she found out root beer was Frank's favorite. Then she started stashing the little treats in places he was sure to discover them. His desk drawer, his coffee mug, *his* shirt pockets.

He'd professed irritation at the time—because he was unable to resist the sugary treats, and it severely pissed him off anytime his willpower failed him. But right now, he'd give anything to once more be on the receiving end of one of those sweet suckers.

Instead it was Angel, that *prick*...

Bill turned toward the railing, resting his elbows on the top rung. "I don't know how to feel about that." He motioned with a jerk of his chin toward the pair laughing and carrying on below.

"Neither do I," Frank admitted.

Bill shot him a sharp glance. "I always kind of figured it'd be you."

"It'd be me what?"

"You know," Bill shrugged. "I figured it'd be *you* who ended up with Becky."

"And why would you think that?"

"Because of the way you two constantly dance around each other like boxers, taking strips out of each other's hide."

Frank made a face clearly stating his belief that Bill must be suffering from some sort of insanity.

Bill rolled his eyes. "Goddamn, Boss. Are you gonna make me say it?"

"I guess so, since I don't know what the hell you're talking about."

"The way you guys continually snipe at each other... it always sort of feels like...I don't know...foreplay."

"Goddamnit, Bill!"

"What? You made me say it. And just because she's my sister, I'm not supposed to notice these things?"

"You're damned right!" Frank barked, embarrassed, incensed, more than a little bit chagrined because, in truth, it always sort of *felt* like foreplay.

"Oh, come on. I'd have to be a blind man."

"Yeah well, I'd never do anything about it." *At least not when I'm stone-cold sober. Give me a few narcotics, and then I can't keep my flippin' hands to myself.*

"I know." Bill nodded, still watching him with too much intensity. "You'd never breach the sanctity of the employee/employer relationship which, God knows, I respect you for. But I just figured someday..." He let the sentence dangle.

Someday. If the guy only knew what'd happened down in the *Patton*'s sick bay...

"She's too young for me," he spoke aloud the mantra that'd circled around in his head for over three years.

"Maybe," Bill agreed, and a new world record for pounds-per-square-inch of pressure was set by Frank's jaw. "But what's a few years when we're talking about amour?"

Aw, goddamnit. He needed to nip this thing in the

bud right here and now. Turning to Bill, he managed to unclamp his teeth and let the man see the raw, profligate heat in his eyes. "Who's talking love, Bill?"

See? See what I feel for your sister? It's straight-up, one-hundred-percent, fuck-all-night lust.

But instead of getting pissed like he should have, like Frank *wanted* him to, Bill simply tilted his head and narrowed his eyes in speculation.

"Drink to me only with thine eyes, and I will pledge with mine. Or leave a kiss but in the cup, and I'll not look for wine..."

"What the hell? You're quoting poetry now? Jesus H. Christ!" *Someone please shoot me!*

"My point is, Boss," Bill stressed, "that what I've seen in your eyes when you look at my sister isn't always what you're showing me right now."

Frank growled and once more faced the railing, silently cursing Bill for seeing too far, too much. After a long moment, he swallowed down his hostility and ventured, "And you'd have been okay with that? With me and Becky?"

"If you loved her?"

He groaned like he was being tortured—which he was. "Yeah, if I loved her."

"Yeah, Boss. I'd be okay with that, but I don't think *you* would."

"You're damned right! It makes me a filthy lecher!"

It was sudden understanding he saw flicker through Bill's dark gaze, a sort of *ah-ha* moment. Though, if Bill was just now light-bulbing the fact that he was too old for Becky, then the guy was a lot slower than Frank ever guessed, and that didn't make a damn bit of sense given Bill was usually nose-deep in a novel the size of a small coffee table.

"I don't think the age gap is problem, Boss," Bill replied. "One, because what's a decade and some change when you come right down to it? And two, because I know you. This has nothing to do with Becky's age or your age and everything to do with that woman up in Lincoln Park."

Don't punch him. Don't punch him. Don't...

"Shit!" he growled as he stomped away from the railing, slamming the door to his office behind him and throwing himself down in his desk chair until the metal springs wailed for sweet mercy.

Instead of punching Bill for his unwelcome insight, he satisfied himself by slamming his palm down on the scarred surface of his wooden desk. He regretted the move when it caused a stack of papers, precariously perched close to the edge, to slip over. The stack fluttered to the floor in a giant, disorganized mess.

"Shit, shit, *shit!*" He yelled and then glared at the lone sheet remaining from the stack. It sat there, partially hanging over the side of his desk, taunting him with its tenacious presence. He imagined that sheet of paper was his ridiculous infatuation with Becky Reichert, hanging on despite the odds and the overwhelming current of events surrounding it.

With a vicious swipe of his hand, he sent it flying down to join its wildly strewn compatriots.

He should've felt better afterward...

He didn't. Especially when he heard Ozzie's voice drift through the closed door, "What the hell did you do to Boss?"

"Hit him with a violent torpedo of truth, I think," Bill replied.

Ozzie barked out a laugh. "Good ol' Charlie Sheen."

Frank had no idea what that meant. Probably something to do with pop culture—of which Ozzie was a master. Still, regardless of the meaning behind the phrase, the truth of Bill's words *had* hit him like a violent torpedo of truth.

Because Bill was absolutely right. If things were different, if Shell hadn't been part of the equation, he'd have given into his base desires months ago. Hell, probably *years* ago. And that made him no better than the man who'd sired him, the man he swore he'd never become.

The rotten apple sure doesn't fall far from the tree, does it? Gee thanks, Dad.

Chapter Twelve

"IT'S UNSEASONABLY NICE OUTSIDE," BECKY ANNOUNCED around a Dum Dum as she popped her head into Frank's office, interrupting the situation report Ozzie was giving to all the Knights. Everyone—excluding Ghost, who was staying with his fiancée, Ali, on the East Coast until she finished teaching the semester's classes—had finally returned from whatever conference, assignment, or mission they'd been tasked with, and the small office was full to bursting with hardened operators.

But there was someone glaringly absent from the group. Who could that be? Oh, right. *Her*.

It irked her to no end that she wasn't allowed in on such meetings. She worked with these guys, and gal— let's not forget Vanessa Cordero, the new hotshot communications specialist—every day. She cleaned their wounds and their underwear. They were her frickin' family, for Pete's sake, but when it came to their missions, she was treated like a nosy civilian, and that just really, really, *really* pissed her off.

Not that she didn't know what was going on with her guys out in the field…

She used the hacking skills Ozzie taught her to break into their computer system and make herself privy to all of the Knights' confidential files. Anytime there was an update on one of the guys out on a mission, she got an email notifying her of their new status, so *yeah*, Frank might try his best to keep her out of the loop, but she was definitely smack-dab *in* the loop and, just to irritate him, she'd made it her life's mission to impinge whenever possible, whenever she knew the information being discussed wasn't critical—like now.

"How nice is it?" Ozzie asked, his blue eyes lighting up like a kid being offered a shiny new bike.

Good ol' Ozzie.

She could always depend on him to have her back, especially when it meant they'd likely get to go do something fun. And a warm day in Chicago in October absolutely demanded that they go do something fun.

She popped the grape-flavored lollipop out of her mouth so she could blow him a raspberry, then grinned and wiggled her eyebrows, surveying the rest of the group. "It's sixty degrees outside, likely the last day it'll be nice enough to take the bikes out. What do you say we all mount up, ride over to Delilah's, and have ourselves some dogs? Frank?" Last night, when she freaked out, he'd held her safe and warm in his arms. But today? Today he was back to treating her like a plague-carrier which was just... perfect. *Not.* "How long before you can't eat or drink?"

"I'm supposed to begin fasting at eighteen-hundred," he grumbled, obviously biting his tongue on the harsh scolding he usually had ready for whenever she interrupted one of their "confidential" gatherings.

Billy was leaning against the wall beside the door. She grabbed his wrist to glance down at his waterproof diver's watch. They had two hours. "So we'll have the blue-hair special. Fine by me. What do you all say? Winter's almost here. This may be our last chance..."

Again, she wiggled her eyebrows enticingly. All the Knights suffered from a form of seasonal affective disorder when winter rolled around. Oh, not because the endless cold, cloudy Windy City days caused them to slip into depression, but because the endless cold, cloudy Windy City days kept them from their favorite pastime...namely mounting a couple of tons of hand-rolled steel and rumbling toward the freedom of the open road.

"But the newbies don't have bikes yet," Ozzie shook his head despairingly, referring to the three newest members of Black Knights Inc. "And Boss can't ride Boss Hog with only one arm. The stretch is way too far."

True. Frank's chopper—the pearl-colored beauty/beast appropriately named Boss Hog—was impossible to operate one-handed. In fact, *all* their choppers were impossible to operate one-handed. Trying to do so was sure to result in a terminal case of road rash.

"Boss can ride with me, and the rest of you can take one of the production bikes," she declared, anxious to get out of the shop and away from the charged atmosphere Frank had created since their return. Or perhaps it'd be more accurate to say the atmosphere had become supercharged. It'd always hummed with electricity any-time the two of them were in the same room together, but now? Man, now the small hairs on her neck were perpetually twanged upright in warning.

It was getting really annoying, this constant feel-ing of being on the precipice of something explosive. If only Frank, the big, dumb dill-hole, would let her apologize so they could go back to being normal, then she wouldn't—

"I'm not riding with you," he sputtered, his left eyelid twitching.

"Well, then ride with Rock. I don't really care," she rolled her eyes.

Although, truthfully, she *did* care. Why did he have to go and look like mounting up behind her on General Lee was tantamount to jumping face-first into a bubbling volcano?

Sheesh. What'd happened between them aboard the destroyer wasn't *that* bad.

"I have a single seat, *chère*," Rock reminded her. "Only your bike and Ghost's have the capability to ride double, and Ghost took Phantom with him."

"So Frank will miss out on all the fun and drive the Hummer," she growled, throwing her hands in the air.

Why was everything always such a production?

Oh, yeah. Because they were all alpha males, pumped up on testosterone and their own sense of self-importance, used to doing every little pain-in-the-ass thing their own way.

God save her.

"Oh, uh," Ozzie scratched his Einstein-esque crop of blond hair, "I forgot to tell you."

She glanced at the guy's grimacing face. "Sweet Lord, what have you done now?"

"So, uh…" His mouth twisted into what Billy liked to call a shit-eating grin, though where that expression came from she'd dearly like to know. Who would eat shit and, more importantly, who'd be grinning about it afterward? "So I was off-roading—"

"Oh, for the love of God! *Ozzie*, I told you not to do that with—"

"Hey!" he interrupted her. "That's what those machines are built for! I was just keeping it in fighting condition."

Yeah, right. It had nothing to do with the fact that he was still a kid at heart and liked to play accordingly. Unfortunately, his games were far wilder and infinitely more dangerous than a happy little bout of hide-and-seek, and those games usually ended with her spending hours fixing one of his "toys."

"Besides," he went on, futilely attempting to smooth down his wild hair as he picked at the peeling appliquéd letters affixed to the front of his T-shirt that read: *My Other Ride is a Constitution Class Starship*, "I plan to help you fix it."

"You bet your ass, you will." She smiled evilly. "And maybe after you've spent days elbow deep in that big engine, you'll think twice before you take it joyriding again, and one other thing—"

"Children, children," Rock interrupted, "let's not get off track. So the Hummer is inop. Christian," he turned toward the former SAS officer who was sitting by the window, avidly watching the byplay, "you'll have to give Boss a lift in your Porsche."

"Ha!" Ozzie slapped his knee. "I'd like to see that one. It'd be like trying to fold a whole tuna into a sardine can."

"I've added racing seats," Christian explained in his well-heeled British accent. "I seriously doubt Boss will fit."

"Oh," Rock scratched his ear, sending Frank an apologetic glance.

"I'll just take the train like we all do when the weather's shit," Frank muttered, clearly unhappy, yet obviously resigned to the outing. Becky resisted the urge to pat herself on the back for having secured this one, small victory. With Frank, she had to count her successes when she could. "Or maybe I'll throw caution to the wind and hail a taxi," he continued. "Problem solved."

"What's wrong, Boss?" Angel rasped, his dark eyes glowing dangerously. "Are you too proud to ride behind a woman?"

Whoa, where the heck did that come from?

The Knights liked to give Frank a hard time on a daily basis, but their ribbing was always in jest. The hard look making Angel's prominent cheekbones stand out like the wings of an F-22 Raptor was anything but playful.

"That's not it at all," Frank growled.

"It isn't?" Angel challenged.

What in the world? Did Angel think he was *helping* her situation by provoking Frank? If so, the guy needed some swift lessons in how things worked around here.

Every pair of eyes in the room swung back and forth between the two men, like the group was watching a raucous ping-pong match—only this contest looked to turn far more physical if Frank's clenching jaw and Angel's clenching fists were anything to go by.

"Is that what you want, Angel?" Frank asked coolly. "For me to ride with her?"

She couldn't read the expression on Frank's face, but Angel obviously could, because the two stared at each other for a very long time. She fancied if she squinted real hard, she'd be able to see little bolts of electricity arcing between the two.

"I want you to do what's right, Boss," Angel finally ground out. "That's all."

What the heck was *that* supposed to mean?

"All right." Frank nodded, his eyes flashing at Angel before he turned toward her. "I guess I'm riding with you then."

"Uh, o-okay," she stammered as Angel said something nasty about Frank's mother beneath his breath.

She was completely, totally flummoxed. There was some sort of strange undercurrent swirling around her, but no matter how hard she tried or how many times she glanced between Angel and Frank, she couldn't seem to determine its cause.

Men, ya can't live with 'em, and ya just can't kill 'em. Sheesh.

━━⌇⌇━━

Frank gingerly mounted up behind Becky, careful to position himself as far back on the double seat as possible—which wasn't nearly far enough.

His big thighs still touched her slim hips, the warmth of her skin still seeped through the thick denim of his jeans, instantly igniting a burning sensation deep in his belly. Ah man, and the smell of her. The smell of sugary candy, acrylic paint, skin lotion…and under it all, the hint of warm lace and healthy, vibrant woman.

This was so not going to work.

He edged back farther, only to stop when she turned to glare at him. "You scoot back another inch, and you'll be sitting on the back fender." The back fender that was painted with the phrase, "I Ride My Own."

Sweet Mother Mary, the woman just slayed him. Everything about her, from her spunky, take-no-guff attitude, to her unbelievable talent, to her tight little body.

"I promise I won't molest you should you deign to

wrap your arm around my waist," she added, lush pink lips twisted in irritation.

Yeah, but could he promise the same?

For the first time in his life, he could honestly admit he wasn't sure. The dark specter of what lay in store for him the next day was playing havoc with his emotions, his will, and…hell, let's be honest, it was royally screwing with his head.

Grinding his jaw, he slid forward until her hips were cradled against his tightening groin. Winding his uninjured arm around her waist, he pressed his chest to her back and realized she was in his arms…again.

It was heaven…and hell.

The sweetest, most erotic thing he'd ever felt. Especially when she fired up General Lee, and the bike started grumbling with barely leashed power.

Holy hell. It was like the two of them were sitting atop a giant vibrator.

And…*wow*, he'd have never guessed her little cafe-style chopper, with its bright orange and black paint job in tribute to the Dodge Charger made famous by the Dukes of Hazzard, would be so flippin', blow-your-hair-back tough.

Although why he'd ever entertained the notion that Becky would ride something less than totally badass was beyond him. The woman lived and breathed motorcycles; *of course* hers would be a mean machine raised to the power of ten. Just because it was small, didn't mean it couldn't pack one helluva wallop.

Kinda like the woman herself.

So yessir, with the bike grumbling beneath him and Becky's slim form against his front, he was in heaven.

He was *also* in hell.

Because in order to keep from springing a boner the size of the flagpole they kept out in the courtyard, he had to picture the razed villages of Herzegovina after they'd been shelled by the VRS.

Okay, that worked.

Well, it worked until she revved the engine. Then all he could think of was the long list of don'ts he'd compiled in his head before climbing on the back of her bike. Like *don't* bury his nose in the soft curve of her fragrant shoulder, and *don't* run his tongue up the side of her graceful neck, and *don't* subtly lift his hand until his thumb caressed the gentle undercurve of her breast.

Like *don't* dwell on the fact that but for a few layers of clothes, he'd be inside her, spreading the sweet, warm globes of her ass to push into something much sweeter and much warmer and—

Damnit.

What an asshole he'd turned out to be. And a *stupid* asshole at that, because he was here, now, living through this torture, simply to give Angel—that prick—a giant middle finger.

He was just about to swing off the bike—he couldn't do this; it was too much—when Bill gave the thumbs up and the group took off, prowling behind Christian and his Porsche like a pride of steel lions as they exited the shop's side door.

They were accompanied by the sound of rolling thunder.

Usually he reveled in that loud, blood-pumping racket, relished the raw power of a V-twin engine in perfect, growling condition.

But not right now.

Because right now that sound meant he was stuck exactly where he was for the amount of time it would take to get to Red Delilah's—approximately ten minutes, depending on traffic. And those ten minutes promised to be the longest, most agonizing of his life.

Chapter Thirteen

BECKY LICKED THE LAST BIT OF CELERY SALT FROM HER FINGERS after having wolfed down a hot dog and frowned toward the end of the bar where Frank was trying and failing not to stare into the Grand Canyon of Delilah's cleavage.

She liked the bar's proprietress and namesake; she really did.

Delilah was clever and fun, and she could double pour a Guinness so it formed the perfect frothy head—a real talent in Becky's book. She was warm and welcoming, always there with a sympathetic ear when a girl had one too many and started lamenting aloud the pathetic path of her love life—or the lack thereof. She had a nearly encyclopedic knowledge of classic rock bands, could diffuse a bar fight with only a high-pitched whistle, and wrangle an uncooperative drunk into a taxi cab…

She also just happened to be built like a living number eight, with a set of curves that defied humanity. And even though Becky generally liked Delilah, right now she was envious as hell of those curves and the nearly hypnotic effect they seemed to have on Frank.

Yepper, maybe if *she* looked like an hourglass, he would finally give her the time of day and let her apologize, because if there was one thing she was sure of, it was she was sick and damned tired of walking on eggshells around him…or having him walk on eggshells around her…or whatever the heck was going on to make the room experience a sudden blast of nuclear winter whenever they both managed to inhabit it.

"Did that satisfy your craving?" Angel asked as he plunked a sweating bottle of Samuel Smith's Imperial Stout down on the polished bar and swung a muscled leg over the wooden stool beside her.

"I could eat two more," she told him, dragging her eyes away from the pair at the end of the bar. "But I just bought a really cherry pair of 7 For All Mankind jeans, and it'd be a shame not to be able to fit into them."

He tilted his head and smiled at her, and she wished she could read whatever it was she glimpsed behind his dark eyes, but…she couldn't. Even after all the hours they'd spent together, he was still such a mystery she couldn't help but wonder if there was anyone on the entire planet who knew what Jamin "Angel" Agassi was really all about.

Not for the first time, she tried to guess what his real name might have been. Maybe it was something cool, like Asher or Raphael. Although, given life's little ironies, it was probably more like Bob or something equally disappointing.

"Who is that man?" Angel/Bob asked, dragging her from her fanciful thoughts.

She glanced in the direction of his gaze but could barely make out the shadowed profile of the man tucked into a dim booth in the far back corner of the bar.

"I don't know. I can't really see him. Why do you ask?"

"He's been watching us."

She squinted, trying to make out the face within the shadows. It was useless. "How can you tell? It's too dark over there."

"I can tell," his raspy voice brooked no argument.

Okay, so Shadow Man was watching them. So what?

"Well, it's not like there's a ton of activity in here right now. We're probably the only thing *to* watch." She took an unconcerned sip of her beer.

And speaking of activity…

She figured it was about time to check in and see just how ol' Frank was making out with the whole trying-not-to-drool-down-the-front-of-Delilah's-V-neck-sweater thing.

When she glanced in their direction, she was pleased to find there was no drool involved, although there was a lot of playful grinning and flirtatious gazing.

Grrr.

"You should call him over here and do it," Angel announced.

Uh, non sequitur anyone? Still, Becky couldn't pretend she didn't know what he was talking about.

"I thought you said I didn't need to. That I should just forget all about it."

"Yes," he sighed, shaking his head in annoyance. "And I still believe that was good advice, but you're not going to be satisfied until you get this apology…how is it you say?…out of the way. And I, for one, refuse to sit here and watch you fidget until you plotz."

"Ew!"

"It does not mean what it sounds like it means." With that, he grabbed his beer and stood up. And before she could stop him, he sauntered to the end of the bar where Frank and Delilah stopped their bantering to glance at him questioningly.

Becky lit up like a campfire when Angel said

something to Frank that caused him to frown so fiercely she was amazed Angel didn't immediately curl into a protective ball. That particular look of Frank's always had that effect on *her*. Angel, however, seemed immune. He just smirked and crossed his muscled arms over his chest, standing his ground.

With a curse that even she, at the other end of the bar, could hear above the beats of the jukebox, Frank pushed past Angel, accidentally hitting the guy's shoulder with his own—yeah right—to stomp in her direction. His big biker boots crushed the peanut shells scattered over the scuffed wooden floor into baby-fine powder.

"What?" he growled, towering over her. She tried to remind herself that he was just a very fit man, like all the other very fit men she worked with, operators who had to keep their bodies in peak condition because their very lives depended on it. But she failed, because despite what she told herself, Frank Knight would always be the toughest, meanest, *biggest* sonofagun she'd ever known.

"What *what?*" she asked, her hackles instantly twanging upright in defense.

"Angel said you wanted to talk to me, so *what* did you want to talk about?"

"What is it between you two, anyway?" she asked, thinking back on all that testosterone-y weirdness that'd gone down in Frank's office.

"*That's* what you wanted to ask me?" he thundered, causing every head in the bar to turn in their direction. Thankfully, given the early hour, besides the Knights there were blessedly few heads.

"No," she hissed, trying to ignore the heat of

embarrassment climbing up her throat to sting her cheeks. "I just don't understand why you two—"

"Becky," he ground out. Well at least he'd moderated his tone so the whole bar was no longer privy to their conversation. For that, she was grateful. Until he continued, "Just spit it out, for the love of God."

Oh, and now it was her turn to make a scene.

"I'm sorry, okay!" she yelled, sudden tears pricking behind her eyes, which only pissed her off further. If she stared bawling right there in the middle of her favorite bar, she swore she'd never forgive him.

"You're...you're *sorry*?" he sputtered. Yep, she'd never before willingly offered up an apology, so she could understand his incredulity now. "For what?" he demanded, still looming over her until she felt the need to shrink down into herself. She had to make a conscious effort to keep her spine straight when her shoulders wanted ever so much to slink up around her ears.

"For the time we...for w-what happened on the *Patton*," she muttered as she darted a glance around the room to make sure no one else had heard that juicy little nugget. "I shouldn't have taken advantage of you like that, and I'm...I just wanted to say I'm sorry, okay? I know you don't want to talk about it, but I want things to be all right between us."

"Sonofabitch." He briefly covered his eyes with his big hand. Then he dragged his palm down over his face and the raspy stubble on his jaw. Taking a deep breath, looking like he'd just aged ten years, he hooked a toe in the rungs of a barstool, yanked it out, and plopped onto the seat with a groan of weariness, or embarrassment, or some other emotion she couldn't name.

Ugh, this was turning out way worse than she ever imagined. Maybe she should've listened to Angel.

Except…hold the phone, Frank's eyes were strangely soft when he finally turned toward her. "It wasn't your fault, honey."

Honey. *Honey?*

If there'd been a record playing, the needle would've scratched across the vinyl surface. *Scccrrriiitch.* Because Frank Knight was not one for endearments. Hell, before the deal they made on the *Patton*, he'd refused to call her anything more informal than Rebecca, much less something as personal as *honey*.

She sat there for a second. Completely pole-axed. All she could think was honey, honey…honey?

Finally, shaking her head like a dog shakes off water, she managed, "Of *course* it's my fault. You were out of your frickin' mind."

"Mmm," he agreed, nodding his head. "Just enough out of my mind to do something I've always wanted to do."

Her heart stopped beating. "What do you mean?"

"Come on, Becky." He sighed, grabbing her pint of Guinness and taking a big slug. She couldn't help but check the glowing neon Budweiser clock above the bar to make sure he wasn't violating his food and drink cut-off time. He still had fifteen minutes. "Don't pick this moment to turn dense."

So Angel was right. He *had* wanted to kiss her.

"But if you've always wanted to kiss me, then why, for Pete's sake, haven't you?" She thought of all the time they'd wasted. Time they could've been loving, living their lives together instead of continually, carefully keeping each other at arm's length.

"Because I'm your boss, and I'm too old for you," he replied, his eyes bleak as they stared straight ahead to the shelves of liquor glinting on the mirrored wall behind the bar.

She couldn't help noticing he made no mention of the woman up in Lincoln Park. So, had she been right about it not being serious? About the woman just being a friend with benefits? Her heart not only began beating, it leapt with hope.

"First of all, you're not technically my boss. My paycheck comes directly from the sale of the choppers, not the U.S. government. Second, thirteen years isn't exactly a spring/fall relationship, Frank. It's more like a spring/summer relationship, if you want to categorize it. Or," she went on, getting more upset by the minute because things could've been so different if only he'd let them—the big, stupid dill-hole, "maybe you could take the enlightened approach and admit that when it comes to relationships, age doesn't matter."

He turned to her then, his expression strangely pained. "But it does, Becky." When she opened her mouth to argue with him, he pushed ahead. "Besides, that's not an issue now."

"What the hell is that supposed to mean?"

"Simply that." He shrugged. "It doesn't matter what we could or couldn't have had now that you have Angel."

Her mind blanked. Simply…blanked. She understood the words that'd come out of his mouth—they were English, after all—but they didn't make a bit of sense.

"What are you talking about?" she cried, then nervously glanced around the bar.

Thankfully, everyone except Angel appeared determined to give them their privacy. Angel, for his part, simply perched at the end of the bar, nursing his beer, not trying to hide the fact that he was narrowly watching their exchange.

Now she really, *really* wished she could read the mysterious Israeli, because somehow he was involved in all this…this…whatever the hell this was.

"I'm talking about the fact that you're in love with the pretty-boy ex-Mossad agent."

It was like he was spewing advanced Calculus formulas. His words were English, but they might as well have been Mandarin Chinese. "I am?"

"Aren't you?"

"No!"

He blinked at her, the scar slicing up from the corner of his mouth going stark white, the big one slashing through his eyebrow puckering and turning vivid pink when he frowned fiercely. The man's face was a brutal, beautiful mess. It was like a roughly detailed map of the harsh life he'd chosen, and she figured she could look at it for the next hundred years and always find something new to admire.

After a long moment, he licked his lips and asked, his deep voice even deeper than usual, "You're not in love with Angel?"

"Of course not. In fact, I'm pretty sure he's carrying a flame for someone back home and…What? What's that look for?" His square jaw jerked back on his neck like she'd punched him, his storm-cloud eyes intently searching her face.

"But…but the way you two have been acting, I thought—"

She held up a hand, stopping him. "And how have we been acting? Like friends? Like colleagues?"

"Like lovers," he growled.

Okay, it was definitely time to call bullshit.

"Whatever, Frank. I haven't treated Angel any differently than I've treated the other guys. Think about it."

"I saw you two cuddling on the couch."

"Cuddling is a bit dramatic, don't you think? It was more like I fell asleep on the poor guy, and he was nice enough not to disturb me even though I was snoring and slobbering all over the front of his shirt."

"But…" He shook his head, trying his level best not to believe her. God only knew why, because *she* sure as heck didn't. "But you two have been inseparable since you got back."

"Uh, *yeah*. Because we've been racing to finalize the plans for his bike, since you just hit me up for another custom job. Surely you remember all the hours you and I spent coming up with the design for Boss Hog?"

Geez, *she* sure remembered them. They'd been the best hours of her life, immediately followed by some of the worst. Because most evenings, after they'd worked all day together, side by side, he'd taken himself up to Lincoln Park. To Chesty McGivesItUp.

Grrr.

"I remember *precisely* what it was like to work so closely with you, Becky. And the two of us certainly weren't laughing and joking around like you and Angel have been doing."

The man was an idiot.

"That's because things are *different* between us, you big, stupid dill-hole! They always have been!"

He opened his mouth to say something when the front door of the bar opened and Samantha Tate, Chicago's newest, brightest, most persistent reporter stepped inside.

Oh, sweet Lord, not now. Becky rolled her eyes and groaned.

The woman had left her about a zillion messages, all of which she'd studiously ignored. Because Samantha Tate wasn't after another quote for her paper on the whole piracy incident. Of that, Becky was absolutely sure. Although just exactly what the reporter *was* after was still murky.

And when it came to interaction with the press, she absolutely hated murky. Scratch that. It was more like when it came to the press, she absolutely hated interaction.

The woman made a beeline for Becky.

Well, this is just frickin' frackin' great!

For the first time in over three years, she and Frank were talking, *really* talking, and then the one thing guaranteed to make the big, bad, I-ain't-scared-of-nothin' Frank Knight take off with his tail tucked between his legs came marching through the door.

Given the clandestine nature of his profession was at direct odds with freedom of the press, she wasn't surprised when he hopped from the barstool and carefully strolled away, leaving her to deal with the reporter on her own.

"What do you want, Miss Tate?" she growled before the journalist could take a seat.

"A follow-up," the woman replied, slinging a hot-pink crocodile carry-all onto the bar and motioning for Delilah as she appropriated the barstool Frank had just abandoned.

"Not gonna happen," Becky shook her head. "In case

you haven't gotten the hint, I've given all the interviews I'm going to give. Told my story as many times as I'm going to tell it and—"

"That press conference the day you returned, and the few phone interviews you've given since, aren't going to satisfy the public's thirst for more detail about your harrowing experience," the reporter declared firmly before turning to Delilah. "I'll take a martini, extra dirty, two olives."

"And I'll take the check, Delilah," Becky announced. "Add her drink to it."

"Thank you."

"You're welcome."

"I guess it's the least you could do after refusing to return my phone calls."

"Like I said, I'm all interviewed out."

"Mmm." The reported nodded slowly, then slid Becky a calculated look that had the hairs on the back of her neck twanging a warning. "So how'd your employee get hurt?"

"What?"

"That big, brutal-looking guy that was just sitting here." She motioned with her chin over to where Frank had joined the rest of the Knights by the jukebox. "He's one of your employees, isn't he? So how'd he get hurt?"

"None of your damned business." If ambition had a scent, it would be called *eau de Samantha Tate*. Becky just hoped like hell the breaking story that boosted Miss Tate to the top wasn't the discovery of a covert group of government contractors operating out of good ol' Chi-Town.

"Why the hostility?" the reporter asked, feigning injury. "It was just an innocent question."

"I've learned no question is innocent when posed by the press."

"True." Miss Tate laughed, shaking her head. "So, was he injured while rescuing you?" She took a big swig of the cloudy martini Delilah plunked down in front of her.

Uh-huh, innocent question my ass.

"Rescuing me from what?"

"The pirates."

"Of course not. He's one of my mechanics. What would he be doing out in the Indian Ocean?"

"What indeed?" Miss Tate lifted a smooth, infuriating brow.

"Thanks," Becky murmured to Delilah after being handed the check. She glanced at the total and fished in her jacket pocket for her wallet, praying she had enough cash to cover the total without having to wait to run a credit card.

Thank you, St. Peter, she did.

Throwing a wad of bills on the bar, she stood.

"I don't know what you want from me, Miss Tate. Like I said before, I've told my story too many times already. And I'm sure people are just as sick of hearing it as I am of telling it."

"Something more happened on that tanker, didn't it, Miss Reichert?" the reporter called after her. She'd already turned to head toward the door. "Something more always seems to be happening when you're around. Tell me, why is that?"

Becky's heart dropped down to her feet, but she managed to swing around and march back toward the bar in order to tower over the nosy journalist—only she was too short to tower so she satisfied herself with glowering instead.

"I've told you everything I know. Now normally, if someone wants to go on a wild-goose chase, I let them. But you're not only wasting your time by barking up this tree, you're also wasting *my* time. And yes, I *know* I mixed my metaphors, so just go ahead and quote me!"

Miss Tate threw her head back and laughed. "I think if things were different, you and I would be very good friends, Miss Reichert."

"Doubtful."

"You never know."

"Whatever."

"Are you used to getting the last word, Rebecca?"

"Always, Samantha."

The woman snorted and saluted Becky with her martini glass. Becky couldn't help it, one corner of her mouth twitched.

Shaking her head, she turned and started toward the door, only to slow her steps when she glanced into the back corner. Even though the features of man in the booth were still concealed in shadow, there was something slightly familiar about the general shape of his face, the hard ridge of his jaw and broad expanse of his forehead.

Hmm...

"Who is that?" she murmured to Frank with a jerk of her chin as he held the front door for her. The rest of the Knights had already exited Delilah's—yep, throw a reporter in the mix, and men whose lives depended on their cover were quick to quit the scene. The rough growl of their engines firing up out on the street nearly drowned her question, but along with a superior physique, Frank also had superior hearing.

"That would be the ex-CIA agent known as Dagan Zoelner," he replied.

Her eyebrows shot up her forehead as she turned to get a better look, only to be thwarted once again by the shadows. Dagan Zoelner had been working for the senator responsible for the brutal deaths of two of the employees of Black Knights Inc., but as soon as he'd realized the senator's treachery, Zoelner had been instrumental in bringing the man down. And the last time she'd seen him, he'd looked like a human punching bag, having withstood a serious ass-whipping by Dan, so it was no wonder she didn't recognize him now.

"What's he doing here?"

"Dunno." Frank shrugged as they stepped out of the dim bar and into the weak October sun. "Guess we'll wait for him to tell us, huh?"

"This day has just been one surprise after another," she observed above the racket of the rumbling motorcycles.

"You're telling me."

She glanced at him sharply. "Did you really think I was in love with Angel?"

"Is that so hard to believe? According to you, the guy's drop-dead gorgeous." The last word came out as a snarl.

"Yep, he is," she admitted and wondered if she should go one step further and just admit the whole kit and kaboodle. *Oh, what the hell.* "But he's not you, Frank."

The man skidded to a halt so fast it was a wonder he didn't slip a disk. When she glanced at his face, his expression was stricken.

"Don't go there, Becky," he ground out, his deep voice so low it was barely audible.

"Why?" she demanded, sick and tired of the games

they'd played for the last few years. "I thought we were finally being honest with each other today."

"Then believe me when I honestly tell you nothing can come of it. I can't give you what you want."

Why did men always think they knew what women wanted? Would they never learn? "And just exactly what is it you think I want?"

"What every woman wants. Everything!"

Ah, the ol' I'm-not-into-commitment excuse. If she hadn't been so mad, or sad, or whatever the hell it was she was feeling, she would've laughed because...well, it was so pathetically cliché.

"God, Frank. Now who's being dense? You think just because there's always been this...this," she motioned between the two of them, "...this *thing* between us, that I'd want *everything*? What happened to good old-fashioned sex just for the sake of sex?"

He looked so startled she almost managed that laugh.

"Don't you tempt me with this now," he groaned. "Not today."

"Why?" she demanded, scowling up into his hard, stubborn, wonderful face. "What's different about today?"

Something frightening flashed behind his eyes and a strange chill streaked down her spine.

"It doesn't matter." He shook his head so forcefully she wasn't sure whom he was trying to convince, himself or her. "I refuse to give in to this thing between us."

Ow. Okay, now *that* stung.

"Your choice," she told him as she stalked toward General Lee.

Shoving her helmet over her head, she tried to ignore the erotic sensation of his big body warm against her back as he mounted up. He dwarfed her, and she realized he was the only man on the entire planet who made her truly appreciate her own femininity.

Most of the time, with paint on her shirt, grease under her fingernails, and a power tool in her hand, she forgot that she wasn't just one of the guys.

But when Frank walked in the room, so large and powerful and *male*, suddenly she remembered that she had breasts and a womb and needs, and, oh for Pete's sake…

Before she started the engine and joined the others out on the city streets, she decided to throw all her cards on the table once and for all. An emotional Hail Mary play. Glancing over her shoulder, she pinned him with a challenging stare. "Should you ever change your mind, you know where I sleep…"

Chapter Fourteen

Grafton Manor
St. Ives, England

THE TRIP HAD BEEN INTERMINABLE, THE PAIN
excruciating, but Sharif clenched his jaw against the
overwhelming urge to lie down in the cool, wet grass
blanketing the expansive lawn and just sleep for the
next century. Instead, he shuffled up the wide, flagstone
steps of the Tudor-revival-style house, and fumbled
with the front door.

He could've rung the bell, he supposed. Phelps, aged,
stoic, and so typically English, would've been quick to
respond to the summons. But he had no stomach for answering the question he knew he'd see in the old butler's
shrewd eyes.

When he stepped into the cool, tiled foyer, with its
precise line of cherrywood pedestals supporting price-
less Ming vases, he heaved a small sigh of relief.

He'd made it.

For a few moments during the flight, when the un-
bearable pain caused his vision to narrow to a tiny, dark
tunnel, pierced only by a small shaft of light, he thought
perhaps he was nearing his end. And he lamented, in a
strange, detached sort of way, the prospect of never seeing the bright green fields of England again. Africa might
have been his birthplace, but England was his home.

Allowing himself one more moment of peace, he finally shuffled toward the immense set of carved mahogany doors at the end of the dark hall. Upon reaching them, he screwed his eyes closed, knocked, and girded himself for the confrontation to come when a deep voice bid him, "Enter."

Born from the brief dalliance between a wealthy English lord and an affluent African princess, Asad Grafton had struggled to make his way between the two worlds. That struggle had molded him into the man he was today. Tough, razor sharp, and completely merciless.

Sharif had had occasion to witness that mercilessness once, and the memory still haunted him...

Pushing open the heavy doors, he stepped into the wide library with its large, cheerfully crackling fireplace and two-story bookshelves filled with first editions. The floors were hand-laid parquet, lacquered to a high sheen so that his reflection stared up at him. The furniture, imposing and ornate, was Sotheby's quality antique Chippendale.

And in the midst of all that opulence Asad sat perusing the latest edition of the *London Times*. He glanced up after carefully folding back one corner of the paper. "You shouldn't have come here. Interpol is after you. My sources say they've already picked up your trail from Kenya to Heathrow. You should've been more careful."

Sharif's mouth twisted with a cynical smile. "It's good to see you're alive as well, *father*."

"Don't be so sensitive," Asad sneered. "You're just like your mother."

Ah, the worst insult the man could conceive of. "I

came because I need information. And I hadn't the time to be more careful."

"Then you should've killed that backward bush pilot you paid to fly you to England. I doubt he waited until you cleared the tarmac before he called the authorities, giving them your description."

Sharif held up his bandaged hand. The movement caused blood to pound in the wound like a second heartbeat, a second heartbeat with sharp, venomous teeth. "That backward bush pilot was twice my size, and in case you haven't noticed, I'm more than a little impaired."

"I heard you lost a finger."

"I could've lost much more," he snarled, feeling a sick sweat break out all over his body. He'd been oscillating back and forth between hot and cold ever since he'd awoken in the Kenyan hospital. "I could've lost my life."

Asad—Sharif didn't think of him as Dad—leaned back in his leather wingback chair, steepling his long fingers under his aristocratic chin. "And you blame me?"

"I would not have been there, out on that tanker, had you not sent me."

"Oh, how selective your memory." Asad smiled like a shark, all teeth and no feeling. "Wasn't it *you* who begged me for a job that would pay enough for you to retire from this nasty business?"

In learning to live between his parents' two worlds, Asad had perfected the ability to live in *both*. He took the wealth he'd inherited from having been born a Grafton and invested it into deals with the contacts he made from being his mother's son. Asad's public business ventures were simply fronts for his private enterprises. Namely drugs, guns, the slave trade, and, most recently, piracy.

"I never thought you'd put me in the direct line of fire," Sharif informed his father coldly. For a long minute, Asad simply stared at him. It was somewhat like being a wounded gazelle, watched by a lazy, satiated lion. You knew there was the potential for quick, painful death, but there was the eternal hope the big cat wouldn't deign to expend the energy.

Finally, Asad spread his arms, indicating the luxury of the room around him. "Do you think I got all this from staying safely behind the line? From never taking my chances and facing the Reaper?"

"I only meant that—"

"Enough!" Asad bellowed, and Sharif briefly closed his eyes as the sound echoed like a dropped anvil behind his fevered brow. "None of this matters now. The operation was a failure, so the only course is to move forward. But first you must leave here. You can't be seen with me."

"And why would anyone ever think to look for me here, *father*," he snarled the word. "No one knows of our relationship."

Like his father before him, Asad Grafton had made a voyage to Africa, and there met a beautiful, exotic woman. But unlike his father before him, Asad had refused to publically acknowledge the child that resulted from the brief, tumultuous affair. Sharif didn't even known he *had* a father until he was old enough to attend school. Then his mother shipped him to England where, with the benefaction of Asad Grafton's money, he received an education—and nothing more.

"Nor will they ever know of our relationship," Asad

said with infuriating unconcern. "Especially now that your face is in the system. And speaking of that, you need to leave England. Immediately. Go to a non-extradition country and have surgery to change your appearance. We'll get you a new identity, that's easy enough." He waved his hand like the forging of passports, personal histories, birth certificates, and any other such legal documents was inconsequential. Which, for a man of his resources and power, was probably true.

"I will," Sharif agreed easily, because that'd been part of his plan all along. "But first I need all the information you can give me on Rebecca Reichert."

"What?" Asad frowned. "Why would you need that?"

Again he lifted his hand, ignoring its protest at the movement. "Because she must pay for this."

"Ah. But revenge for such an insignificant wound seems a bit self-indulgent, don't you think?"

"Insignificant!" he raged. "I'm permanently disfigured! This isn't something a plastic surgeon can fix!"

"Yes, but you can hardly blame the woman. From the reports I've received, you had a weapon to her head, threatening to throw her over the side of the tanker. Did you expect her to go willingly?"

How Asad came by his information, Sharif would dearly love to know. The man was like a God, endowed with omnipotence.

"She insulted me at every turn. Surely, you of all people understand that I cannot let that stand."

"She's American," Asad declared, as if that excused her behavior.

"She's a mouthy bitch, and I want her silenced, *permanently*."

"Mmm." Again with that indulgent, knowing smile. It'd always made Sharif's skin crawl. Now was no exception. "And in what way will you make her suffer before you silence her permanently?"

"I don't know, father," he sneered. "Perhaps I'll make her suffer the same way you made my mother suffer."

Sharif had been finishing his sixth year at boarding school when his mother made her first trip to England to visit him. She'd been weak and haggard, a mere shadow of the beautiful woman he'd left behind.

The civil war in Somalia had decimated the country and left its population starving and destitute. He hadn't known it at the time, but his mother had been desperate. And that desperation had led to her death, because she badly misjudged Asad Grafton. When she tried to blackmail Asad, promising to go public with the story of his illegitimate son, Asad simply responded as he responded to any obstacle in his path, decisively and permanently.

Coming back to the dormitory where his mother promised to await him following his last class, Sharif had arrived to find his father waiting instead. On the drive to the hotel, he'd been deliriously happy, thinking his parents were going to get married, thinking his father would save his mother and make everything all right.

As it turned out, the salvation of Nadifa Garane was the very last thing on Asad's mind.

To teach his son the lesson that no one crossed Asad Grafton and lived to tell about it, his father tied him to a chair in an opulent room at the Savoy in London and made Sharif watch as he first raped and then strangled his mother.

It was a lesson Sharif learned well, but even with the fear of his father's vicious disapproval, he could think of nothing save making Rebecca Reichert pay for what she'd done to him.

Asad chuckled at his reference to what'd happened in that hotel room all those years ago. "You liked that, didn't you? Watching the power a man has over a woman?"

No. He hadn't liked it at the time. He'd cried until his eyes swelled, screamed behind his gag until his throat was raw, and struggled to get free of his bindings until his wrists bled.

All to no avail, of course.

But the thought of doing to that blond American bitch what his father had done to his mother made his manhood swell with blood. So, perhaps his psyche had broken that fateful day, or maybe it'd simply been warped beyond all redemption. Unfortunately, he was coming to believe the truth of the matter was that he was more like his father than he ever imagined.

"I want the information," he declared, resisting the urge to wipe the cold sweat from his brow. It would be a sign of weakness, and he'd learned never to show weakness to his father.

"And you shall have it," Asad reached into the side drawer of his desk, pulling out a file, offering it to him. For the first time in his life, Sharif thought perhaps there was a spark of pride in his father's eyes.

When he opened the file, his blood boiled. There she was, her laughing face captured in a full-color, eight-by-ten photograph.

Rebecca Reichert.

I'm coming for you...

What the hell am I doing here?

It was the third time in as many minutes Frank had asked himself that exact question as he stood in the dark, empty hallway on the third floor of the shop, his forehead pressed to the outside of Becky's bedroom door.

It was oh-one-hundred. Everyone had turned in hours ago, including him, and despite his belief that he wouldn't, he'd managed to fall asleep. But he awoke sometime later with a violent start, his shoulder throbbing, chills racing down his spine, the certainty that tomorrow he'd see his last sunrise absolute.

So what did he go and do?

He jumped out of bed like the mattress was on fire, threw on a pair of old jeans, threaded one arm through a button up shirt, pulling the other half over his bandaged shoulder and sling, and padded down the hall to stand... outside the one door on the entire planet he shouldn't be standing outside of.

That invitation...holy hell, he couldn't get it out of his head...

"If you ever change your mind, you know where I sleep." It kept swirling around and around inside his heated brain, right along with, *"Whatever happened to sex just for the sake of sex"*

And right behind all of that, a little voice would whisper, *It doesn't matter. You're still her boss. She's still too young for you. And think of how this will hurt Shell.*

Unfortunately, with morning and his shoulder surgery creeping closer, that little voice was growing fainter and fainter while another voice, a more tempting voice, grew louder and louder.

That voice was telling him by tomorrow night he

might be dead, and it was asking him which he would regret more. One night in the arms of the woman he wanted more than his next breath? Or the betrayal of someone he loved?

In answer, a memory flashed behind his closed lids…

It was a bright, sunny June day, and he was riding with the windows down in the passenger seat of his father's teal-blue Thunderbird. He was ten years old and on his way to get "ice cream." That was the code Robert Knight used when he was going to see one of his *lady friends*, as he liked to call them.

The "ice cream" runs were always the same.

His father would buy him a double scoop of Rocky Road and a new comic book and plunk him down on the stoop of whatever apartment building Robert's current lady friend happened to inhabit. An hour later his father would emerge, his step jaunty, his dark hair mussed, and they'd go home, both smiling at the little deception because it was fun to have *guy* secrets. Things they shared, just the two of them. Things the girls in the family didn't know about.

But that fateful June day things were different. Because that fateful June morning Timothy Murray, Frank's best friend and next-door neighbor came over crying, wailing that his parents were getting divorced because his dad was having sex with a woman other than his mother, and a light bulb went off in Frank's head.

For the first time, it occurred to him that maybe his father wasn't simply drinking Coca-Colas, smoking Marlboros, and playing poker with his lady friends.

"Do you have sex with them?" he asked when they pulled up to a little clapboard house with a covered porch and a patchy lawn. At one time, the house had been white, but it'd deteriorated to a peeling, faded gray. And even ten-year-old Frank recognized the smell of desperation hanging in the air like the fumes from a refinery.

"What do you know about sex?" his father replied, leaning a muscular arm on the windowsill and pushing in the lighter on the console.

Robert Knight was one handsome devil—that's what everyone said.

Frank didn't know about all that, he only knew that his father was bigger, meaner, and tougher than most men. And he felt absolutely dwarfed, especially with the hot air inside the car suddenly vibrating with the tension stretching tight as a piano cord between the two of them.

"I know enough about sex to know you're not supposed to have it with anyone but *mom*," he answered sullenly, throwing his ice cream cone out the window, watching it splat on the sidewalk below, the pointed cone sticking up like a sad, little party hat.

This was no cause for celebration, and eating that ice cream would mean Frank was complicit in his father's actions.

The thought made him feel dirty in a way he never had before, like he needed a good scrubbing with a gallon of bleach.

"Who says I'm not supposed to have sex with anyone but your mother?" his father queried quietly.

"Everyone!" Frank yelled, his face hot with embarrassment and anger.

He didn't want to be the son of philanderer—he'd heard that word on one of the soap operas his mother watched in the afternoons, and when he asked what it meant, she'd explained that it was a man who stepped out on his wife and kids despite his promises to be loyal.

His father didn't so much as flinch at his outraged roar. He simply grabbed the lighter and lit the fresh cigarette clamped between his big, white teeth. Dragging the smoke into his lungs, he blew it out and lazily watched it circle around the felt ceiling of the car before he softly posed, "Have you ever heard the saying 'what you don't know won't hurt you'?"

"Yes." Frank crossed his arms over his scrawny chest, for the first time in his life wanting to punch something, surprised that that something should turn out to be his own father. "But just because mom doesn't know, that doesn't make it right. What you're doing is *wrong*."

His father shrugged. "But who's it hurting? I pay the bills. I put a roof over her head. She's happy with her women's groups and her pretty dresses and her shiny, new car. I'm discreet with my lady friends…you know what discreet means, don't you?"

Frank nodded.

"Okay, then, so again, who is it hurting?"

He didn't know how to answer, because his father was right. His mother *was* happy, and she'd *stay* happy as long as she never found out.

He suddenly realized he was trapped. Trapped in his father's deception as neatly as a spider traps a fly in its silken web.

"I'm going in now," his father announced after a prolonged silence, and Frank glanced toward the house. A woman stood in the doorway, dressed in cut-off shorts and a little lace top.

It was the first time he'd ever seen one of his father's

lady friends, and he was shocked by the sight of her. When he thought of a *lady* friend, he pictured the type of women his mother liked to invite over for tea and bridge. Round, soft, mom-like women with fine wrinkles at the corners of their eyes and hints of gray showing through their hair.

The girl standing in the door was none of these things.

First of all, she was skinny, as in *skin-ny*. Her ribs showed in her chest like the bars of a xylophone. Secondly, even despite her emaciated appearance, she was still one of the prettiest women he'd ever seen, with high cheekbones, big, heavily lashed eyes, and a mouth that made him realize for the first time that there was something utterly compelling about a woman's lips. Her skin was a smooth, flawless, milky color and her hair a shiny, lustrous red.

"How old is she?" he asked before his father could step from the vehicle.

"Eighteen, I think."

Frank recoiled at the thought of his father having sex with someone the same age as the girl who sometimes came over to babysit.

His father chuckled at his reaction. "The great thing about being a man is we get better with age. We may get older, but the women who want us never do. And you'll come to realize there's nothing sweeter than a girl in her first bloom."

With that parting bit of advice, his father slammed the door and sauntered up the cracked walk, flicking his cigarette butt into a motley clump of grass.

That was the last time Frank went with his father for "ice cream," but neither did he reveal his father's secret.

Two years later, he caught one severe case of strep

throat after another until his doctor sent him in to have his tonsils removed, and that was the day Frank's life changed forever. When things went bad on the operating table and he almost died, Robert Knight conveniently used the excuse of the crisis to declare his dissatisfaction with family life and finally abandon them once and for all.

Frank shook his head now, pushing the painful memory away as he shoved back from Becky's door.

What the hell am I doing here?

The question once more flashed through his aching head, but he didn't have time to answer it before the door suddenly opened. And then he couldn't remember his own name much less the answer to the question, because his mind blanked.

Full stop.

No thought whatsoever.

Because there she stood. The woman of his dreams, grumpy and disheveled, and warm and rosy from sleep.

He'd never been a devotee of anything that didn't come with an extra clip or have the ability to be sharpened to a razor's edge, but right now he wanted to prostrate himself at the baptismal fount of red lace.

Oh man, that top she was wearing…

It was cherry-colored satin, trimmed along the collar with soft lace that lightly brushed the smooth mounds of her unrestrained breasts and, yessir, those were her nipples lightly pebbled, pushing against the silky fabric.

"What do you want, Frank," she grumbled, rubbing the sleep from her eyes, squinting up at him as she flicked on the light inside the bedroom.

It illuminated her messy hair, the pillowcase marks

on her smooth, still slightly discolored cheek, and the fact that all she was wearing besides that ball-tightening top was a pair of soft red-and-green flannel boxer shorts.

Was it Christmas?

Nope. Not for another ten weeks.

But looking at her, especially in those colors, he felt he'd been given the greatest gift on Earth.

What did he want?

Um…nothing…but…sex.

Yessir, sex.

It was the only answer that came to him in the span of a few infinite seconds, during which time he couldn't move, just stood there staring at her nipples, then down to her boxer shorts, then further to her sleek, bare legs and those brightly painted toenails that always drove him absolutely crazy.

"Um," he managed to drag his eyes up to her face, though the effort it required was tantamount to Hercules having to slay the Nemean Lion, "I couldn't sleep thinking that I hadn't told you what a good job you did today with that reporter."

And yeah, so sign him up for the Dumbass of the Year Award right here and now.

"Huh?" She yawned and stretched with the sleek grace of a cat. Her shirt drifted up, revealing the circle of stars she had tattooed around her dainty belly button.

Okay, and that was it. He had to get out of there. Now. Two minutes ago…

"I just wanted to tell you that you did a good job deflecting that reporter's questions today," he whispered as he started backing down the hall.

"Frank," she called after him, leaning out of the

doorway. The sight of her shirt dipping down to reveal the soft globes of her breasts froze him to the spot. "Are you nervous about the surgery tomorrow? Do you want someone to talk to about it?"

He made himself hold her worried gaze—*stop staring at her boobs, stop staring at her boobs*—as he shook his head.

The skin across her cheekbones tightened and turned pink as something hot sparked behind her dark eyes.

"Then would you like to come in for another reason?" She backed up and held her door wide.

Yes. Oh, honey, please yes!

"It'd be a bad idea," he ground out and tried—and failed—not to let his eyes once more angle down to her breasts and the press of her nipples against the satin of her top.

"That isn't a *no* I'm hearing," she whispered in her phone-sex-operator voice, and before he knew what she was about, she reached for the hem of her shirt and whipped it over her head.

Becky wasn't a big-breasted woman, not by any stretch of the imagination. She was small and soft, her breasts high and round and creamy skinned, topped by light, peach-colored nipples.

In a word: perfection.

He tried to say something; he had no idea what, probably just another reiteration that this was a very bad idea, but the only thing that came out of his strangled throat was a weird choking sound.

Then she did something even more preposterous.

She hooked her thumbs in the waistband of her boxer shorts and shoved them down the smoothly tanned

length of her legs, kicking the material back into her
bedroom in the same direction she'd thrown her top.

Kee-rist. There she was. Five feet away. Completely,
wonderfully, starkly naked. And he could only stand
there gaping like a flippin' dipshit, because the word
perfection no longer seemed adequate. He didn't *have* a
word to describe the radiant, glorious, female beauty of
Rebecca Reichert in the nude.

"Well, Frank," she murmured, smiling that smile
a woman smiles when she knows she's got the upper
hand, because the man has completely stopped thinking
with the head perched atop his shoulders and has started
thinking with the one that usually dangles between his
legs. "It's your move. Are we finally going to do this
or not?"

Something inside him broke, just snapped and tore
free like all the ligaments and tendons in his shoulder.

He didn't care that he was her boss or that she was
too young for him. He didn't care about his father and
that he was about to commit the same sin Robert Knight
had committed over and over and over again. All he
cared about was that this was what he wanted. This was
what he was finished denying himself.

This woman. This night.

It was all that mattered.

Besides, after tomorrow it might all be over anyway…

Chapter Fifteen

OH, GEEZ. DID I JUST MAKE A FRICKIN' COLOSSAL MISTAKE?
Becky asked herself as heat washed from the top of her head to the tips of her toes.

She'd been so sure when she'd been awakened by the sound of someone outside her room. Sure that Frank had finally overcome whatever it was that'd been holding him back from her. And when she'd opened the door to find him standing there, she'd been 100 percent *convinced*.

But instead of grabbing her and bum-rushing her back into her bedroom to throw her on her bed, he was just standing there, raking in ragged breaths. Instead of crushing her mouth with a kiss to burn her soul, he was hanging on to the waistband of his jeans like some sort of lifeline.

Come on, Frank. Make your move.

But one heartbeat turned into ten and he continued to just… *stand* there.

Well, if he was going to reject her, *again*, she was going to make sure this moment was burned into her memory like a brand. Because she'd played her hand, gone all in. There'd be no next time after this time. So she let her eyes drink their fill and really let herself look at him.

He was so big and beautiful.

Her eyes traveled up from his toes, over his calves and thighs and lean hips. With his shirt only half-on, she got a view she was rarely privileged to see. Frank's chest. Coarse, dark hair spanned his bulging pectoral muscles only to narrow to a thin line that ran down the corrugated muscles of his belly and disappear into the waistband of his jeans—the waistband he was *still* holding onto like maybe his pants were about to fall off.

As if I could be *so lucky*, she thought.

And just when she was sure she'd miscalculated, just when she was about to back up and close the door in his face—a woman could only offer so much, take so much rejection—something changed in his expression.

He went from looking like a torture victim to looking like a hungry hawk that just spotted a wounded mouse hobbling through the tall grass.

Her heart nearly exploded with happiness when he took two big steps in her direction, pushing her back into her room, softly closing and locking the door behind him.

―⁓―

He wanted to rip open his jeans, bend her over the desk, and sink himself into her until his heated balls smashed against her smooth ass.

That was one part of him.

The other part of him knew he only had this one night. This one night to make it count.

He reached out to touch her hair, reveling in the sight of his thick, callused fingers against the smooth, golden strands.

He'd always loved her hair, especially like this. She usually had it pulled back in a ponytail, all slick, contained and do-not-touch. But it was certainly advertising "touch me" with the way it fell around her shoulders and down her back in a messy, golden curtain.

He moved to her cheek, rubbing a gentle thumb over the slight bruise that remained there, shuddering when he remembered the absolute terror that'd squeezed his heart when he thought she was going to go over the side of the tanker and the burst of overwhelming relief and joy when his fingers managed to grip her slender ankle.

Lightly he traced the smooth column of her throat, stopping at her rapidly beating pulse-point and feeling the head of his dick pound in rhythm to her heart.

Two hearts beating as one. He'd heard that said somewhere. At the time, he'd thought it a big ol' load of hooey-gooey nonsense, but now? Oh yeah. He got it. And it wasn't hooey gooey at all. It was erotic as hell.

She must've thought so too, because she was breathing heavily, her big, soft eyes wide, staring with such trust and hope and *hunger*.

He licked his lips as he let his fingers drift lower, over her delicate collarbone, and further still. Until he brushed the tight, peachy bud of her nipple. She shuddered and an answering ripple of sensation ripped up the length of his spine.

"Frank," she whispered, trembling openly now.

He didn't know exactly what kind of sex she wanted. What kind of sex she expected from him…

Most times, he liked sex that was slow and hot, a little bit naughty when his partner was willing, and a whole lot unrestrained regardless. But what kind of sex did Becky want? Because, despite the fact that this was *his* one night, all he cared about was being perfect for *her*.

She moved toward him then, apparently through

waiting for him to act, and wound her slim arms around his neck, standing up on tiptoe to try and reach his lips. Even with the added height, she was still too short, God love her. So he bent his head and marveled at the smoothness of her lips when they brushed against his own, the taste of her tongue when she boldly licked into his mouth. He couldn't help but angle her chin with the palm of his hand and return the gesture and—

Watermelon.

That must've been the flavor of the last Dum Dum she ate.

It was ambrosia. Nectar of the gods. And she was a goddess.

Especially when she moved closer, pressing herself against him. Breast to chest. Hip to hip. Skin to skin.

She was so hot, so smooth and supple and so very, very female.

Yes, yes, yes, yes…

That's all that was going through his head. Just that one word over and over again, because it was a stupefying, mind-blowing sensation having Becky, naked, in his arms. Even more mind-blowing when she hooked a heel behind his knee and ground her hips against the hard length of his swollen cock. And when the warmth of her belly pressed against the sensitive head of him, where he was peeking from the waistband of his jeans, he froze…

"Becky—" He tried to pull back from the kiss, pull back from the grip of her sweet arms, but she just pressed herself closer, sighing her approval of the resulting growl that issued from the back of his throat and the hand suddenly grabbing her ass, anchoring her to him as he ground his hips into the wet warmth between her legs.

He'd been about to ask her something, but he was having a hard time remembering what. Especially since her hands were everywhere, in his hair, rubbing over his chest, reaching around to squeeze his ass, and then she was unbuttoning his jeans...

Kee-rist!

It was too good. With her tongue in his mouth and his hand full of her breast, her hard nipple rasping under his thumb.

If he didn't ask it now, he'd get too carried away, and then he'd be in no position to ask at all. "Becky, what do you want?"

"I want you to keep kissing me, keep touching me," she breathed, licking the side of his neck and driving him insane.

Yeah, well, that's *a given.* So much so he had to laugh. "But *specifically* what do you like. What kind of kisses, what kind of touches, how do you—"

She devoured his mouth. That was the only way to describe it. She grabbed his face, sealed their lips, and feasted like a starving woman even as she reached between them again, spreading the halves of his fly apart in order to stroke him.

And her hand...

Her sweet, calloused hand—Becky's hands weren't soft; she worked with them, and it showed—felt so unbelievably wonderful that his balls hitched up close to his body and a telltale prickle of warning teased at the base of his spine.

Yes, yes, yes, yes. The chant resumed its cadence

inside his brain and pulling her fingers from around his cock was the hardest thing he'd ever done. But he somehow managed. Then he kissed the lush curve of her lower lip when she stuck it out, pouting like a child relieved of her favorite toy.

—~~~—

Becky was dying.

She wanted to rip off his jeans and impale herself on the smooth hardness she'd just held in her hands—it was either that or she was going to shimmy up his big body, wrap her legs around his head, and insist he wear her around like a government-issue gas mask. But he was determined to draw out the moment, to slow everything down when all she wanted was hard and fast and now, now, *now*!

Because they were there. Finally. After all the years of wanting and denying that wanting, they were finally grabbing onto each other with both hands. Literally.

Well, not *quite* literally. Frank could only use one hand, since the one in the sling was pretty much re-strained from much wandering.

"Frank," she moaned his name, "stop stalling."

His deep chuckle was exhilarating given that it rumbled through her breasts where they pressed tightly against his chest. The sensation zinging across her nipples made her eyes cross.

Okay, so scratch the gas mask idea. She'd just straddle his chest while she tickled his ribs. That'd certainly work.

"I'm not stalling." He ran his teeth down the column of her throat. "I'm trying to get a few facts straight."

"Fact one," she said and shivered when he sucked at the junction of her neck and shoulder, "I want you. Fact two, you want me. Fact three, I'm not fragile. I'm not going to break, so there's no reason for you to worry you need to be careful or that you need to hold back." Because, yeah, she could feel him against her, so big and hard and *big*. And she knew Frank, his mind was going to be making sure she was okay, that he didn't do anything to hurt her or scare her or make her uncomfortable.

And that just wasn't going to work.

She didn't want him holding back, staying in control, reining in his lust.

She wanted *him*. She wanted *sex*. No-holds-barred *sex*.

She tried to convey this by grabbing his ears and re-claiming his mouth, by boldly reaching between them to caress him.

God, she couldn't help but moan at the contact, he was so hot and smooth and pulsing and so completely, utterly *male*...

She dipped her chin in order to look at him there, spearing unapologetically from the V of his undone jeans.

Well, hello.

Okay, so Frank's goods were...fearsome. Long and thick, violently red and rock hard. The veins roping up the length of him stood out in harsh relief, the head broad and weeping.

She went to her knees then. It's all she could suddenly think about. Tasting him, getting her mouth around—

"I'll never make it," he growled, grabbing her shoulder and hoisting her up against his chest, slamming his mouth over the top of hers until the only thing she knew was him, his hands and skin, teeth and tongue, the hot, spicy smell of hungry man filling her flaring nostrils.

He was backing her up, edging her toward the bed, and when the back of her knees hit the mattress she grabbed his waist and twisted until it was *him* who fell backward onto the bed.

With his shoulder confined to the sling, she didn't want him straining to hold himself above her. All she wanted was for him to *feel*, because she knew for a fact, that's all *she* was going to be doing.

———

Just look at her, Frank thought as he lay back on the bed, watching her through heavy lidded eyes as she grabbed the waistband of his jeans, pulling them down over his thighs, whipping them off his feet, tossing them over her shoulder. *She looks like a huntress claiming a kill.*

So fierce and proud and determined. So unapologetically female with her slim, smooth limbs, tiny little waist and flaring hips.

"Becky, please just tell me what you want. Tell me what to do to make you feel good." The last two words came out as a strangled growl, because she'd dropped a knee to the mattress and started climbing on top of him.

For a brief moment, he was filled with doubt. Wondering if what he was doing was right. The answer, of course, was *no*, but, then again, just how wrong was it?

Not very, because, number one, she wanted this. She'd said as much. And number two, she'd grabbed his hand and pressed it between her legs.

It was the only kind of answer she gave him. The only

kind he needed really, because yes, what he felt against his fingers was so soft and smooth and warm.

It was also soaking wet.

She was wet for him. For this. For whatever he could give her and, baby, he was determined to give her everything.

Now.

No more stalling.

He watched her face as he slid first one finger and then another inside her, watched a blush of heat rise from her breasts to her throat to her cheeks, watched as she licked her lips then caught the lower one between her teeth.

She was everything a woman should be. Hot and wet and wonderful. Abandoned as she raised her own hands to her breasts and lightly pinched at the hardened nipples.

The sight went all through him, making his hungry dick jump up and down against his belly, like it was shouting, "look at me, look at me, look at me!" She caught the movement and reached down to stroke him, softly, lazily.

She moaned at the same time he did, arching her back and opening her legs wider. With his thumb, he located the little pearl at the top of her sex. Rubbing against it, he watched, fascinated, as her color deepened.

Sweet Lord, she was so unbelievably delicious, so completely perfect.

"Oh Frank, I'm going to…"

"Yeah, honey," he growled, working his fingers faster, "come for me."

"No." She shook her head and a heartbeat later—less really because he sure as hell hadn't seen it coming—she was straddling him. Angling him toward her entrance and sinking down.

His whole world exploded.

With a burst of pleasure so intense he thought maybe he'd come, she impaled herself on him, surrounding him with her wet heat, taking every inch of him in one long, steady glide.

He didn't know if it was minutes or hours that passed as the two of them remained motionless, reveling in the sweet sensation of two bodies joining so elementally it seemed impossible they'd ever part. But then she leaned forward, kissing him, swinging her hips up only to drive them back, and two things occurred to him. One, he hadn't come—*thank God*. And two, he wasn't wearing a condom.

He tried to tell her this very important fact as her short nails bit into his chest. She was clinging to him as if she was afraid they both might just blow apart.

He wasn't so sure she wasn't right. Which was why he needed to open his goddamned mouth and—

"Becky," he managed to grind out, even though his eyes were crossed, his toes curled, and his brain focused, completely *focused* on one very specific part of his anatomy.

It'd never felt this good. Never. Not even the first time when he was fifteen and so horny he actually thought he'd die from it.

"Becky," he tried again as her hair hung on either side of his face, smelling fresh and clean. For days he could have waxed poetic with descriptions of her hungry mouth and darting tongue, written sonnets about the sweet grip of her smooth thighs around his hips as she once more angled her pelvis back only to drive forward, composed symphonies about the soft smoothness of her breasts pressed against his chest, about the firm roundness of her ass gripped in his hand.

But he didn't have days. Because he was seconds

away from coming, and that would be bad on so many levels, the worst being he *wasn't wearing a condom!*

She pulled her mouth from his. "Oh, Frank, I'm going to—"

Yeah, he knew exactly what she was going to do, because her muscles tightened around him and if he let her...Well, he'd follow right behind her, no ifs, ands, or buts about it.

With superhuman effort, he gripped her hips and lifted her from him, ignoring her cry of anguish and biting down on his own tongue to stop the same when he slid from the hot heaven of her body.

"Condom," he managed to growl.

They stared at each other for a few ticks of the clock, then Becky scrambled over to her bedside table and pulled out a blue rubber dildo—*hello!*—which she hastily tossed over her shoulder before heaving out a box of condoms.

He didn't know why he felt so goddamned gratified when he noticed the box was unopened.

"New box?" he asked, just so he could hear her affirmative.

"Not really," she said, and he frowned. "I bought it three years ago."

Something wonderful and terrible exploded inside him. It was possessiveness and something more...something he refused to name.

She ripped open one foil package and looked over at him. "I'm not sure I got the right size."

"It'll fit," he assured her.

With stunning speed, she rolled the condom onto him, once more straddled his hips, and drove herself down his length.

His neck arched, and he knew he should never have doubted what she wanted. Never have worried about *giving* her what she wanted. Rebecca Reichert wasn't the kind of woman to wait around for a man to make the moves. She *took* what she wanted, damn the torpedoes and full speed ahead!

He was pressed so deeply inside her, as far as he could possibly go, and she was hanging above him, her arms braced on either side of his shoulders, her face mere inches from his.

"If I move," she whispered, gazing down at him, the heat in her eyes enough to make him come on the spot, "I'm gonna lose it."

He wished he could tell her it didn't matter, wished he could promise he'd make her lose it a hundred times more. But that would be a lie.

"I wish I could tell you something different, honey." He laughed regretfully. "But you're not even going to *have* to move because I'm going to come in about two seconds."

She groaned and then she moved and—

"Becky," he gasped, heaving beneath her when her inner muscles clamped down on him, pulsing and sucking and—

Holy hell! He exploded. Lights flashed behind his eyes, his spine snapped back, his world became a kaleidoscope of sharp sensations that burst through him like electrical charges.

He finally understood why some people referred to an orgasm as a shattering experience, because he was blown to pieces, rocketed apart and reduced to his elements, every part of him a shimmering molecule of ecstasy.

When his body put itself back together sometime

later, he opened his eyes to find Becky laying on top of him, a satisfied little smile playing at her lips.

The wanton minx, he chuckled, gently lifting her off him, tucking her next to his side so that her cheek pillowed on his chest and he could run his fingers through her hair.

"So, uh, what's with the toy?" he asked.

"Mr. Blue?"

He couldn't stop the snort that escaped his lips. "Is that what you call it?"

"Yepper." She ran her fingers through his chest hair. He could feel her mischievous grin. "Blue because, you know, he's *blue*. And Mister because, well, he's a *boy*. He's been handy to have around all those times you and I went at each other, verbally that is, and then I didn't have any way to work off the frustration."

He groaned at the thought of her lying in bed, using that absurdly colored toy on herself while fantasizing about him. Funny, he'd probably been three doors down doing the same thing. Oh, not using a toy. He had an experienced right hand for that, but there'd no doubt been endless times they'd both been thinking of the other while pleasuring themselves.

The idea was sexy as hell.

"Don't worry," she said, reaching beneath the covers to palm him. "Mr. Blue holds no comparison to the real thing."

God love the woman.

───※───

Becky woke sometime later to feel of Frank's large, callused fingers fluttering across her nipples.

"Mmm," she moaned and stretched, cracking open

her eyes to glance at the clock on her bedside table. At some point, he must have gotten up to turn off the light because the red digital numbers glowed dimly in the surrounding darkness.

"It's three-thirty in the morning, Frank," she mumbled, sucking in a breath when his lips closed over her left nipple. The hot spear of his tongue against the swollen bundle of nerves had her eyes rolling back in her head. "You've got to be up in another two hours. You need to get some rest before surgery."

"I'll sleep when I'm dead," he grumbled, the sound strangely menacing and strangely...*meaningful*.

She didn't have time to try and figure out what that meaning was, not when he shifted closer and the hard, hot length of him pulsed against her hip. She reached down, grasping him, marveling in the silkiness of the skin she found and the marble hardness it covered.

"Oh, that's you," she giggled when he groaned at the contact. "For a minute there, I thought I was in bed with a baseball bat."

"Mmm, very funny," he murmured, moving to her opposite breast.

Oh, this is perfect, she thought, stroking him softly, her womb contracting at one particularly strong pull of his lips. *This is how it was always meant to be.* The two of them, laughing, teasing, making love.

Why had they waited so long?

Okay, she knew the reason. It lived up in Lincoln Park, but she wasn't going to think of that now. She refused to think of that...

Tomorrow was for reality.

Tonight...tonight was for fantasy.

And the truth of the matter was, her fantasies didn't come close to the reality of Frank. So big, so warm and strong. His skin was smooth—except for the hard ridge of the occasional scar. His muscles hard—no exceptions there. And his smell…

It was the sexiest thing she'd ever encountered, because it wasn't applied or contrived. It was all clean, healthy male, and every time she sucked in a breath, a delicious little tickle trilled through her belly.

"No," she complained when he pulled away, his mouth leaving her nipple and his hard penis slipping through her ambitiously working fingers. "Don't go away."

"I'm not going anywhere you won't like, honey," his voice grumbled through the darkness. A second later, his mile-wide shoulders were pressing her legs apart.

Oh, no. He was right about that. He certainly wasn't going anywhere she wouldn't like. "Mind holding this leg up so that it doesn't bump against my shoulder?" he asked, as he pushed her knee back until it hit her chest.

Was he kidding? She'd tie herself in a bow if that'd help him in this little endeavor.

"Happy to oblige," she said as she hooked a hand behind her knee, keeping her leg out of the way, "assuming that it's, uh, gas mask time," she finished, chuckling.

"What?" she felt him glance up.

"That's what I was thinking when you first came in here, when you were just standing there, driving me crazy, touching me but barely touching me all at the same time. I was thinking if you didn't get naked and get inside me, double quick, I was going to climb you like a cat climbs a tree, wrap my legs around your head, and make you wear me around like a government-issue gas mask."

"Christ, woman," he groaned, but his chest shook between her legs, and it wasn't long before his deep laughter echoed around the room.

"Now if you start *that*, I'm going to throw you on your back, straddle your chest, and tickle your ribs until I can't see straight."

"I'm almost afraid to ask," he murmured, placing a kiss on the inside of her right thigh, his breath hot, moist and altogether too far away from the spot she most desired it.

Bull's eye, Frank. Go for the bull's eye.

"Well, in case no one's ever told you, when you laugh it vibrates through your chest."

"Still not following." He licked another hot kiss higher up on her trembling thigh.

Getting closer…

"Well if I were to sit on your chest while making you laugh, it'd be like straddling a giant, furry vibra—oh!"

Bull's eye!

"Forget it," she breathed as his tongue speared into her, only to retreat and swirl at the top of her sex, tapping rhythmically against her clitoris as his thumb entered her and stroked in and out. "This is so much better."

"Mmm," he growled his agreement, and the added vibration made her toes curl.

She knew it'd be good. She'd *always* known it'd be good. But this…this went beyond good. Maybe the simple explanation was that it felt so much better because they'd held back for so long, or maybe they had some sort of weird chemical compatibility, some sort of animal synergy, because this was…

"Oh, Frank, I'm going to come," she breathed, and

everything inside her tightened into a painful ball
of pleasure.

...this was transcendence!

"Frank!" she screamed his name, curling her fingers in his hair and pressing him against her as ecstasy
snapped her head back, pulsing from the base of her
spine out, toward her extremities, and then rebounding
back again.

The fingers of her free hand curled in the sheets, her
knees instinctively hitched higher.

Oh, oh, *oh* this was going to be a good one.

A thousand explosions detonated inside her, a thousand colors swirled behind her screwed tight lids, a
thousand sounds beat against her eardrums. She'd never
lost touch with her mind before, but it was gone. She
was nothing. Nothing but a bundle of firing nerve endings, pulsing muscles...

"I love the way you announce you're about to come,"
he chuckled as he started kissing his way up her body.

Was he talking?

Why was he talking?

One did not speak after an orgasm like that.

"Ah," he murmured before sliding the head of his
penis inside her. He must've donned a condom at some
point, the crafty, multitasking sonofagun. "I never
thought I'd see the day." He kissed her, delving his
tongue inside her mouth.

Frank slid in a little farther, stretching her wonderfully, deliciously, insisting her female body submit to
his male intrusion.

But the funny thing was it didn't feel like intrusion.
It was more like she'd been achingly, yawningly empty,

and now things were as they should be. Sweetly, spectacularly full.

"I've rendered you speechless," he murmured, kissing her shoulder as he drove those final few inches, seating himself to the hilt and rocking her softly against the mattress.

"Oh, Frank," she moaned at the feel of him inside her, above her, all around her. She was drowning in him, and it was the sweetest sensation.

"Ah, so your oral faculties have returned."

"I'll show you my oral faculties later," she promised, wrapping her arms around his back, pulling her knees up around his hips and hooking her heels beneath his surging buttocks. His hips drove smoothly and rhythmically, like the pistons in a well-oiled engine.

"Sweet Lord," he growled, and she grinned as he pulsed inside her.

So, he likes the thought of that, eh? Yeah well, what man didn't?

She whispered hot words against his lips as he pumped inside her, describing exactly what she'd do to him when she got her mouth on him. Then she could no longer speak because her world shattered once more, and she was left glorying in the feel of him following right behind her.

Later, after a little catnap, she held true to her promise and devastated his control with her oral faculties. And after that, he returned the favor, and she…well, she was certain to make her little announcements.

Chapter Sixteen

BECKY MOANED GRUMPILY AND SLAPPED A HAND DOWN ON her screaming alarm clock. "It's time," she murmured, rubbing the sleep from her eyes and stretching as Frank sat up and swung his long legs over the mattress.

Clicking on the lamp, she scratched her head and smiled sleepily at the sight of his broad back. The hard muscles on either side of his spine flexed as he bent to retrieve his shirt.

Oh, and what a butt. When he pulled on his jeans, she avidly watched his high, tight ass disappear into the denim. Grinning, thinking back on all they'd done mere hours before, she wolf-whistled her appreciation of the show.

He darted a brief look in her direction, then went back to buttoning his fly.

Uh-oh.

Sitting up, she whistled again, and even though he flashed her his wonderfully lopsided grin, it was impossible to misread what was written all over his face.

In a word: regret.

Oh God. She'd convinced herself this wouldn't happen, convinced herself that once she tore down all the barriers he'd erected against her over the years, he'd realize that what had *finally* happened between them was inevitable. That it was good and real and, more importantly, *right*.

Wow. She was turning out to be a cock-eyed optimist and, worse, a complete and utter dumbass.

Her heart started pounding, and a strange buzzing sounded in her ears as she threw off the covers and padded over to her dresser. Wrenching open a drawer, she grabbed some panties and stepped into them, then fished for the matching bra, wrestling herself into it and calling herself one hundred kinds of fool for ever thinking this had any chance of working out.

Oh dear, sweet Christ, she'd seduced him.

She'd propositioned him, stripped naked in front of him, and completely, recklessly, *willfully* seduced him, thinking she could be his new go-to girl, his brand spanking new Chesty McGivesItUp.

Of course, it took two to tango, as they say, so she wasn't the only guilty party, but what red-blooded male could resist the woman he'd freely admitted to fantasizing about for over three years when she shucked her drawers and spread her legs in invitation?

None that she could name.

So, yep, he'd surrendered, but with the light of day and the reality of what'd they'd done sinking in, it was obvious one night of passion with her didn't change the fact that he had no plans to make her a regular in his heart, mind, or bed. She was the one who'd asked for just sex, and that's precisely what he'd given her. The best sex of her life.

But that was it. End of story.

The two of them weren't going to ride off into the sunset together. She was obviously not going to replace the original Chesty, and the fact that she'd even considered that a possibility was so absurd it was almost laughable.

She would've laughed too, had herself a real knee-slapper, had her heart not been breaking into a thousand little pieces.

"Hey." His voice was as gentle and warm as the hand he laid on her shoulder after she shimmied into a pair of jeans. "Are you okay?"

No, I'm not okay. I talked big about sex just for the sake of sex, but that's all it was. Talk.

"Yeah." She grabbed an AC/DC T-shirt out of her top drawer and pulled it over her head because firstly, she no longer felt comfortable being naked around him—and, okay, after what they'd done to each other it was a classic case of closing-the-barn-door-after-the-cows-escaped, but she couldn't help it—and secondly, because pulling the shirt over her head allowed her to avoid his gaze. "I'm great. How are you?"

"Becky...honey..." He softly forced her around by the shoulder, grabbing her chin between his thumb and forefinger, making her look at him.

Don't cry, you stupid, stupid woman. If you cry, he'll know all that talk about sex for the sake of sex was nothing but a boatload of bullshit.

"I wish things were different." He shook his head, the look on his face enough to pulverize her already wounded heart into a fine powder. "I wish..."

He didn't finish, just sighed regretfully.

"It's all right, Frank," she told him, using the excuse of locating her boots to slip away from him.

Of course, it was anything but all right.

"But I want you to know that I—"

"It was sex for the sake of sex, Frank. Isn't that what we agreed on? And it was great, way better than anything I ever imagined, but you don't need to explain anything."

"That's where you're wrong. I want you to know how—"

"Hey, if you don't mind," she quickly interrupted him,

because she sure as hell didn't want to hear the words about to come out of his mouth. Her pride could only take so much, "I'd like to leave for the hospital a little early to stop by Starbucks. That waiting room coffee is worse than the sludge we brew around here and—"

"I don't want you to go to the hospital. You can come, uh, after…" Some strange emotion flashed across his face, and his deep voice broke before he continued, "but not before."

Her stomach tied itself in knots, and she wondered just how stupid a woman could be.

She briefly closed her eyes as she pushed her feet into her boots, swallowing the hot ball of misery clogging her throat before gathering all her strength to glance up at him and smile. "Okay, then. I guess I'll just wish you good luck."

"Becky, I—" His voice sounded miserable.

"You better get back to your room if you want to catch a shower and change before you have to leave," she interjected before she stood and marched to her bedroom door, ignoring the sight of her rumpled bed and the memories that came with it.

She unlocked the door and held it wide.

He wasn't a dummy. He knew a get-the-hell-out when he saw one. Still, before he stepped into the hall, he stopped beside her. Scanning her face, his lopsided smile was a parody of its usual self. When he brushed one finger down her cheek, to her horror, hot tears climbed up the back of her throat, and these weren't the kind she was going to be able to stop.

He needed to leave. Now.

"I'll see you in recovery," she told him, closing her

eyes when he bent to place a soft kiss on the corner of her mouth.

"You're one of the most wonderful women I've ever met, Rebecca Reichert," he grumbled hoarsely. "No matter what happens, I want you to remember that."

She threw her arms around his neck, hugging him tight, allowing herself one last moment of holding him and pretending he was hers to keep forever.

—~~~—

"Hi, I'm Michelle or Shell if you prefer. Frank's sister. He's told me so much about you all," the tall, chestnut-haired woman said as she shook hands with Dan Man.

Bill choked on the swig of Pepto he'd just taken.

Boss has a sister? He couldn't believe it. He'd known the guy for over three years and never had he heard anything about a sister...

"Well now, he hasn't told us a thing about you, sweetheart," Ozzie drawled, wiggling his eyebrows and resembling—with his all-American good looks, mad scientist hair, and *Star Trek* T-shirt—some strange combination of Casanova and your typical audio/visual class president. Standing and vigorously pumping Michelle's extended hand, Ozzie leaned in to whisper in mock conspiracy, "And now I know why. He knows us well enough not to dangle a treat such as yourself under our noses."

"You must be Ozzie," Michelle laughed, then as she made her way around the waiting room at Northwestern Memorial Hospital in order to shake the hands of the Knights who'd gathered there to wait for Boss to get out of surgery.

"And you must be Wild Bill." She came to stand in front of him, extending a long, elegant hand. "I'm very glad to meet you."

"It's a pleasure," he replied hoarsely, still coughing, still having trouble believing…

He was just about to open his mouth to ask her if he'd heard her right, if she was really Boss's sister when his own sister breezed through the door, weighed down with an armful of snacks from the vending machine.

Becky stumbled to a halt when her eyes lighted on Michelle. A bag of Cool Ranch Doritos fell to the floor.

"Becky," he said, bending to retrieve the chips, "this is—"

"I know who she is," Becky interrupted, her eyes glued to Michelle's face.

"You do?" he asked, perplexed.

"Yeah." She nodded, pasting on a smile. "Isn't it obvious?"

He glanced at Michelle. Okay, so she and Boss *did* share the same eyes and similar hair coloring, but that's where the similarities ended. Because Michelle was the beauty to Boss's beast.

"I *guess* it is." He scratched his ear.

"You must be the amazing Rebecca Reichert." Michelle went to shake Becky's hand but was thwarted by the mound of snacks.

Becky walked to the plastic coffee table pushed in front of the sofa where four of the Knights were lounging. She dropped her load on its surface, bracing herself on its edge for a second as if she was dizzy, before coming back to take Michelle's hand. "Call me Becky," she said. Her voice gruff.

Bill peered at her closely but could read nothing on her face. Something was wrong with his sister…

Probably just nerves over Boss's surgery combined with too much caffeine, he assured himself with a mental shrug.

"Mama, mama!" A little boy about three years of age came running into the waiting room, the soles of his tiny sneakers lighting up with each step, a Chicago Cubs baseball cap pushing his ears out from his head. "Can I eat it? Can I?" He was holding a bite-sized Hershey's candy bar as if it were the Olympic flame.

"Sorry." A nurse scurried after him. "He saw the basket of candy sitting on my desk, and I just couldn't resist his little face."

Michelle bent and scooped the boy into her arms. "It's perfectly fine. What do you say, Franklin?" she prompted, and Bill turned to his sister when he heard her drag in a strangled breath. She immediately started coughing, and he reached over, pounding her on the back.

"You aren't coming down with anything, are you?" he asked.

"No." She waved him off as she struggled to catch her breath, staring at the little boy in Michelle's arms.

"Thank you," Franklin dutifully told the nurse before turning and catching his mother's cheeks between his dimpled hands. "Now can I eat it?"

"*May* I eat it."

Bill watched Franklin's little chest expand on a deep sigh of exasperation. "*May* I eat it?"

"Yes you may," Michelle grinned, "but first I want to introduce you to some nice folks." She turned toward the group, rolling her eyes when the bundle of energy suddenly turned shy and tucked his head under her chin, peering out at the gathering of strangers. "Everybody, this is Franklin. Say hello, Franklin."

"H'lo," Franklin mumbled, refusing to look at any of them, his candy bar suddenly an object of intense study. Bill noticed the kid had the same eyes as his mother. The same eyes as Boss. Obviously, they were a family trait.

"Mr. Knight is ready for visitors," a short, plump nurse in pink scrubs announced from the doorway.

"Oh good." Michelle hoisted her purse higher on her shoulder, positioned Franklin on her hip, and started following the nurse down the hall. The Black Knights trailed behind her like a line of train cars, Becky slowly bringing up the caboose. "Can you believe that loser had himself convinced he was going to die?" Michelle threw over her shoulder, helping Franklin tear open his candy bar wrapper.

"What?" It was Christian who asked the question they were all thinking.

"Oh yeah. He's only been given general anesthesia once, as a kid, and it nearly killed him. *Did* kill him, as a matter of fact. He died on the operating table, but they were able to bring him back. I guess that's a given, huh?" She chuckled again. "Anyway, apparently he metabolizes narcotics in a weird way, and it's easy for him to overdose. Ever since then, he's been petrified to go under again."

Hmm, well that would explain—

"I, uh, I...I forgot I'm supposed to meet Eve," Becky announced from the back of the line.

"What'd you say, sis?" Bill asked as the group stopped to turn and look at her.

"Yeah, I...I'll pop in to visit Frank later. But,

uh...but until then, you all give him my best. Tell him I'm glad everything turned out." She smiled, her face white as a sheet, before spinning around and marching in the opposite direction, her hands fisted at her sides, her back straight.

What in the world was wrong with her? *Was* she coming down with something?

"Where are you going?" he demanded, not liking the idea of her and Eve traipsing all over the city by themselves, especially with that damn pirate still on the loose. Of course, he comforted himself with the knowledge that the Somali making it onto U.S. soil when the entire international community was hunting him was slim to nil.

"I'm meeting Eve for drinks at Delilah's," she called over her shoulder, repeatedly pushing the button for the elevator. The doors opened with a ding, and she jumped inside like the hounds of hell were nipping at her heels.

He shook his head, glancing around at the perplexed faces of the Knights. "What's gotten into her?" he asked and was met by a series of shrugs.

―⁓―

"Delilah! *Uno más!*" Becky crowed, smiling crookedly and holding one wobbly finger up for the lush, redheaded woman working behind the bar. The last word came out sounding more like *mosh,* and Eve stifled a giggle.

After a small hesitation, the bartender refilled their shot glasses, the brown liquor sparkling like agate under the bar's low lights.

Becky lifted the glass and Eve wondered what they'd drink to this time. They'd already run through health, happiness, prosperity, world peace, and all the other usual toasts. "To your suber—suter—" Becky made a face causing Eve to snort a laugh, "*super* cute leggings."

"Cheers." Eve clinked her glass against Becky's, threw the liquor to the back of her throat and swallowed, hissing as the hard burn hit her belly.

Slamming the shot glass down on the bar, she woozily turned to her friend. "My knees are still a mess. I can't stand the way they look, so skirts are out. And jeans hurt too much which means…" She made a rolling motion with her hand. "…it's leggings or nudity. I've been choosing leggings."

Becky gave her a sympathetic look before leaning one elbow on the bar, cupping her cheek in her hand. "Can you believe we were held hostage by pirates? It all seems kinda like a dream."

"A nightmare, you mean. And speaking of…"

"Say no more." Becky lifted a hand. "I had a doozie the other night. Ran out into the hall with my pistol loaded."

"I wish I had a pistol," Eve declared hotly. Maybe then she wouldn't feel so scared all the time. Maybe then she'd be able to scrub out the images of those six terrible days from her sleep-deprived brain. "I also want to start taking self-defense classes."

"I'll drink to that. Delilah!" Becky grinned sloppily, holding up that finger again, "Uno mosh!"

"No way." Eve shook her head, actually feeling the last four shots of rot-gut whiskey sloshing around in her belly as she hopped from the barstool. "I can't take another shot, or I'm going to barf."

"Hehehe. The über ch…chic," Becky hiccupped, "and oh-so-classy Eve Edens just said barf."

"It's a word, isn't it?" She looked around blearily, surprised to see so much leather and so many tattoos and so much facial hair...

Where in the world am I?

Oh yes. A biker bar on the east side of the city.

She, Eve Edens, queen of Bergdorf's, was getting hammered on cheap whiskey in the diviest of dive bars, filled with the scariest of scary types, and listening to the crappiest of crappy Def Leppard songs. Every time she heard this one, all she could think about was hot, sticky sweet feet.

Ew!

Something had to be done. Immediately.

Stumbling over to the jukebox, she fished in her pocket for a couple of bills and, after smoothing them out on the edge of the machine, slid them into the cash slot. And even though Red Delilah's was the dive-iest of dive bars, she was pleased to find it sported one of those fancy jukeboxes that connected to the internet so she could pick any song her little ol' heart desired.

And what did her little ol' heart desire?

Why, Chaka Khan, of course.

Just stand aside, Bridgett Jones!

She paid the extra fee to have her song jump the others lined up in the music queue, and spun away from the jukebox, swinging her hips and waving her arms in the air as the driving beat blasted from the huge speakers that hung from the every corner of the bar.

"*I'm every woman,*" she belted at the top of her lungs and motioned for Becky to join her out on the dance floor, er...she glanced down at her feet and the crushed peanut shells beneath them. So maybe this wasn't a dance floor, but it was a *mostly* clear space, and that's all she needed to get her groove on.

Becky vigorously shook her head, and Eve quickly decided she was having none of it. Chaka absolutely demanded dancing.

She ran over and tried dragging Becky off the barstool, which turned out to be far more difficult than she ever dreamed. The woman was small, but she was strong.

"You might as well go dance," the redheaded bartender told Becky, "because I'm not serving you another drink for at least an hour."

Becky gave her a scowl which blatantly said, *ya big party pooper,* and opened her mouth to reply, but Eve interjected, "Come on. Can't you hear that? Chaka's on the jukebox!"

"Listen to your friend," the bartender advised. "She's wise beyond her years."

Uh-huh. Except a wise woman would have laid off the shots three pours ago.

"But I don't want to dance," Becky grumbled petulantly as she grabbed on to the edge of the bar, stubbornly anchoring herself there as Eve tried to pry her fingers away.

"We have to dance," Eve insisted. "That's why God gave us parts that jiggle."

"What's gotten into you?" Becky demanded, one eyelid drooping lower than the other.

"Whiskey."

"Oh yeah." Chuckling drunkenly, Becky hopped from the stool, and together the two of them stumbled out to the "dance floor." For the next few minutes they danced, sang and laughed at the catcalls they received from the peanut gallery like they hadn't a care in the world. Becky had to shoo away some guy named Buzzard when he came to grind up against Eve, his big beer belly pushing into her back until he almost knocked her over in his fervor.

Just when the song was about to end and she was digging in her pocket for more money to reload the tune, Becky suddenly raised her hands to her eyes, her shoulders trembling.

Thar she blows!

Okay, so they were finally going to get down to the business of what had brought them here, to this seedy bar in a bad part of town in the middle of a Tuesday afternoon.

When Becky called earlier, voice strangely tight, begging Eve to meet her here, she'd dropped everything. Because Becky didn't ask for help unless the situation was dire, and although Becky'd been all smiles and laughing demands for shots up until this point, Eve knew it was only a matter of time before whatever was tearing her friend apart on the inside broke through to the surface.

It appeared the breakthrough was in full effect.

Finally.

Whew. One more shot and she was sure she'd find herself flat out on the peanut shell-strewn floor. And talk about one place in the world a girl would not want to end up. Especially if she didn't fancy catching a terminal case of ptomaine or hepatitis.

"Shh." She wrapped a comforting arm around Becky's trembling back and started herding her toward the rear of the bar and the booth pressed far into a shadowy corner.

"I...I promised myself I," *hiccup*, "wasn't g-going to do this h-here," Becky sobbed.

"It's okay," Eve assured her and tried to keep them both upright as they unsteadily wove their way around tables and chairs and the occasional five-gallon paint bucket filled with salted peanuts. "We're almost home free."

Just as she said it, they reached their destination, and she pushed Becky onto the red vinyl seat of the corner booth before throwing her purse on the table. Sliding in opposite, she was happy to be sitting because the blasted room suddenly decided it was a grand idea to do a slow tilt.

She should *not* have taken that last shot—or the previous four. She had to grab on to the table to keep from sliding under it.

"I can't be-believe I'm crying in the middle of Red Delilah's," Becky sniffed as she looked around for something on which to wipe her nose. Finding nothing, she used the back of her hand, and Eve figured a good friend would make her way up to the bar and ask for a napkin, but right now she was doing her level best just to remain sitting upright.

"It doesn't matter," she said, frowning when the second word came out sounding more like *dushn't*. "Nobody's paying us any attention except for maybe that guy." She hooked her thumb at the man sitting in the booth opposite them. He was wearing a baseball cap that obscured his eyes and most of his face.

Becky swung her bleary gaze over, and something changed in her face, her eyes sharpened. "Hey, you—"

Just as she said it, the guy got up, grabbed his beer and ambled off in the direction of the men's room.

"Hey!" Becky yelled at his broad back, and Eve shushed her.

"What are you doing? Leave that poor man alone."

"I think I know 'im," Becky said, shaking her head. "He's ex-CIA, and he's been hangin' around here and… oh, what does it matter?" She moaned before planting her forehead on the table in front of her.

Ex-CIA? Mr. Baseball Cap? He certainly didn't look like any government agent Eve'd ever seen. Where was the black suit? The dark shades? Of course, she'd recently learned a man's appearance meant nothing when it came to his job, because *Billy* was apparently some sort of government agent and he looked more like a poster boy for the WWE so, like the saying went, there's really no telling a book by its cover.

Billy. Oh, dang. She wasn't going to think about him, because then they'd *both* be bawling their eyes out.

She reached across the table to pat Becky's shoulder. "So, come on, spill. Why'd you invite me here?"

"We did it last night."

"Huh?"

"It, it, *it!* Me and Frank."

"Oohhhh." Eve was strangely sober all of a sudden, or maybe she was just strangely somber. It was hard to tell…

"Yep. *Oohhhh* is right."

Eve couldn't imagine. The man was so big and… scary-looking and…*big.* "So, uh, how was it?"

Becky glanced up, her brown eyes bloodshot, her eyeliner smeared until she resembled a drunk raccoon. "Wonderful…*awful!*" She groaned again and replanted her forehead on the table.

"Well, which was it? Wonderful or awful?"

"The sex was wonderful, *beyond* wonderful," she mumbled into the scarred surface of the table. "It was transhen-transcendent really."

Transcendent sex. Another thing Eve couldn't imagine. "So, then, explain the awful part."

"The awful part happened this morning!" Becky wailed. "When I met the woman I thought was just a friend with benefits! But she's not that. She's so much more, and I think he must love her because they have a little boy together! Oh, God!" She buried her nose in the crook of her arm to stifle the sound of her hard sobs.

What? "Back up. Back way, *way* up. He's in love with another woman?"

Becky nodded into her arm, sniffling loudly.

"Well then, I don't understand what the heck he was doing having sex with you."

"I sedush-seduced him, Eve," Becky admitted tearfully, raising her head and blinking so quickly Eve knew she was having trouble focusing. "He came to my room to talk to me about some stupid reporter and I...I stripped."

"*What?*"

"Yep." Becky wiped her nose with the back of her hand again. "I just whipped off my sh-shirt and shorts and stood there in my birthday s-suit, all but daring him to walk away."

"You stripped in front of him?"

"That's what I just *said*."

"I know. I know, it's just..." Eve shook her head, having a hard time imagining anybody, even Becky, being that audacious. Wow. "Uh, okay. So you stripped in front of him, all but daring him to walk away, and I guess he…I guess he didn't?"

"Nope."

Yes, because what man would? Becky was lovely and, despite her chosen career, infinitely feminine. Plus she had that rebellious streak and a couple of tattoos, so she pretty much embodied that quintessential combination of good girl and bad girl that all men found irresistible…

"But he's in love with someone else? Did you know about her?"

"Sort of."

"*What?* What does that mean?"

"It means I knew he was seeing someone. He's… he's," Becky hiccupped again and made a face of frustration at her body's inability to control itself, "he's been seeing her for a few years. But I figured it c-couldn't be that serious. I figured maybe it was just a friends-with-benefits type deal, and hey, if that's the case, why couldn't that friend be me, you know? But then, as we were all waiting to see him after he came out of his shoulder surgery, I met her and she's…she's…" Becky buried her head in the crook of her arm again, muffling her voice. "She's really beautiful, Eve. And nice. And funny. And did I mention he must love her because they have a s-son together? But I didn't know. I swear I didn't know or I never would've…How could I have known? He was supposed to list them with JSOC back when he was still with the Teams, but he didn't!" When she looked up, her expression was devastated.

"What do you mean he was supposed to list them—"

"Doesn't matter." Becky cut her off. "What matters is that he has a son. And the little guy looks just like him, *just* like him." In her mind's eye, Eve saw a little boy with linebacker shoulders and a bevy of scars. "Well, he looks like Frank must've looked at about three or four. All rough and tumble with these huge, soulful gray eyes…"

"Geez Louise, Becky."

"I know! And to make matter w-worse, come to find out Frank thought he was going to die today so…yep, that explains everything."

"What?" Was it Eve's imagination or had she been using that word a lot during this conversation?

"According to Michelle, that's her name by the way, *Michelle*, just like that Beatles song, 'Michelle ma Belle,' and she *is*, Eve."

"You aren't making a lick of sense."

"Belle. Pretty. She's so pretty."

"Becky, that hardly has anything to do with anything at this point." Eve wasn't sure if it was her level of drunkenness or Becky's level of drunkenness, but this was one of the most difficult conversations she'd ever tried to follow. "Why did Frank think he was going to die today?"

"Oh yeah, uh…because he did once before."

"Did what once before?"

"Die. Are you paying any attention to what I'm saying?"

"I'm *trying*." Lord knows she was trying but—

"I guess he's got some weird allergy or something, and he's had a bad reaction to anesthesia before and ended up flatlining only to be brought back, so he convinced himself he wasn't going to live through this surgery, which is why he…why we…oh, sweet Jesus!" Becky covered her face with her hands, choking on a sob.

Cheese and rice, and Eve thought *her* love life was a disaster…

"I'm going to have to quit, " Becky said after a few minutes. "I can't see him every day, know he's sleeping down the hall from me and—" Her voice broke, but this time she didn't give in to her grief, didn't let another teardrop fall.

Leave it to Becky to only allow herself about ten minutes to fall to pieces before she started cementing herself together again. The woman gave new meaning to the phrase, "tough as nails."

"But, you love that job."

"I know, but I just…I can't do it."

Eve wasn't sure she wanted the answer to this next question, but she asked it anyway. "Do you love him?"

When Becky met her gaze, Eve figured she had her answer right then and there.

"I love him," Becky admitted and sighed so heavily she appeared to deflate like a circus tent after the show. "I've loved him for over three years, but it doesn't matter. I know that now. There's no way it's ever going to work."

Eve couldn't help but agree. She didn't know Frank Knight very well, but she figured she knew enough of him to know he wasn't the kind of man to leave his son and the woman he loved behind while he took up with his hot, young boss. Or was he *her* boss? It was all very confusing. But regardless of who ran what, Eve was still surprised he'd given in to Becky's seduction. He just didn't seem the type, especially given everything Becky'd told her about him.

Of course, when faced with death, people did strange things…

"I'm going to the bathroom," Becky suddenly announced.

"I'll come with y—"

"No," Becky waved her off when she started to stand. "I'm fine. I don't need a witness as I pee, puke, and try to repair what's left of my make-up. Especially considering I have no idea in what order those activities will occur."

Eve nodded and watched her best friend sway toward the long gloomy hallway that led to the restrooms and back door.

Poor Becky, she thought, her heart breaking for her friend.

Mr. Baseball Cap turned to eye Becky's progress from his new position at the bar, and Eve sat up straighter, trying to make out his partially concealed features.

CIA? Really?

Good grief, was *no one* what they appeared to be nowadays?

She watched him curiously for a few minutes before she made the decision to go over and introduce herself—she'd never met a real, live CIA agent, ex or otherwise. She clumsily stood from the booth, and her movement caught his attention. For a second, something hot and calculating entered his eyes. Whatever it was, it kept her rooted to the spot, a startled hand fluttering up to her throat. Then a brief smile touched his lips, and she wondered if the lights from the bar had been playing tricks on her, making his amiable, handsome face appear hard and deadly.

She took a step in his direction, but before she could manage a second one, something down the hall snagged his gaze. He jumped from the barstool, dropping his beer in the process. In the blink of an eye, he barreled toward the darkened hall and the dingy restrooms.

For a second, she just stood there, staring in stupefied surprise at the shattered beer bottle and the foaming liquid spilling onto the wooden floor, watching as two peanut shells caught in the beer and briefly turned into little brown sailboats, merrily floating their way across the dusty slats. Then her mind caught up with her eyesight and she raced after Mr. Baseball Cap, ignoring the spinning room and the strange lassitude making her legs a pair of anvils dragging behind her.

She skidded around the corner in enough time to see Mr. Baseball Cap smash through the back door. The high pitched squeal of a car peeling out in the alley blasted into the bar, momentarily drowning out the sound of the jukebox.

What in the world?

She pushed open the door to the women's restroom. "Becky?" she called, an uneasy feeling swirling around in the pit of her stomach—it had nothing to do with the whiskey. "Where are you?"

No answer.

She peered into the three stalls. All empty save for a plethora of colorful graffiti. Spinning toward the bathroom door, she pushed it open just as Mr. Baseball Cap came thundering back down the hall.

"Call for help!" he hissed as he ran past her. "Some black guy with a bandaged hand just grabbed your friend and stuffed her in the trunk of his car. It's a black BMW sedan."

"Wha—"

Mr. Baseball Cap didn't stop to explain any more. He just burst through the front door. A mere heartbeat later, she heard the sound of a big engine firing up. The shrieking wail of burning rubber followed in the next breath.

Stumbling down the hall and over to the booth and her purse, she fumbled with her phone and didn't stop to wonder why the digits she dialed weren't nine-one-one.

Chapter Seventeen

"You love her, don't you?"

"What?" Frank turned toward Shell, wondering if his pain meds were causing him to have auditory hallucinations. He wouldn't be surprised. In fact, he'd never be surprised again given he sustained the biggest whammy of his life when he actually woke up in the recovery room a few hours ago.

He'd made it through surgery. He still had trouble believing it. He'd been so sure he probably wouldn't that he—

"Becky. That young woman you have working for you. You love her, don't you?"

He quickly glanced at the door through which Wild Bill and Rock disappeared mere moments earlier to make a coffee run—the rest of the Knights having returned to the compound long ago. Then he peered at little Franklin who was curled up in an armchair, taking his afternoon nap. Carefully adjusting himself on the narrow hospital bed, he ventured, "What makes you think that?"

"Because hers was the first name you uttered when you came out of anesthesia." When he shot her a startled look, she explained, "The nurse told us."

Goddamnit, whatever happened to doctor/patient confidentiality? Did that have no bearing on nurses? If not, someone should really inform patients of that very salient little fact. *Shit!*

"Because of the terrible look on your face when you realized she wasn't here," Shell continued. "And ever since the guys told you she'd stop by later, you've checked the clock on the wall every two minutes."

Okay, so he'd apparently been playing the role of Captain Obvious.

"I'm just worried about her, he hedged." I can't shake the feeling we haven't seen the last of the pirate who got away."

"Bullshit, Frank." Shell grabbed his good arm, squeezing gently. "It's an easy enough question. Do you love her?."

For a split second, he considered lying...*No, I don't love her. I care about her like I do all the guys but*...No. He'd never lied to Shell before, and he wasn't about to start. Oh, not because he was opposed to lying as a general rule. In his line of work, he told more untruths than truths. Hell, come to think of it, his whole life basically was one giant untruth, so, no, lying wasn't the issue. It was the lying to his sister that was the issue.

"Yeah," he sighed heavily against the restraint of his half-body cast, and the motion caused his newly rebuilt shoulder to grumble in protest. "Yeah, I love her."

It was the first time he'd admitted it aloud. The first time he'd ever really admitted it to himself.

And the truth will set you free? Whoever came up with that gargantuan load of bullshit was a frickin' jackass, because now that the truth was out there—just hanging out there like a whore's underpants on a hot Friday night—he felt so, so much worse. Because *Shell* was going to feel bad for ever making him—

"So what's the problem?"

He turned to gape at her. "You know what the problem is. She's barely twenty-six!"

"So?" Shell shrugged. "Last I checked, twenty-six is officially considered way past the age of consent in every state in the union."

Well, thank God for that, because even if twenty-six wasn't past the age of consent, he didn't think he'd have been able to resist Becky last night. Not when she whipped off her clothes and stood in front of him so naked and...

No, she hadn't been naked. Naked was a way to describe any Joe Shmoe sans a good set of threads. When he shucked his clothes, *he* was naked, all hairy ass and knobby knees and wrinkly balls hanging out for the world to see. But Becky...man, Becky had been *nude*.

Wonderfully, perfectly, artistically *nude*.

Kee-rist. What the hell had he been thinking? What the hell was Shell thinking now?

"Have you completely forgotten my promise?" he bellowed and then flinched when Franklin stirred sleepily, rooting around his fist for his thumb. When the little guy found it, he shoved it into his soft, cherubic mouth and settled back into sleep with a shaky sigh.

"I haven't forgotten one word you've ever said to me," Shell whispered, tucking a thin hospital blanket around Franklin's sturdy little shoulders. "But I have no idea what you're talking about now."

"I promised you I wouldn't turn out like him, and, by God, I won't! I refuse to!"

"For the love of...*Frank*, would you *please* start making sense?"

"I promised I wouldn't turn out like Dad, and I don't—"

"Wait." She held up a hand, interrupting him. "Wait

just a minute. How does your loving Becky have anything to do with your promise not to turn out like our father?"

"Because she's so much younger than me, and she's so—"

"Dad's *lady friends*," Shell made the quote signs with her fingers while rolling her eyes, "were young?"

Frank frowned, nodding. Of course they were young...

"You never told me that."

He hadn't? So then...

"How young were they? No—" She held up that hand again, shaking her head. "Never mind. I don't want to know. I have a lifetime's worth of disgust for that douche bag already. No need to add more fuel to the fire."

"So then what did you mean when you asked me to make that promise?"

The look she gave him clearly questioned his mental acuity. "I meant I wanted you to swear that when you grew up, when you became a man, you'd find someone to love. Someone you could give your whole heart to without ever looking back, without ever having regrets. Someone you wouldn't be tempted to cheat on. I meant simply that you should be a good man. A good husband. And a good father, if it ever came to that."

"Yeah, I got all that. But I also thought it had to do with his particular penchant for younger women."

She slapped him on the back of the head.

"Ow! What was that for?"

"For being a jackass. Why would I have you promise not to date younger women? That's absurd!"

"I was only twelve, Shell," he mumbled in his own defense, rubbing at his sore noggin. "Jesus, you think you'd have more sympathy for a man fresh from surgery."

"I have very little sympathy for fools, fresh from surgery or not."

For a moment, they sat in silence, each contemplating the ramifications of a promise made between two kids, two siblings who'd had nothing but each other to depend on after their father disappeared and their mother decided to hide her shame behind contiguous bottles of Stoli.

Finally, Shell ventured, "So besides your moronic misconception of what your promise to me meant, is there anything that's keeping you from going down on one knee and begging the lovely Rebel Reichert to love you forever and ever, amen?"

"Did you just quote Randy Travis?"

"Maybe."

"Where did I go wrong?" He glanced toward the ceiling, grinning when she pinched his arm.

"So I'm a little bit country and you're a little bit rock'n'roll. What's wrong with that?"

"Hell, I think I liked it better when you were quoting ol' Randy."

"Oh, don't pretend like you didn't love Donny and Marie. I seem to remember you had a life-sized poster of Marie Osmond stuck to your ceiling. What was it doing up there, Frank?" Shell batted her eyelids with such fervor, he worried she might start losing lashes.

"Can it, creep," he grumbled.

Chuckling like only a little sister can chuckle when she's got her big brother over a barrel, she asked, "*So?* What's stopping you?"

"What's stopping me from what?"

"Ugh, the problem with you men...scratch that. Let

me rephrase. One of the problems with you men is that you can never follow a conversation. So, what's stopping you from going down on one knee and professing your love for Becky?"

"It's not that we can't follow conversations," he told her in defense of every male on the planet. "It's just that we're linear conversationalists. When we veer off track, it takes us a while to reorient ourselves."

"Just answer the damn question."

"What's stopping me from going down on one knee?"

She nodded.

"Bad knees?" he offered.

Folding her arms in the huffy pose she'd perfected in childhood, she tilted her head and watched him as he considered the question.

So, what's stopping me? What's stopping me now that—

And suddenly, like a bolt of lightning from the clear blue sky, the answer struck him. He glanced at his sister in slack-jawed astonishment. "Well...nothing, I guess. I..."

Holy shit. There was nothing standing in his way. Nothing keeping him from finally claiming the only woman who'd ever managed to touch his jaded heart, the only woman he could envision walking down the aisle with, the only woman he could ever see growing round with his children, the only woman he could look at and imagine growing old with...

Holy, holy, *holy* shit!

So he *could* still be surprised, because suddenly the universe—in the form of his beloved sister—had just handed him the one and only thing he'd ever coveted, the one and only thing he never dared dream could be his.

She chuckled at the look of shock, hope, and sheer *joy* plastered all over his face.

"I was beginning to think I'd never see the day." She squeezed his arm, and he was so overcome, he jerked her against his chest, hugging her tight—damn the pain in his shoulder. He barely felt it.

"Oh man, Shell," he whispered over and over again.

"Oh, Frank," she murmured, smacking a loud kiss on his ear. "I'm so happy for you." She pushed back, her smile watery. "I really like her, you know. I mean, I only just met her, but she seems really spunky." She made a face. "She'd have to be to put up with you."

"She's great, Shell. So smart and talented and *kind*. She feeds her cat too damned much, and she's too nosy by half, but she's got the biggest heart and she's so flippin' brave it kills me and…what?"

Shell was shaking her head, laughing. "You really are in love, aren't you?"

"Yeah," he sighed, feeling like the world must've leapt into a closer orbit with the sun. Suddenly everything was warmer, brighter…"I'm really in love."

"What are you two grinning about?" Bill asked as he shouldered into the hospital room, juggling a cardboard carton full of Starbucks and a bag of fresh-from-the-oven blueberry muffins.

He was struck again by the sight of Michelle.

Shit, all this time he and the rest of the Knights had thought Boss was sneaking up to Lincoln Park to see some Pamela Anderson archetype when, in fact, the man had been visiting his *sister*. It was so absurd, he couldn't help but snicker.

Of course, now the small smile that flickered over Rock's mouth whenever the subject of Boss's lady love was raised made a whole helluva lot more sense. Rock was the only Knight who'd been with Boss before the founding of Black Knights Inc., and the squirrely son-ofagun had obviously known all along what the deal with Michelle really was.

Bill glanced over at Rock and vowed to give the cagey bastard an earful for letting them all make such fools of themselves...

"It's a brother/sister thing," Michelle explained, and he had to remember what he'd asked her. Oh, yeah. He'd asked what they were grinning about.

"Ugh, I understand those," he groused, and she flashed him a warm smile of thanks as he passed her a tall white-chocolate mocha, extra whipped cream. The woman liked her coffee sweet. God help her if she ever came to visit the shop. He lifted the lid on his own house blend and blew across the steaming liquid. "Only the brother/sister things Becky and I share usually end in insults, minor injuries, or yelled promises of retribution."

"Oh, Frank and I have our fair share of those, too."

Bill turned to eye Boss and the monstrous blue cast that wrapped from his waist and chest up around his shoulder and extended down his entire arm, keeping it frozen in an awkward angle away from his body. The surgeon said it was a *species* cast or a *spica* cast or some such thing. Bill didn't care what it was called, because what it looked like was some maniac's idea of medical torture.

"So when are they letting you blow this joint, Boss?" He fished in the bag and pulled out a muffin, dropping it in Boss's greedily outstretched fingers.

Food was the first thing the big guy had requested after coming out of the anesthesia...

Well, that wasn't entirely true. According to the nurse, the *first* thing Boss had requested was Becky, and that really threw Bill for a loop. He couldn't help but wonder if things had changed between Boss and his sister since he'd had that little chat with the dude back at the shop.

He hoped so.

Because despite whatever little flirtation she had going with Angel, he knew Boss was the only man on the planet who could make her truly happy, since Boss happened to be the only man on the planet with big enough balls not to be intimidated by a woman of her particular talents and...uh...call it *moxie*.

Not to mention, Boss was the only man she happened to love...

Oh, she tried to hide it, and perhaps she did—from the other guys. But a big brother knows when his little sister gets a particular look in her eye. And she'd had that particular look in her eye since the first day she'd been introduced to Boss.

"They say they want me to stay overnight," Boss replied around a mouthful of muffin. "Something about keeping an eye on my pain meds."

"That's probably—"

Somewhere a phone rang; the tone was the opening jingle to Blue Oyster Cult's "Don't Fear the Reaper."

"That's me," Boss said, and Bill chuckled. He figured

if he had to have a brother-in-law, he could do a lot worse than Frank Knight.

"Where are my pants?" Boss asked.

"Here." Michelle opened the little closet and pulled out Boss's worn jeans. Digging in the hip pocket, she retrieved his phone and tossed it to him. And even loopy on medication, Boss's reflexes remained those of a cat.

He caught the phone one-handed, punched the "talk" button, and held it to his ear. "Well, I'll be damned. Dagan Zoelner, I was wondering when you were going to give us a call...*what*?"

Bill frowned when Boss's eyes sharpened, his expression turning murderous. Automatically Bill reached to make sure his Sig was safely nestled at the small of his back, because he'd seen that look on Boss's face before and it was usually when they were neck-deep in bad guys.

"Goddamnit!" Boss yelled, and everything began happening at once. Franklin woke up and started bawling, Boss ripped out his IV-lines and scrambled from bed, Rock asked, "What's up?" even as he checked to see that his two extra clips were full, and Bill's phone started vibrating in his pocket.

Pulling out his cell, he glanced at the caller ID and lifted a brow. Whether he wanted to admit it to himself or not, he'd been waiting for this call, but it was not a good time.

"What?" he barked impatiently, watching Boss push Michelle away as he started trying to hop into his jeans using only one arm.

"Billy?" Eve's strangled voice sounded through the receiver. "He's...oh God!" Her voice broke on a pitiful sob. "He's got Becky!"

Sharif could not believe how easy that had been.

Snatching Becky had been as simple as waiting for her to appear alone from the safety of the high-fenced complex in which she lived, following her city bus as it slowly wound its way through the traffic-clogged streets of Chicago, hiding out in the men's restroom of that sleazy bar while she got pissed on cheap whiskey, and lying in wait for the moment when she excused herself to the loo—because ladies always eventually excused themselves to the loo.

Hitting her with the stun gun had been a cinch; she hadn't even seen him slip from the men's restroom.

He'd been on her, pressing the electrical prongs into the side of her neck and squeezing the trigger, before she ever knew what hit her. Of course, his error had been in not realizing what a jolt of that magnitude would do to a small, inebriated woman. Instead of simply incapacitating her, the shock had knocked her out cold.

Still, he couldn't help but think it'd all worked out for the best.

Having her unconscious certainly made it easy for him to hoist her over his shoulder and stuff her into the trunk of his rented vehicle—the vehicle he'd been able to secure on the stolen passport his father proudly handed him before he walked out of the house in St. Ives. Having her unconscious had also solved the problem of transferring her from the trunk into his abhorrent little room in a fleabag motel way out on the south side of town. He simply backed up to the door, opened the trunk, threw the discolored comforter he swiped from the queen-sized motel bed over her, and carted her inside.

No one had given him a second look.

Which was just one of the three reasons he'd chosen that motel...its location in a neighborhood where a woman's screams were so *de rigueur*, nobody gave them more than a passing thought. The second reason was the metal bed. It was absolutely perfect for what he had in mind. And the third reason was loitering across the street at the petrol station. A group of pathetically dressed gangbangers who'd no doubt sell him the cocktail of street drugs he knew it was going to take to make this ordeal last, and last, and last...

Oh, Becky Reichert was going to beg for death before he was finished with her. *Beg for it!*

"We're going to have some fun, you and me," he promised her, tightening the last rope around her slim wrist. Having her unconscious had made the process of tying her, spread eagle on the bare, stained mattress, just that much easier as well.

So it'd all worked out for the best, except...

He frowned at her T-shirt and heavy jeans. This little endeavor, this waiting for her to wake-up so he could revel in the fear and pain and anger in her dark eyes, would be so much more enjoyable if she were naked, if he could gaze at her pale breasts and supple thighs.

But he didn't dare untie her, and even if he did, he still wouldn't be able to undress her one-handed.

Looking around the room, he realized he'd forgotten one crucial piece of equipment. Something he could use to cut away her clothes.

Bollocks! He usually wasn't so absent-minded,

usually made sure to cross all his Ts and dot all his Is before he embarked on any assignment, but he'd been feverish and weak and obviously both had interfered with his mental processes.

Well, what was done was done. He needed to figure out a way to rectify the situation.

Scissors would be his best bet. Less gratifying than a knife maybe, but so much easier to wield one-handed.

With a frustrated shake of his head, he moved to the dingy window and pulled back the dusty blinds. Eyeing the rundown petrol station across the street, he wondered what the odds were on them carrying a pair of scissors.

Fifty-fifty he decided as his eyes pinged over to the group of hoodlums lounging on the chipped curb.

He needed to go score some blow, anyway. A little angel dust to keep his cock hard and his mind bright so he could enjoy every last minute of Beck Reichert's delicious misery. And while he was out doing that, he'd swing by the petrol station and find *something* he could use to cut away her clothes.

Glancing one last time at his pretty little hostage, he smiled.

This was going to be such splendid fun.

—⁓—

"What do you mean you've lost her!" Frank's heart jumped into the back of his throat and pounded there like a bad toothache. His roar filled the small interior of his sister's Hyundai Elantra. After Shell realized trying to keep him in the hospital bed was about as futile as pissing in the wind, she did the smart thing—she'd always been a smart girl—and tossed him her car keys.

The doctors had been a bit more difficult to convince, shouting how they'd have security come strap him down if he didn't return to his room.

He wasn't sure, but it might've been his murderous face, along with his thunderous description of just how the CPD would find their dismembered bodies at the bottom of Lake Michigan should they attempt any such maneuver, that eventually managed to overcome their objections.

"They exited off I-94 onto South Vincennes Avenue about six minutes ago, but I've lost them on the side streets," Zoelner replied, and Frank would worry later about what the ex-CIA agent was doing hanging around Chicago and more specifically Red Delilah's. For right now, he was grateful as hell the guy had been on the scene—even if he had lost sight of the vehicle in which Becky was being held hostage.

"Keep looking," he barked, cussing and slamming a fist into the little car's roof when Bill, who was doing his best impression of Mario Andretti over in the driver's seat, hit a particularly vicious bump that caused Frank's injured arm—kept stabilized in a diabolically awkward position by his bright blue spica cast—to knock against the front windshield.

"I'm going to sign off and call Ozzie," he told Zoelner after he could unclench his teeth against the pain eating at his shoulder and the base of his skull like a starving sewer rat. "I'll see if he can ping her cell phone. In the meantime, if you spot that vehicle, you call me on the double. Our ETA is fifteen minutes from your last position at the Vincennes Avenue exit."

"Roger that."

Sweet Jesus, honey, just hold on. Stay tough. Stay strong. Stay smart. Don't let—

"I can't believe that goddamn pirate had the cojones to come take her right out from under our noses!" Bill slammed a palm against the steering wheel, even as he whipped around a slow-moving Comcast van, garnering him a single-finger salute from the pissed-off driver. "Where the hell was Interpol when that bastard was going through immigration? And what the hell does he want, anyway? He has to know he can't hold her for ransom here in the U.S. without us finding—"

"Come on now," Rock interrupted from the small back seat. "He probably got through immigration with a fake passport, and I'd bet my bottom dollar it's not ransom he's after. The only thing that would bring 'im here is revenge."

"Yeah, I know. *Shit*," Bill hissed, taking one hand off the wheel to reach into his jacket pocket. Snagging a little bottle of Pepto, he unscrewed the cap with his teeth and knocked back half the bottle as Frank punched number nine on his speed dial.

Yeah, Bill's stomach wasn't the only one giving him fits. Frank's was doing loopty loops like he was on a goddamned roller coaster, and despite the coolness of the Chicago day, he was pouring sweat. His jeans were chockablock full of nut soup. He wished he could blame it on the meds, but he was pretty sure he'd be experiencing these same symptoms stone-cold sober because the woman he loved, the woman he wanted to spend the rest of his life with, was, according to Zoelner's reports, drunk, unconscious and stuffed in a filthy pirate's trunk and—

"Ozzie," he wheezed a breath of relief when the kid answered the landline back at the shop, "I need you to ping Becky's cell. Zoelner's no longer got eyes-on and we're going to—"

"Already on it, Boss," Ozzie said. Frank could hear the kid's fingers flying over a keyboard. "But it's going to take five to ten to get a lock."

"Make it five," he clicked off without waiting for Ozzie's reply.

Make it five, kid, he prayed, *because every second counts.*

Chapter Eighteen

OH, MAN, WHY DO I EVER DRINK?

Becky didn't want to open her eyes, didn't want to see the room spinning, didn't want to lift her pounding head for fear it might just fall right off her neck, didn't want to shift her thousand-pound legs off the mattress because it was really, *really* iffy whether or not they'd support her weight.

Basically, she didn't want to move one teeny-tiny muscle.

Of course, she needed to do all these things, in short order too, because her tongue felt like it was wearing a wool sock, and she had to get a drink of water. Now. Or she might just shrivel up into a Becky raisin.

"Ugh," she kept her eyes screwed tightly closed, "worst hangover in the history of the world." On a scale of one to ten, this hangover was a solid eleven.

Do the crime, and you do the time, sis. That'd been Billy's sage advice on her twenty-first birthday, the first time she'd ever tied on anything more than a cozy little buzz. She'd barely resisted the urge to kill him then. Now she figured she'd do better to kill herself. Just end the misery. Of course, if she didn't get some water in her system pretty soon, her body might do the job for her and call it a day.

"Yowza, how Dan manages to handle this on a daily basis is beyond me," she told the room, then grimaced

when the sound of her own voice made the little de-
mons pounding inside her head exchange their ham-
mers for pickaxes.

Water! her body cried out again, and she could no longer ignore the painful thirst making her throat ache like
she'd swallowed all the sand on North Avenue Beach.

"Okay, okay," she grumbled and sat up—

Uh, no she didn't. She *couldn't*.

Her eyes flipped open, and the first thing to meet her
blurry vision was a giant water stain on a filthy popcorn
ceiling. *Where in the world…?*

And then it came rushing back to her, a tidal wave of
memory surging through her bleary mind.

She'd been at Delilah's and had just come out of ladies' room when a familiar smell cut through the clouds
of stale beer, strong whiskey, and sawdust. It was a
man's cologne, overwhelming and unusual and for some
reason the scent made her skin crawl and…

It took her all of a half second to remember where
she smelled that particular cologne before, and that was
obviously a half second too long, because then she'd
gone supernova. Like a dying star, every particle of her
being was squeezed down to a single point of intense
pain before exploding outward in the next instant. *Blam!*

Then…lights out. Nothing.

And now she was in some filthy motel room if the
queen bed, window unit, and cheap plywood furniture
were anything to go by, not to mention the acrid smell
of stale cigarette smoke and the underlying aroma of
sweaty bodies and…yuck, that was definitely sex lingering in the air along with the tang of urine.

Oh yeah, and the really big float in this Macy's Day

Parade of Disastrous Hits was the fact that she was trussed up like a Thanksgiving turkey.

Sharif, you asshole!

She'd have screamed it into his butt-ugly face if he'd been in the room. But he was noticeably absent.

Not that she was complaining. Heck, no.

If he'd somehow managed to, oh, let's say, get himself run over by a CTA bus or gunned down by a gang of Southside Latin Kings, she'd be really hard pressed to shed a single tear. Of course, that would just be way too easy, and her luck, of late, certainly wasn't running in any direction that could be considered even remotely easy.

So…yep, he was likely somewhere gathering God only knew what kind of paraphernalia, and she should be scared. She *knew* she should be. Two seconds after meeting the guy she knew there was something really wrong with him. Something missing in his fathomless black eyes.

Had it been the spark of human kindness? That elusive kernel of light that despite race, color, creed, or religious affiliation all humans harbor within the depths of their souls?

Whatever it was, Sharif lacked it. And she suffered under no delusions then that he was a psychopath, capable of taking her life without batting a lash. Now she suffered under no delusions that not only was he capable of taking her life, but he was going to *enjoy* doing it. A guy didn't tie a woman, spread eagle, to a bed unless he had very specific, very obscene plans in mind.

Which just brought her back around to the fact that she should be scared to death. Shaking in her boots. Ready to—

Hold the phone…

Shaking in her...*boots!*

"Oh, you wonderfully incompetent moron!" she choked on a dry laugh.

The dumbass had tied her ankles, but he'd done so without removing her heavy biker boots.

What a bonehead. Still, she couldn't help but send a small prayer skyward that Sharif had been graced with a questionable IQ.

Wiggling her right leg, she was able to slowly, inch by excruciating inch, shuffle her foot out from inside her boot. When her heel finally popped free, she wanted nothing more than to pant and rest like a dog in the summer sun. Her head was doing its best impression of an open wound, but time was working against her, so she immediately hooked her toe into the top of her left boot and pried her remaining foot free. Then she toed off her socks and plunged barefoot back into her left boot, feeling around for the one thing that just might save her life.

Frank, you big wonderful dill-hole, you may love another woman, but I'm gonna kiss you smack on the lips next time I see you.

She'd been totally kerflummoxed two years ago when he presented her with a deadly looking knife with all the pomp and circumstance she was used to seeing when a guy presented her with dozen red roses.

"Ya never know when you're going to need it," he'd said after insisting she store it in her boot.

She hadn't been able to conceive at the time, especially given her propensity to surround herself with highly trained operators, just what horrific course of events could possibly culminate in her needing a USMC "Bulldog" Tactical Combat Knife with a hollow ground 440C high chromium martensitic stain-less steel blade.

Well, now she knew. It was the scenario where she was kidnapped and hogtied by a fancy-talking Somali pirate.

Wrestling the knife from its hidden sheath, she hooked the Madagascar rosewood handle between her toes. Folding at the waist, she lifted her feet above her head. Thank God she'd been keeping up with her Pilates, or this little maneuver would've been impossible. Still, she needed to start buying bigger jeans if she planned to make a habit of turning herself into a human taco...

Gripping the blade tightly between her toes, she sawed at the rope securing her right hand.

Monkey toes. That's what Billy called them. Given her short stature, it'd be natural to assume she'd have small, stubby toes, but hers were long and thin. Well, now she thanked the good Lord for blessing her with monkey toes. Because along with Sharif's bumbling incompetence and Frank's insistence she always be armed, her toes might just be the key to her making it out of this situation alive and—

Bingo!

The thin rope frayed and snapped under the razor sharp edge of her blade, and she wasted no time palming the knife and putting it to work on the restraints around her bruised left wrist. The rope gave way almost instantly and, blessedly free, she raced to the window, carefully pushing aside the edge of one dusty, smoke-stained curtain. She stumbled back in shocked horror when she saw Sharif's ugly face through the dirty window.

He was right there. Right at the door. In the process of pulling out an old-fashioned room key.

Time warped and slowed.

She reeled toward the bathroom, her limbs moving as if they were submerged in water.

An out-of-body experience. That's what she was having. Because she was watching herself from a distance.

She saw herself fling open the bathroom door. Saw herself catalog the moldy shower curtain, stained floor tiles, and chipped toilet. Saw herself dispassionately scan the dripping faucet and used-to-be-white-but-now-sickly-yellow motel towels stacked on the shelf under the sink.

And then she was shot back into her body like an arrow from a bow, her heart plummeting to the bottom of her stomach, because the one thing she wished to see, the one thing that would've given her a chance of escape was glaringly absent.

The bathroom had no window.

She refrained from screaming her disappointment only because she didn't have time for the breakdown she so richly deserved after this hellacious, surely-it-can't-get-any-worse, oh-wait-it-can day. She didn't have time because the doorknob rattled as it turned.

Oh God, oh God, oh God, oh—

Sharif stepped over the threshold and blinked in confusion at the empty bed. Then his dark face contorted into a mask of such horrible rage, she knew she'd see that vicious look on the backs of her eyelids for years to come.

If she lived that long.

And she was determined to live that long.

Just as it slowed to a snail's pace, time suddenly reversed directions. The next few moments passed in the blink of an eye.

Sharif noticed her standing by the bathroom door and instantly dropped the plastic grocery bag in his hand, fumbling for the matte-black handgun shoved in the waistband of his pants.

She took a loose grip on the rosewood handle of her knife, steadied her breath, and let her USMC "Bulldog" blade fly—just like Frank'd taught her.

"Ozzie's got a lock on her," Frank said after thumbing off his cell phone and taking a steadying breath lest he pass out. Wild Bill finished screeching around a corner, causing his injured arm to slam against the passenger side door. "Her cell is located on the corner of 109th and South Wentworth," he managed through clenched teeth.

"That's only five blocks away. Hang on."

Yeah, hang on. Easy for Bill to say.

Frank squeezed tight the ol' peepers and just let the pain wash over him when Bill took another corner on two wheels—Shell's Elantra was never going to be the same—and his newly repaired arm once more made jarring contact with the car door.

Fuck-fuck-fuckety-fuck!

When he dared to reopen his eyes, the smell of burning rubber wafted in from the vents and added to the prescription soup of narcotics, mind-numbing agony, and gut-twisting fear to have blackness closing in on the edge of his vision. His skin prickled like he was covered in bugs, his whole body flashed hot and cold. Just when he thought he was going to sink into Zzz-Town whether he wanted to or not, just when the blackness began to completely take over, the vibrating of his phone dragged him back from the edge.

"Go," he barked, listening intently as Zoelner quickly relayed his location and the fact that he'd found the black BMW.

"It's parked in front of room six at the Lazy Suzanne Motorway Motel," he repeated Zoelner's words to Bill, "Corner of 108th and Wentworth."

"One block closer. That's even better," Bill muttered, flying through a red light and narrowly missing being sideswiped by a rusted out jalopy that looked like perhaps it'd been an El Camino in a previous life.

The last block and the dilapidated buildings on either side of the street whizzed by in a blur of sagging stoops, drooping roofs, and dusty yards. Frank registered the rundown gas station with its requisite South Side gangbangers hanging out on the corner just before Bill whipped into the parking lot of the Lazy Suzanne. The three of them poured out of the vehicle at the same time Zoelner leapt from a silver SUV. All four men palmed their weapons, holding them out and at the ready.

Bill, Rock, and Zoelner ran low across the lot, each quartering the area, scanning for threats.

Frank just ran.

"You bitch!" Sharif screeched as the knife she'd sent flying lodged in the meaty part of his shoulder. He dropped his weapon and it hit the orange shag carpeting with a muted thud.

Becky saw her chance. It was *now!*

She lunged for the weapon at the same time Sharif

charged like an enraged bull in her direction. She narrowly missed the swipe of his arms by ducking and launching herself at the handgun like a Major League base runner diving toward home plate. With a skid and a grab, she was able to snatch the Glock, roll, and leap to her feet. Aiming the Glock at Sharif's head, she curled her finger around the trigger.

"You so much as twitch, and I swear to God I'll squeeze this trigger until the clip's empty," she warned, panting, trying to quiet her racing heart in the same instant she tried to still her shaking hands.

She'd never met the devil, never really believed in demonic possession, but the absolute hatred on Sharif's face made her realize she must be looking at Satan's close cousin. There was no other word but *evil* to describe the dark light glinting in Sharif's hard eyes.

She tried to swallow past the lump of fear and dread that had taken up permanent residence in her throat.

"Don't make me do it," she pleaded when he reached up and grabbed the handle of the tactical knife protruding from his shoulder.

Please don't make me do it.

All the marksmanship lessons Ghost had taught her, all the coaching she received about separating herself from the target, had sounded really good in theory. But now that she was there, looking into the face of a man—albeit an evil man—it was hard to dismiss the fact that his heart was pumping blood through his veins, his lungs sucking in oxygen, his brain synapses firing. It was hard to dismiss the fact that he was alive, and it was within her power to take that life away, snuff it out in an instant with nothing more than a series of muscle contractions in her pointer finger.

With a bellow that had white spittle gathering at the corner of his mouth like a rabid dog, Sharif yanked the knife from his arm and lunged toward her.

God forgive me, she prayed.

Three pounds of pressure and a half-breath later, it was all over.

"No!" Frank roared, his heart exploding inside his chest a split second after the hard bark of a .45 rent the cool Chicago air and a muzzle flash briefly illuminated the dingy window of Lazy Suzanne's room six.

He took two lunging steps, planted his size-sixteen biker boot in the center of the door, and used his momentum and every bit of his two hundred forty-five pounds like a human wrecking ball. The already-warped door flew off its hinges, landing inside the dim room with a splintering, teeth-rattling crash. Frank stumbled in right behind it.

And he saw it all in an instant.

He saw Becky blowing like she'd run a race, standing with her bare feet shoulder width apart, her left hand supporting the edge of her right palm, her head tilted slightly so that her eye lined up with the Glock's sights. He saw Sharif lying in an expanding pool of sticky, crimson blood, the top of his head completely gone, his left leg twitching like a beheaded snake.

"Frank," Becky panted, barely giving him a look as she continued to draw down on Sharif. What did she think? That the bastard might jump up and come after her again despite the fact that a good portion of his skull was missing and most of his brains were slowly sliding down the opposite wall? "You should be in the hospital."

If he hadn't been on the verge of breaking down and crying like a goddamned baby, he would've laughed.

She was alive, wonderfully, gloriously *alive*, and she was issuing opinions in that dusky Demi Moore voice of hers and…sweet, sweet, Jesus!

He did two things then. He dropped his weapon and fell to his knees, barely able to hold back the hard sob of relief building in his chest.

That-a-girl, was all he could think. *That's my tough, wonderful girl.*

"Becky!" Wild Bill cried as he charged through the door, stumbling to a halt when he took in the gruesome scene. "Oh, thank goodness, sis. Thank goodness," he repeated as he slowly made his way past Frank's kneeling form and over to Becky's side, gently removing the .45 from her trembling hands and shoving it in the waistband of his jeans.

Bill had to take her by the shoulders and physically turn her away from the horrific sight of Sharif and that twitching leg, and even then she kept glancing back, her beautiful eyes huge and filled with shock.

Yeah, Frank was somewhat of an authority on terminal ballistics. They were never pretty. And head shots? They were the ugliest of all. The movies always portrayed them as a nice, neat hole smack-dab between some sorry bloke's glassy, sightless eyes. What Hollywood usually failed to include was the mess that bullet made upon exiting.

The skull was like a melon, hit it with a hard object, and it tended to just bust apart into a terrifying hash of blood, bone, and gray matter. And when you added in the lovely little electrical pulses that continued to manipulate muscles like strings animating a marionette, yeah, it was pretty much the stuff of nightmares.

The distant wail of sirens was the just the sound Frank needed to pull himself out of Nadaville. With a hard shake of his head and a big, steadying breath, he managed to get his brain and his legs moving again. Pushing to his feet, he screwed his eyes shut when a bout of dizziness almost had him taking a header.

A hard hand on his shoulder steadied him.

After a brief moment, when he was pretty sure he wasn't going to pass out or puke, he turned to face Zoelner. "What the fuck are you doing ghosting around Chicago?" he demanded, even as stars skipped happily in front of his vision.

Rock poked his head into the room from his position guarding the door and reported, "Local PD comin' in hot. ETA is two minutes."

Frank nodded before turning back to the mysterious ex-CIA agent.

"Johnny Vitiglioni, that greasy Las Vegas mobster, has put a price on all of your heads in retribution for Ghost killing his boys," Zoelner said. "I figured the least I could do was keep a close eye on your backs. You know," he shrugged and holstered his weapon under his arm, "just a little reparation for getting involved in that whole mess in the first place."

"Goddamn. If it's not one thing it's another."

On top of everything else that'd happened today. Frank was going to have to deal with Johnny Vitiglioni.

Of course, that'd have to wait. Because, for now, he had to take care of something else.

Like the not-so-insignificant fact that Becky was

ghost white and staring in abject horror at Sharif's dead body. The guy's leg had stopped dancing around like it was full of Mexican jumping beans, but the stuff oozing out of his ruined skull just kept getting worse and worse.

It was obvious that now that the adrenaline was wearing off, the enormity of what she'd done, namely killing a man, was setting in.

His heart lurched at the sight of her huge eyes and quivering lower lip. It made him want to scoop Sharif's brains back into his shattered cranium and shock the bastard back to life just so he could kill him all over again.

"Get her out of here, Bill," he commanded as he reached in his pocket for his cell phone. He had to make a call into Chief Washington and beg the guy for another favor. Lawrence P. Washington was a former marine sergeant turned CPD police chief. He was solid as a rock, cranky as a wet cat, and the only man in the city who had even a slight inkling—very slight—as to the truth behind Black Knights Inc. Which put him in the inconvenient position of having to cover the Knights' tracks when their activities intersected with the mean streets of Chicago.

"No, I'll, uh," Becky swallowed convulsively, "I'll stay. The police are going to need a statement."

She glanced back at Sharif and shivered.

Frank wanted nothing more than to grab her up, press her head against his shoulder, and make it all go away. Just turn back the clock so he made it to the motel thirty seconds earlier. If he had, if he'd had that extra half-minute, it would've been his bullet ending Sharif Garane's malicious existence and not hers.

Sharif *Garane*. Oh yeah, Interpol had finally been

able to identify the guy, thanks in large part to Becky's sketch. Fat lot of good it did them in catching him before he got the chance to strike.

"The police *are* going to need a statement," he told her, "but not from you. You were never here."

Her wide eyes jumped to his face. "But I...I," she pointed to Sharif, unable to go on.

"Listen to me, Rebecca. For weeks your face has been splashed across the evening news. If this incident gets out, the press will be on us like flies on a shit-wagon. And you know as well as I do, we can't afford that, not so soon after Patti and the whole piracy incident. If people find out you were here, they might start to wonder why you and Black Knights Inc. are always slam-bam in the middle of trouble. And if they start to wonder, then they'll start to investigate. Lord." He ran his hand through his hair, all manner of horrific paparazzi scenarios swirling through his head. "Can you imagine what Samantha Tate will do? You thought she was a nuisance before? Well, if she gets wind of this, you're going to need a restraining order to keep her away."

"Okay, but Frank I—"

"Just *go*, Becky!"

She flinched, but he hadn't time to console her like he wanted, he hadn't time to wrap her in his arms and tell her he loved her, because the sirens were closing in and he needed to put in that call to Chief Washington two minutes ago.

Chapter Nineteen

BECKY SAT IN HER FAVORITE LOUNGE CHAIR IN THE DIM courtyard, a blanket over her shoulders and a hot cup of cocoa clutched between her shaking hands. There was a fire roaring in the fire pit but, strangely, she couldn't feel its heat.

Maybe it was because her hair was still a little wet from the extra scrubbing she'd given it in the shower. The shower where all she'd been able to think, over and over again, was *I killed a man*.

"You did good, sis," Billy told her, chafing her arm as he sat on her left.

Yeah, he could probably tell by her chattering teeth, she was having trouble getting warm. She was beginning to wonder if she'd ever get warm again. Perhaps killing someone chilled a person down to the very depths of their soul.

"I did what Ghost taught me," she mumbled, watching a mini marshmallow slowly melt into her hot cocoa. "Slow, smooth, straight, steady, squeeze." They were the five S's of marksmanship. She'd obviously learned them well considering she'd hit the bull's eye, or the fatal t-zone as Ghost called it.

"We're gonna make an operator of you yet," Ozzie said from across the way, stoking the fire until it rumbled and snapped and the fragrant pine logs glowed bright orange.

She gulped, looking around the courtyard at the sup-
portive expressions on all the Knights faces and wondered why the concept of becoming an operator didn't
sound nearly as appealing as it had just that morning.

She'd done the right thing. Sharif would've killed her
if she hadn't killed him first. It was self-defense. Self-
preservation. But she just couldn't get that image out
of her head. That horrific slideshow of bullet leaving
barrel, head shattering, fluid and flesh spraying, body
crumpling, leg twitching…

Sweet Mother of Mercy. No matter how many reports
she'd read on the Knights' missions, nothing had prepared her for the actual carnage of a .45 bullet impacting
a human skull.

She shivered, and Billy chafed harder. She'd be lucky
to have any skin left on that arm after he finished…

"What happened to Eve?" she asked, suddenly remembering the poor woman she'd been made to abandon at Red Delilah's.

"When Bill called and said he was bringing you
home, I went and fetched her from the bar. I took her
back to her apartment," Angel, who was sitting in the
lounge chair beside hers, explained.

"Was she okay?"

"She was shaken and still very drunk. But once I explained that you were fine, once she realized Sharif had
not managed to harm you, she seemed okay. The last I
saw of her, she was curled on her sofa with an afghan, a
bottle of water, and two aspirin."

"Thank you so much." She reached over to squeeze
his hand.

"Anytime."

She smiled sadly, took another sip of cocoa and thought, *Let's hope there's not a next time.*

Why couldn't she get warm?

"Becky?" Angel murmured softly, and she glanced up into his beautiful face. "I once heard it said that one man can change the world with a bullet in the right place. The same applies to one woman."

She shuddered at the thought of her *bullet in the right place.*

"You saved lives today by taking his. Next time you are doubting yourself, doubting the rightness of what you did, you remember that."

Hot tears stung the back of her throat and filled her eyes. She reached for his hand again, holding it tightly.

Rock's phone jingled to life, and all heads turned in his direction, giving her the opportunity to casually wipe away the wetness threatening to spill down her cheeks.

"Are you pullin' my leg, Manus? He...he said his name is Snake?" Rock sputtered into his phone. "Yeah. Hell, yeah. Send him on in."

"Who's Snake?" Becky asked, but Rock just waved her off as the back gate opened and a tall, movie-star handsome man with shaggy, golden hair and a really bad Hawaiian shirt strode into the courtyard.

"*Mon Dieu*," Rock said, grinning as he stood to take the mystery man's hand. "It's good to see your face again, *mon ami.*"

"I'm here for Shell," the man said, a muscle twitching in his jaw.

Huh? Who was this guy Rock allowed to stroll so casually into their compound? And who the heck was Shell?

Then she forgot all about ascertaining the answers to those questions, because the mumble of male voices sounded from around the corner and she closed her eyes. She'd managed to push the thought of what was about to happen to the back of her mind, but now there was no more avoiding it.

The shit, as they say, was about to hit the fan.

Because she'd gone and done it again. Despite trying her level best to avoid it, trouble had found her. And that trouble once more threatened to shine a spotlight on the Knights—a group of men whose very lives depended on anonymity.

And for the past hour, instead of lying in a hospital bed being fed a nice little cocktail of intravenous pain-killers, Frank had been out cleaning up her mess, insuring the Knights and their covers remained intact.

So add all that up with the fact that she'd seduced him on the one night when he was at his most vulnerable because he thought he was going to die, pretty much insured that, yepper, he'd had it right all along. Rebecca Reichert was the bane of Frank Knight's existence.

Apologize.

First and foremost, that's what needed to come out of her mouth. An apology. Not explanations, not words of defense, just a straight-up, no-holds-barred, "I'm sorry."

Frank, I'm sorry. Frank, I'm sorry. Frank, I'm sorry.

She practiced it over and over as she set her coffee mug on the little wrought-iron table beside her chair and stood, slowly making her way toward the gate so she could address Frank face-to-face as he deserved. She wasn't going to cower behind Billy or Angel or any of the others.

Frank, I'm sorry. Frank, I'm sorry.

Although, considering how much trouble and heartache she'd caused him over the last twenty-four hours, those three words sounded feeble at best, downright vapid at worst.

She could hear his big boots clomping against the blacktop.

Twisting her hands together, she practiced tactical breathing just like Ghost had taught her. Three short breaths in, one long breath out. It was supposed to steady your nerves before you squeezed the trigger on a target. She wasn't fingering a trigger, and she sure as heck didn't have a target, but she needed steady nerves.

Lord knew she needed steady nerves…

Just when she was about to give it another go, because the first bout of tactical breathing hadn't done anything but make her dizzy, Frank rounded the corner.

"Zoelner's out front," he said. "Make him at home, Ozzie."

Ozzie took one look at Frank and jumped to do as commanded, rushing past Becky where she stood awkwardly by the gate.

"Christian, I'm gonna need you to call General Fuller and fill him in on what's happened," Frank continued. "Rock, you'll have to…" He stopped when his weary eyes alighted on their newest arrival. "Well, I'll be damned, Snake" he said, shaking his head, a tired smile playing at his lips. "You picked one helluva time to make an appearance, but it's good to see you again."

"You might not feel that way after I tell you what I'm here for."

"Oh?" Frank's smile faded.

"I'm here for Shell," the mysterious man announced again, and Becky watched Frank take a deep breath before slowly blowing it back out.

"Okay then." He ran a hand through hair that looked liked he'd already run his fingers through it a hundred times before. "I guess I'll deal with that later. Don't think I'm rude, but there's something I gotta do right now." He turned to her then, and her heart started pounding.

Because even though he was white as a ghost, that didn't detract from the expression on his face. The one that held her rooted to the spot.

Oh, geez, this was so much worse than she expected. He looked like he wanted to kill her...

"Frank, I—" That's all she got out before he scooped her up in his good arm and pushed her back against the shop's back wall, slamming his mouth over hers.

...or kiss her?

Eve was right. It was hard to know which he had in mind when he wore that particular expression.

For a second she was frozen, her eyes blinking and crossed as she tried to see his face. Then his hot tongue plunged between her lips, and he pressed his big body up against her and all thought flooded right out of her ringing ears as she wrapped her arms around his neck, kissing him back with everything she had.

Too soon he pulled away, his gray eyes fierce as a winter storm. "Come with me," he growled at her. "Now."

Bill smiled as he watched Boss drag Becky out of the courtyard. And when he turned back, he was surprised to find Angel mirroring his expression.

"What the hell are you grinning about?" he demanded. "The big Boss Man just made off with your girl."

Not that Bill was complaining, of course. It was about damn time Boss and Becky acted on the love that'd been growing between them for years. And he wanted nothing more than to see his little sister happy.

That being said, he figured he could've gone the rest of his natural life without bearing witness to the gut-turning spectacle of Becky getting body-slammed and lip-locked. Then again, if some guy was going to grind his sister against a brick wall, he could think of much worse options than Frank Knight.

Angel Agassi being one of them.

"We were never anything but friends," Angel mused, taking a sip of the cocoa Becky'd left behind, absently watching as Rock escorted their visitor through the back door of the shop. The rest of the Knights followed the pair, no doubt keen to find out who the mystery man was. Bill was curious about the guy as well. But he was even more interested in Angel's response.

Never anything but friends?

Yeah, my ass, he thought. "So what was with the perpetual pissing contest between you and Boss?"

"A mistake," Angel admitted with a shrug. "I thought I was protecting her." His face twisted in a wry grin. "I didn't realize the woman Boss was courting in Lincoln Park was his *sister*."

Bill felt himself soften a bit toward the enigmatic Israeli. After all, the guy had risked his life to save Becky once, and now it seemed he'd been willing to risk his job, risk being thrown out on the unforgiving streets of Chicago, just to safeguard her virtue.

Maybe he and the rest of the Knights had been too hard on the man. Oh, not that anyone had overtly introduced their fist to the guy's face or left a boot-print on his ass, but heaven knows they certainly hadn't welcomed him with open arms either.

"I guess I should be thanking you, then," he admitted, offering a hand. "For that, and for seeing Eve home earlier."

"You are welcome on both counts." Angel accepted his hand and gave it a hard shake.

"And speaking of Eve," he mused, suddenly restless, "I should probably give her a call and check on her, make sure she's all right."

"She told me she planned to turn off her phone. She said she needed approximately twenty hours of sleep. I doubt you'll be able to reach her." Angel tilted his head, his dark eyes seeing too much in Bill's tightly controlled face. "So, Eve Edens? I can't help but feel there's history between the two of you."

Bill ran a hand over his face and sighed, planting his ass on a lounge chair. "It's a very long, very stereotypical story. You know, rich girl, poor boy, Daddy doesn't approve."

"Well," Angel looked around the empty courtyard and shrugged, "it would appear we have all the time in the world."

Before Bill even realized what he was doing, before he realized he even *wanted* to spill his goddamned guts, he opened his mouth, and the words just started tumbling out like road apples from the south end of one of Chicago's northbound carriage horses.

"Becky, Becky," Frank whispered over and over again between kisses as he backed her into his bedroom.

He reveled in the knowledge that there were no more barriers standing between them...well, unless you considered their clothes, but even one-handed, he was doing a pretty fair job of disposing of those.

Becky was no slouch herself. She'd already pulled off his hospital gown and was going to work on the buttons at his fly.

Love. He couldn't believe it, but he was in love. And it was so damned good, because he'd never realized it before but love was life. He was alive! He was in love, and he was alive and if he was any more happy he'd probably burst. *Kaboom!* He could just see himself exploding into a colorful mist of heart- and dove-shaped confetti.

He managed to whip her shirt over her head and unhook the back clasp of her bra, and—*God love the woman*—she stepped out of her jeans and panties and stood in front of him and—

Sweet kee-rist, she was gorgeous.

And she was his. All his.

He couldn't help himself; he lowered his head to press a kiss to one of those amazing nipples, smiling when it hardened against his tongue. Her fingers were in his hair, his name was on her lips, and when she pushed him back on the bed and straddled his hips, he forgot all about telling her the one thing he'd meant to tell her the minute he walked through the door.

Then, suddenly, she was gone.

―❦―

She couldn't do it.

She really, *really* wanted to. But she couldn't. Not after meeting Michelle. Not after staring into little Franklin's eyes.

What was this thing she was feeling?

Guilt. That's what.

And it was so cliché it was almost laughable. Who didn't suffer recriminations after having elicit sex with a man who happened to love another woman, another woman who happened to be the mother of his child?

For crying out loud, she was the *other* woman. One giant, walking stereotype. And she wanted to delay the next few moments for as long as she could, because, God, the come-to-Jesus talk she needed to have with Frank was going to be awful….

Don't be a coward! her conscience yelled at her and, prodded by that shrill inner voice, she made herself meet his confused gaze as he sat up on the bed.

His endearingly crooked grin stopped her from saying the words on her tongue, and she couldn't help herself, she reached forward to trace the thin white scar on the edge of his lips. "How'd you get this?" she whispered.

"I got it courtesy of my father."

"What?"

"It's a long story," he leaned in for a kiss, but she backed away. "One that begins with my father's cheating and ends with a ridiculous childhood promise I thought I made to Michelle." He frowned at her reaction to his move.

And there it was. That woman's name. Thrown out there so casually and carelessly.

Becky's heart shriveled down into a hard stone and

pulsed inside her chest like a bad tooth. She swallowed. So much for putting off the come-to-Jesus talk. "What are we doing here, Frank? How can you love her and make love to me?"

"I don't see what one thing has to do with the other."

Men. The insufferable assholes!

"You can't understand how wrong it is to be in love with Michelle while you diddle me?" She couldn't help it, the last few words came out on shriek of outrage.

She bent to grab her jeans, stepping into them and angrily pulling them up her legs even while she searched for her bra.

Where was the stupid thing?

Oh yes, hooked over his lamp.

Another cliché.

Man, she was really racking them up today.

"First of all," Frank said, scowling, as he watched her wrestle herself into her clothes. "You and I do *not* diddle. We make love. Secondly, I *love* Shell, but I'm not *in* love with her. I think there are laws against that."

"What are you talking about?"

"I'm talking there are no flowers in my family's attic," he said as he shoved himself back inside his jeans and fumbled one-handed with the buttons.

She raised a brow. The man had obviously lost his mind.

He rolled his eyes at her look of confusion. "Let me see if I can explain it another way. Are you in love with Bill?"

He *had* lost it. No question. "No, of course not. He's my brother."

"Well, there you go."

"What are you saying, Frank?" she demanded, hands on hips. "Are you trying to tell me that—" A picture of long, tall, sable-haired Michelle flashed through her frazzled brain. "Michelle's your sister," she breathed, shaking her head as she made the connection, not knowing whether to laugh or cry or both.

"Of course she is."

Of course *nothing*. "You mean to tell me you've been sneaking out for over three years to go visit your *sister*?"

"Well, I wouldn't call it *sneaking*, but, yeah. Wait... did you think...? Ha!" He slapped his knee. "So that's why you jumped up like someone bit you in the ass and started dragging on your clothes in a huff? You thought I was two-timing you with Shell?"

"Why isn't she in JSOC's database from back when you were with the Teams?" she demanded.

"What the hell are you doing hacking into JSOC?"

"Answer the dang question!"

"It's not an easy answer, goddamnit! There's a long, *classified* story behind it. But, suffice it to say, I had a buddy in Delta Squad whose family was targeted because one of his enemies was able to hack into JSOC and get that information. Now I don't tell anybody anything more than is absolutely necessary."

"Okay, but," she shook her head, "at least you could've let us know about her. It's not like she'd be in danger from the Black Knights."

"And that's where you're wrong," he told her, his tone brooking no argument. "There's a sad tale surrounding Shell's involvement with operators, and I promise I'll fill you in on all the hairy details. In fact, given Snake's arrival, I'm gonna have to deal with all of that sooner rather than later."

I'm here for Shell…Suddenly, the mystery man's declaration made sense.

"But for right now," Frank continued, his eyes hot, "I don't want to talk about anything besides the fact that you're wearing too many clothes."

—⁓—

The land-speed record for shucking one's drawers was broken by Becky Reichert, and before Frank knew it, she was nude once again—*thank you, sweet Jesus*—and looking at him with such determination and lust and *joy,* he couldn't help but drag her onto his lap as he lay back on the bed.

"God you're beautiful," he said as she knelt above him, her long hair falling like two halves of a golden curtain between them.

And nope, that hadn't been what he'd meant to say to her when he walked in the door, but it seemed to work, because she kissed him to within an inch of his life and fumbled with the buttons at his fly. When his erection sprang free, she sank down onto him and words completely failed him.

All he could concentrate on was how right it felt when she rode him sweet and fast and hard, taking him so deep inside her that he wasn't sure where he ended and she began.

"I love you," she whispered, leaning forward to kiss him, her mouth hotly demanding, and *those* were the words he'd meant to tell her as soon as he saw her, but all he cared about was hearing her say it again.

He reached up to push her hair away from her face so he could see her eyes. "One more time."

"I love you," she murmured, immediately following that up with a groan as she swiveled her hips, grinding against him, and that's when it happened.

He blew apart.

Just disintegrated into a cloud of heart- and dove-shaped confetti, because he'd suspected Becky's love for years, but hearing the words on her lips was more beautiful than anything he could've imagined.

Oh man, he wasn't going to last another thirty seconds.

"I need to—" he tried to work his hand between their bodies and finally managed to press his thumb into the top of her sex.

"Oh, Frank, I'm going to come."

And *those* were the words he needed to hear because, "I'm right behind you, honey."

Locking her arms around his neck, Becky cried his name as she slipped over the edge, and, true to his word, he immediately followed.

———— ∿∿∿ ————

"I still can't believe you thought I was two-timing you with my own sister," Frank chuckled, and Becky nipped at the flat, brown nipple lying so close to her cheek.

"No one uses the phrase two-timing anymore," she declared, her heart so full of love, she thought it might burst. "It's too old-fashioned."

"Well, *I'm* old-fashioned."

"Frank Knight," she pushed from his chest and stared into his beautiful, stormy eyes, a kernel of hope glowing in her chest since she realized there wasn't another woman standing between them, "you're the least old-fashioned man I know."

"Wanna bet?"

"What do you mean?"

"I mean I don't think it's right for a couple of people in our, uh, situation to be living together under the same roof and reveling in unprotected sex without the writ of a judge. So what say you we make this thing between us official?"

She jerked back as though someone popped her on the chin. The kernel of hope in her chest started to blaze. "Are you asking me what I think you're asking me?"

"I don't know," he grinned, all lopsided and wonderful. "Do you think I'm asking you to marry me?"

Marry. Me.

Dear Lord, they were just two words. Two little words. But they managed to make her heart sing. Then again, those two words hadn't been preceded by the requisite three words.

Oh yeah, she hadn't forgotten about that.

With tears filling her eyes and the promise of forever burning in her chest—she certainly wasn't cold anymore—she leaned toward him. Stopping with her lips a breath away from his.

"You skipped a part," she murmured, running a hand through his hair, marveling in the texture, amazed that she'd be free to do this, just this simple thing of running her fingers through his hair, for the rest of her life.

"I'll get down on one knee if you want me to, but I'm gonna look pretty silly doing it in this cast."

"That's not the part I'm talking about." She threw a leg over him, straddling his lean, naked hips, careful to avoid bumping into his cast. "I'm talking about the profession of certain feelings that are usually made before a proposal of marriage."

"Oh, that…"

"Yes, *that*." She lightly bit the tendon in his neck.

"I love you," he said. Just like that. Plain and simple.

Well of course, that's how he'd deliver it. He was Frank Knight, after all. No-bullshit, no-prevarication Frank Knight. What did she expect?

The tears that'd been hovering burst free, and she buried her nose in his neck with a sob. "It's about damn time," she mumbled when she could find her voice.

"Yeah well, are you going to answer my question or not?"

"Yes," she whispered through her tears, sitting up to look into the most brutal, beautiful face she'd ever laid eyes on. "Yes, I'll marry you. On one condition."

He grinned as he rolled his eyes. "I guess if I'd wanted a nice, biddable wife, I should've looked somewhere other than a tattooed, sharp-tongued, Harley-riding, motorcycle designer."

"I'm serious," she sniffed, reaching to wipe the tears from her cheeks.

"So am I," he said with a scowl.

She punched him on his good shoulder, eliciting a bark of laughter from his deep chest.

"Okay, okay," he held up his hand in surrender when she narrowed her eyes. "Whatever it is, whatever your condition, just name it."

"I don't want to be treated like a nosy civilian. I want in. On *everything*."

For a minute, he just stared at her. Then he closed his eyes and grimaced like someone was shoving hot needles under his fingernails. Finally, he said, "It's going to kill me, you being out in the field, but if that's what it takes to make you happy, then you can be an operator—ah!" He pressed a finger over her mouth when she started to interrupt him. "But before I let you out on an assignment, I'm going to test you on everything from weapons to recon to field dressings, and if you don't measure up, I'm keeping your sweet ass at home."

"Can I talk now?" she burbled around his finger, joy and peace and so much happiness filling her up that she wanted to shout her triumph to the walls.

"That depends."

She lifted a brow.

"Are you going to argue with me?"

"You said yourself you didn't want a biddable wife," she continued to have to talk around his finger, because he'd yet to remove it. The arrogant, fabulous dill-hole.

When he frowned and looked like he was mentally gearing up for a fight, she relented. "But in this case, I'm not arguing."

It was his turn to raise a brow.

"I'm not arguing, because I don't want to be an operator." He got very still. "I just want to be let in on what's going on with you and the guys when you're out in the field. I don't want to be treated like the unloved stepchild. You and the Knights, you're my family, blood or not, and I deserve the right to hear the good, the bad, and the ugly. We're a team. All of us. It's time you realized that."

He reached up and thumbed away a tear that lingered on her cheek, the look in his eyes so warm and full of love she almost started crying all over again.

"You don't want to be an operator? But you've

worked so hard. What changed your mind? Not that I want you doing that kind of work, or course, but I just want to make sure it doesn't have anything to do with what happened today. Because you gotta know you did the right thing in that motel room."

"I know," she told him as she tucked her head under his chin, sucking in the smell of soap, leather, and warm, healthy male. "I know I did. But I don't want to make a habit of it."

"Not all ops require—"

"I don't care about being an operator, Frank," she pushed her nose into his neck, a niggle of desire heating her blood when her lips brushed against his hot skin. "I'm not sure I ever really did. What I cared about was being *included*." She sat up. "Are you going to include me?"

"Well, that depends." He grinned when she rolled her eyes.

"I guess if I'd wanted a nice, biddable husband, I would've looked somewhere other than an ex-Navy SEAL turned private covert operator. So go on, what's your condition?"

"That you marry me," he said, catching her lips in a kiss so hot her ears burst into flames.

"I think we're going around in circles here, Frank," she told him when she could catch her breath.

"Are you going to marry me, or not, Rebecca Marie Reichert?" he demanded, and he looked so cute and fierce, she couldn't help herself, she bent to nip at his full lower lip.

"I am," she breathed against his mouth. "And are you going to let me in on the meetings? Let me officially become part of this team?"

"I am," he told her, reclaiming her mouth at the same time his hand landed on her ass, grinding her against him, and that was the third best thing he'd said to her today. Right after "I love you" and "marry me."

Author's Note

For those of you familiar with the vibrant city of Chicago, Illinois, you'll notice I changed a few places and names, and embellished on the details of others. I did this to suit the story and to better highlight the diversity and challenges of this dynamic city I call home.

About the Author

Deep in the heart of the Windy City, three things can be found at Julie Ann Walker's fingertips: a keyboard, a carafe of coffee, and a sleepy yellow Labrador retriever. They, along with her ever-patient husband, keep her grounded as her imagination flies high. Visit her at www.julieannwalker.com.

Acknowledgments

First of all, I'd like to give a big literary kiss to my wonderful husband for supporting me, encouraging me, and nodding enthusiastically—even though sometimes his eyes glaze over—when I drone on and on and *on* about the minutiae of my writing career. I couldn't have done this without you, sweetheart. You're my rock and my inspiration. (Wink, wink. Nudge, nudge.)

Secondly, I'd like to give a shout-out to Sean Flynn for his beautifully written article, "Pirates in Paradise," which ran in the May 2010 issue of *GQ* magazine. That article was so wonderfully written and so amazingly informative; it inspired me to pen this book. You're a rock star, Sean. No doubt about it.

And, finally, *thank you* to our fighting men and women, those in uniform and those out of uniform. You protect our freedom and way of life so we all have the chance to live the American Dream.